Enigma Books

Also published by Enigma Books

Paolo Mastrolilli

The Italian Brothers

A Documentary Novel of World War II

Translated by Robert L. Miller

Enigma Books

Copyright © 2007 by Paolo Mastrolilli

Published by arrangement with Agenzia Letteraria Roberto Santachiara

Copyright © 2010 Enigma Books for the English translation

Original Italian title:
Adelfi

Translated by Robert L. Miller

First English-Language Edition

Printed in the United States of America

ISBN 978-1-929631-92-6

Library of Congress Cataloguing in Publication Available on Request

The Italian Brothers

1.

Had it been only up to him, Alberto would have said no. A fancy-dress ball was the last thing he needed on that carnival night. His brother insisted however: we must go out, and see people; for one night at least he could try to forget the awful memories of the war. So Alberto finally agreed to go out with him, to avoid further arguments and make his life even more miserable. But it was a mistake. The people were all dressed up in costumes like a masquerade, and the smiles they wore for the occasion appeared sadly tragic rather than funny to him.

He returned home, to the apartment on the Lungotevere Flaminio, without finding the courage to bid his brother farewell. Taking advantage of the excitement at the party, he left him with a small group of girls who were sipping their drinks while their eyes remained hidden behind small black masks.

He went up the stairs slowly, looking downward, lost in his usual thoughts. He opened the door and went straight to his room. He took his naval officer's formal dress uniform out of the closet, the one with the medal for military valor that he had earned for the landings in Albania, and the battle stars for the various campaigns he took part in during the war. He placed it neatly on the bed thinking of what it meant to him, after those years at the academy filled with fervor and illusions, up to the terrible accusation of treason for the massacre at Cape Matapan and the months spent in the clandestine Resistance while Rome was under Nazi occupation. He put the uniform back in the closet more out of respect than modesty.

He went into the bathroom and looked in the mirror for a brief moment. Then cocked the pistol and aimed at his head, while his finger pressed against the trigger.

2.

"The Attorney-at-Law Alberto Conte, son of Luigi and Annita born May 13, 1911, residing at Corso Garibaldi 26 at Lucera, in the province of Foggia, is hereby admitted to the regular course of study at the Royal Naval Academy at Leghorn. He is expected to report for duty on October 19, 1936."

"This time it's for real," thought Alberto, as he closed the envelope from the Ministry of the Navy: it meant the end of a quiet little provincial life as the door to the rest of the world was thrown wide open.

He called his brothers into his room: Giuseppe the oldest, Federico and the youngest one, Vittorio, who was still a teenager. He showed them the letter with some satisfaction:

"Boys, I'm going to say good bye!"

"Naval officer" read Giuseppe in awe "congratulations this is a great honor."

Federico poked fun:

"It's the best spot for a sophisticated dandy like you. Think of all the girls when you'll be out on the town all decked out in your blue uniform."

Alberto smiled and put his hand on Vittorio's shoulder, who was looking at him with a mixture of envy and admiration:

"This letter means that there will be opportunities for all those who want them, believe me." He elbowed his younger brother who laughed at last: "Leave some for me" he asked, "once you become an officer."

Alberto gave Vittorio a friendly smack on the arm.

"That's all you ever think about. Ever since Eve appeared in the Garden of Eden women have never ceased to inspire men. A symbol of beauty and an invitation to courage and responsibility. Not a number in some brothel."

The little brother shrugged his shoulders.

"If you took me to the brothel I swear I'd be ready to kiss a pig's ass in front of everybody."

Alberto shook hands with Vittorio as he put on his overcoat:

"Then it's a done deal. After I introduce you to the first girl, you will kiss a pig's ass the next day and in front of witnesses."

He laughed as he went down the steps and opened the front door.

The streets of central Lucera moved with the laziness customary for a provincial town, still uncertain about its true identity: should it remain a tiny little village or behave like a very small city, since it was an archdiocese and the seat of the local courthouse. The Romans considered it almost as being equal to the imperial capital, to the point of granting it a coat of arms with Senatus PopulusQue Lucerinus, and a few years later Frederick II of Swabia had also built a castle there. But the peasants who worked on the *Tavoliere* that Mussolini --the Duce-- referred to as Italy's granary, had either forgotten about all that or most likely never even knew it.

Alberto hurried to his father's office, the notary Luigi Conte, who also functioned as a public confessional not very different from the town's cathedral. Waiting patiently on the benches of the anteroom was one of the town's important citizens in an elegant black tail coat, along with many other ordinary people who came asking for his advice: before marrying off a son or a daughter, or buying a piece of land, they all wanted to have Don Luigi's thoughts on just about everything. If behind his tiny gold rimmed eyeglasses he would shake his round balding head, it was clearly better to give the matter a lot more thought.

When his eldest son Alberto walked in, the clients in the waiting room recognized him and raised to a man, deferentially, hat in hand. He was tall with deep blue eyes framed in a thin face and light brown hair, always elegant and even very much the dandy. You couldn't miss recognizing him. He went to law school only to keep up the family tradition, but never dreamt of becoming a lawyer and had certainly no intention of following in his father's footsteps. He was really only attracted to music and literature, besides women, that remained a corollary to all his passions. He played the piano and spent his free time giving lectures on classical poetry within provincial social gatherings. His brothers would tease him as some romantic intellectual, but they were really very envious.

"Please excuse me" said Alberto to his father's clients "but it's urgent." He knocked on the door of the study, but got no response. So he knocked again. Not a sound. He didn't dare touch the door knob and sat down to wait patiently with all the others, feeling rather embarrassed. Finally the notary's long time assistant opened the door just as he was shaking hands with a peasant farmer, who had that typical darkened sun baked face that looked like the hard crust of the earth of the Tavoliere. He noticed that Alberto was there waiting and turned politely toward the clients to say: "Please excuse him." He led Alberto into his father's study. The notary took his glasses that were resting on his desk and put them on again.

"Were you knocking on the door earlier?"

Alberto came closer,

"I am sorry but this just arrived in the mail. I thought you should read it as soon as possible."

Luigi looked at the envelope and opened it as quickly as he would when examining an official document for a client seeking advice: "Naval officer. Obviously it's a good position. But it is a very risky job these days. If that's what you want, my son, I must congratulate you. And may God protect you. But now you should go and tell your mother who will feel very saddened by this news, more than anyone else."

Baroness Annita didn't just possess a mother's sixth sense, she could also count on the connivance of her other children and naturally of the servants. When Alberto returned to Corso Garibaldi and knocked at the door of her room there was no need for words. She kissed him on his forehead with tears in her eyes, just like the first day he went off to school.

***

Leghorn is a large metropolitan center compared to Lucera. The traffic, the harbor, the larger crowds and the infinite sense of possibilities that always accompanies the sea. Alberto got off the train and had trouble following his orders to report directly at the Academy. He felt like putting on his hat, straightening his tie and taking a walk through the streets in the center of town, to see if could meet any interesting people.

The barracks were about one kilometer from the railroad station and he made sure he took the longest possible way to get there. He went toward the Fortezza Vecchia surrounded by the Fosso Reale, that he had read somewhere was the work of Sangallo. He wanted to visit the part called "New Venice" because of its crisscrossing canals in the marine area. Busy looking people were bumping into him as he wandered through the streets like an amazed tourist. But Alberto paid no attention and just smiled. He knew that once he passed through the gates of the Academy, if all went well, he would have no more than a single day off every two weeks: 'shore leave' as the cadets liked to call it. So he tried to commit the main sights to memory, in order to return to them as quickly as possible. Even the dives patronized by the rough stevedores, where he imagined he would find the seafaring legends that made him decide to wear the blue uniform.

As he went down the Viale Italia to report to the barracks his eyes were already filled with the sights of a city as he had never seen one before. He was proud to serve a hard working country that was now demanding at last to grab its reward. Those were his thoughts as he reached the entrance of the three story building that since 1881 welcomed the cadet officers about to join the Italian Navy. He looked at the clock tower knowing that it would be keeping his time for months: the officer cadets were not allowed to carry watches because they were to learn to move to a man by simply following the sounds of the clock tower. He noticed the two fasces of the lectors sculpted in granite around the big dial and he felt like walking faster.

Admiral Malceri, the commandant of the Academy, wanted to shake hands with each and every new cadet. So as soon as Alberto went through the gate he was lining up in the Cadet's square, the large quadrangle at the center of the barracks over-looking the Tyrrhenian Sea. With rough waves noticeable in the background he could see the masts of the buried Brigantine, the ship rebuilt in the courtyard and used for training. Every midshipman knew about it since it was the designated venue for all punishment. Anytime a cadet makes a mistake he must do "bar turns", meaning that he would have to climb up thirty meters on the main Brigantine mast, go over the top and come back down on the opposite side, as many times as his commanding officers ordered.

The Commandant with his emaciated and austere face looked at the cadets one by one: "If you think you're here to show off with stars on your uniform, then you have picked the wrong place. If you got in because of some kind of favoritism that's going to be too bad for you: sooner or later you will regret it. The Italian Navy has had a brief but glorious history. We intend to extend it further. Our country is engaged in an enormous effort to make sure that we can compete with the Great Sea Powers and it needs young men who are capable of fulfilling that task and will not disappoint. Gentlemen: that's why you are here. Don't you ever forget it."

When Malceri had finished the older cadets took over the recruits, who at that point were just clumsy civilians unable to march properly without tripping. They lead them to the stores for the clothing rituals: a dark blue uniform, and a dagger with a handle of real mother of pearl.

"Cadet, present yourself."

Alberto stuck out his hand: "My pleasure, I am Alberto Conte."

The older cadet lost his patience.

"Where do you think you are, on some pleasure trip with your friends?"

"No."

"No...what?"

"I mean I'm not going for a ride."

"You don't mean... beans! Haven't they taught you how to answer a superior?"

"Politely, I believe."

The older cadet turned toward his colleagues: "Fellows, this one came here deciding to be a wise guy!" His face suddenly came only one centimeter from Alberto's.

"On the floor, right now! Twenty push-ups."

Alberto looked around flabbergasted.

"I said on the floor, now!"

Alberto put his coat on the floor and without even unbuttoning his jacket began doing his push ups.

"Get up, now: a officer candidate doesn't sweep the floor with his tie. When I or any other superior asks a question you must always answer: "Yes Sir! or No Sir!" If I ask you to introduce yourself you do not extend your hand: you stand at attention and shout: cadet officer so and so. The shape of things is their actual content: get that through your head. And always remember one thing: in here, you count for nothing. Only your rank has any meaning and right now it's at the bottom of the list."

***

Life at the Academy was hard and the nights were even worse. Reveille came at 5:30 in the morning while it was still dark; lights were out at 9:30 at night. During the day you had to follow the drill instructors and quickly learn to become military men - with extensive calisthenics and fencing, sailing, rowing like galley slaves and up and down the length of the pool in ice cold water, 100 meters at a time. Then these were classes: trigonometry, navigation astronomy, naval artillery firing, the chemistry of explosives, thermodynamics. The booklet *The Cadet's Day* preached barracks etiquette and was the equivalent of the Gospel: study hours were to be spent in total silence in individual seats. "It is forbidden to speak or to move." Whoever fails to follow those orders ends up on the masts of the buried brigantine or under arrest at the "Villa Miniati," the brig where you were forced to sleep without sheets. Then at night you had to follow the older cadets who after months on duty wanted to have some fun at the expense of the latest arrivals. At best you could sleep for about one hour on a drenched mattress: "Have you come here to be at sea, cadet?"

"Yes sir."

"Well, here comes the sea." And you would get thoroughly sprayed with salt water.

Alberto managed to make it through that ordeal. He also knew he could write. That was his strong point and he made the most of it when the time came to produce papers. One title was: *The Totalitarian States, the Great Democracies and the Principle of National Economic Autarchy.*

He put his head down and began: "The authoritarian or totalitarian states today are Japan, Germany and Italy. In discussing the so-called Great Democracies the names mentioned are usually England, France, the United States and Russia. These same nations may also be viewed according to a different set of political and economic criteria: on one hand those who enjoy national economic independence thanks to their own natural resources, their colonies and the control of raw materials; and then the nations that do not have access to that kind of independence. According to this classification the nations that occupy a key privileged position because of their control of raw materials are: the United States, the British Empire, and Russia; with France at some distance behind them. The countries that remain in a significantly inferior condition among the Great Powers are: Italy, Germany and Japan. In the final analysis the rich countries are the ones having a liberal democratic internal constitution, while the poor nations have basically authoritarian internal regimes." Following that preamble, came the provocations: "It may be debatable whether the democratic states truly represent democracy. It is possible that, in fact, they are usurping that definition which is based on the residual conception of the past that originates in parliamentary regimes. It very well may be that true democracy such as it appeared after the war —understood as a populist regime, where social classes are abolished, thereby creating equality among individuals and groups - has found its highest expression precisely within the totalitarian regimes and in the concepts of fascism and National Socialism. I would therefore like to ask the question: why is it that rich States are democratic while the poor States are totalitarian? Had Italy not had Mussolini and Germany not had Hitler, could we even speak of totalitarian States today? In other words, are the totalitarian regimes in Italy and Germany a creation of Mussolini and Hitler or do they represent instead an ideological and political evolution that Italy and Germany would have reached naturally in any case because of their economic conditions?"

Alberto looked up for a brief moment at the faces of his fellow cadets, who appeared to be seeking an elusive sort of inspiration from outside the windows. Then he returned to his text.

"The great democracies are very critical of the totalitarian States but the autarchic efforts they are making are not subjected to as much criticism. Perhaps this is because the democracies lack the courage to deny the efforts to avoid famine on the part of an entire nation. Using the economic weapon, the great democracies think they can dominate the world."

These ideas were making headlines in the newspapers and were repeated during the lessons at the Academy. And again he wrote:

"Italy, Germany and Japan do not want to isolate themselves economically and in a sense they cannot; it would be contrary to a policy that proclaims itself as imperial. But they must set their policy on autarchy until things change radically, meaning that the current international organization, that doesn't exclude but actually expects war as a distinct possibility, is replaced by a different system that will reset the course of history."

Not a sound emerged from the Gothic columns that were holding up the old classrooms of the Academy. Alberto's pen went racing to the closing lines: "To deny a people its rightful access to economic autonomy is equivalent today to denying it the right to arm itself for its own defense. To accept such a state of affairs would mean to condemn it to suicide or a form of more or less open international slavery."

Alberto was the first one in the class to turn in his paper. Two days later he found out that Admiral Malceri liked it: "Good work," he marked it eighteen out of twenty, practically the top grade on his first test. Now he could go back to those "bar turns" in front of the upper classmen or sleep on a drenched mattress. Why would it matter? He could sit on the pier of the small port of San Jacopo, from where the Academy's ships set sail, and look as far out as he could at sea.

His first time on board a military vessel came on November 30, 1936: it was a destroyer of the "Navigatori" class *Lanzerotto Malocello* of the 9th Battleship Division of Admiral Bergamini. It was a little jewel of a ship 107 meters long, at 2380 tons, launched in 1929. The very same one that in 1931 had served as the ocean escort for Italo Balbo, during his "Atlantic Cruise" with a flotilla of sea planes to Brazil. As soon as he went on board ship, Alberto wrote in his diary: "The integration of Navy and Air Force. This will be the key to the future for us to keep up with the great powers."

On June 30, 1937 his early youth was over once and for all and he had become an adult: Alberto had completed his courses at the Royal Naval Academy at Leghorn and graduated with the rank of Second Lieutenant. His first real commission was on board the heavy *Zara* under the command of Captain Ferreri.

As soon as he found a moment he mailed a letter back home. "This is a dream. It is the most modern ship in our navy: 182 meters long, 14,530 tons when fully loaded, 8 big guns at 203/53 and 16 guns 100/47, 2 airplanes, a speed of 32 knots and a crew of 841. They said when we built it that it was in violation of the limits set by international rules: I answer thank goodness it is. It's high time we started to defend ourselves. Now we are a country that the other powers must respect."

3.

My dearest Federico, I must thank you for all you have done and you will still need to do for your brothers who, it appears, have found you to be a great help. I'm not referring to that oddball Vittorio, who has some good qualities but whose brain doesn't always function the way it should: I couldn't understand why he was summoned to the Military District since he had already provided form 45 some time ago!"

The notary Luigi reread the letter he was writing to his son Federico who had also volunteered to Acqui as an officer candidate. It was the end of 1938 and the political climate was not at all reassuring. The Munich Conference had just assigned the Sudeten territories of Czechoslovakia to Germany according to the appeasement policy, which British Prime Minister Chamberlain was convinced would have placated Adolf Hitler. Mussolini came out of that four power summit as the indispensable man to hold together the balance of power in Europe. He was beginning to ingratiate himself with his German ally by passing the racial laws that were officially announced by the "Manifesto on the purity of the Italian race" on July 14.

Luigi was worried about his boys: "Alberto, that dear son of mine, has not yet been able to overcome his innate apathy toward those things that concern him directly and will certainly affect his future. He also jumps very quickly into certain silly situations that he should be avoiding! Do you remember his dogged involvement in local politics? I am convinced that had he not left Lucera -something I have deeply regretted - he would have ended up compromising himself!! Last Sunday he spent a few hours with us and told me that by the end of the month he would be leaving the *Zara* for another assignment or go aboard another ship. I will not dwell on the other stupid thing he did in Naples during his stay in that city, when the Führer was visiting it: he rented a car with a few other officers (nothing wrong with that) and insisted on driving it himself! In such cases your brother sets aside his usual apathy! Since he is not exactly well versed as a driver, especially in a large urban center, he slammed into a street car! Miraculously only the car was smashed while he could have been injured and I then would have received a very ugly telegram! Meantime I had to handle the necessary repairs that cost me the tidy sum of lire 2000! I repeat, may we thank God that the damage is only financial. Did he have to be the one driving, thereby taking on the responsibility towards the other passengers, who were also his friends? You tell me whether this is the way to act when you are away from home? What kind of fun and games are these anyway? Naturally with those kinds of hits his balance sheet doesn't look good at all!..."

Vittorio, jackass that he was - as his father would say - had not yet managed to kiss a pig's ass, simply because Alberto had not found the time to introduce him to those young ladies. But he was quietly attempting to catch up to his older brother who was busy smashing rented cars in Naples. The notary couldn't conceive of the application to the Military District, when Vittorio could have easily obtained a student deferment. But his youngest son volunteered for military service in May without saying a word. The answer came on November 5, 1938: "Admitted as an officer candidate at the 12th Regiment of Pola, infantry specialty: Bersaglieri."

Luigi had just finished the letter to Federico when the baroness Annita told him that Vittorio wished to speak to him. "A hot head" as his mother called him, when her motherly affection was overcome by her anger. Terrible pranks, racing horses and parties with his friends were the only activities that he would put his entire heart and soul into. To prepare for his high school diploma exams his father had the left side of his hair shaved off to next to nothing, to keep him at his desk for the minimum amount of time required for him to study. But that also proved useless. Vittorio spent his days throwing pebbles at passing carriages from his tiny garret on the top floor, until he finally managed to fail the exam. At wit's end Luigi was forced to pack him off to a boarding school run by the Jesuits, who had the good sense of getting rid of him as quickly as they could, so that his diploma would not be too obviously obtained through favoritism.

"What has he done this time?" his father asked.

"I don't know." answered his mother, as she once again attempted to protect him.

"Don't waste my time with the usual crap of you defending him. He managed to sneak into a hearse where he played dead, until he suddenly revived during the procession and frightened the senior citizens in attendance? So, tell me what kind of jam he got himself into and what we must do to get him out of trouble."

"I swear that I don't know. But he looks rather pleased."

The notary shook his head: "That sounds even worse. Tell him to come in."

Vittorio, with his blue eyes, his tie undone and his blond curly hair messed up, winked at his mother then stood at attention: "Dear Dad, I present you the officer's candidate Vittorio Conte, 12th Regiment Bersaglieri stationed at Pola."

"Candidate to what? What about your studies? And your student deferment?"

"I'll just request an interruption for my studies. What's the matter? Why aren't you pleased? You were the first to say that I wasn't much of a student anyway."

"And the job I got you at the Banco di Napoli?"

"They paid so little and wouldn't let me do anything in any case. This way I can make myself useful rather than going to waste time around here."

***

To be stationed at Pola, at the tip of the Istrian peninsula, was more than just being in the army. It meant defending the "lost lands" that Italy had won back during the First World War. The regime's rhetoric, but also the logic of many professors of history, viewed that conflict as the Fourth War of Independence and the young officer candidates were being sent up there to learn a patriotic gospel, besides being taught how to use a model '91 Musket. "The functions of a citizen and a soldier" - as the Duce said - "are one and the same."

Vittorio, who was matriculated as a student in business and economics at the university, had never traveled north of Naples before. And Naples had just been an excuse to live in town. Once he reached the officer's candidate school they told him to line up and march in his regular civilian shoes that immediately cracked open like slippers.

"You look like a crazy caterpillar" screamed the drill instructor. Vittorio was assigned to a bunk in the common barracks. For the first time he heard accents and dialects he had only learned about from relatives who had traveled to other parts of Italy. In front of the bunk, on the right, he saw another young man sitting on a metal stool looking very confused. On the left bunk there was another boy who couldn't stay put.

"Hi, I'm Vittorio."

The fellow on the right looked up rather surprised to hear a voice that was not screaming at him:

"Hello, I am Antonello."

The one on the left stopped punching his hat and came closer:

"My name is Leonida."

"Like the Greek general!" said Vittorio teasing him.

"Well, my real job is to write." he answered.

"Me too" said Antonello, "Not professionally, but when I have time I jot down some poems. Last year I also took part in the Littoriali of culture."*

"This is really something!" complained Vittorio. "Here I am, running away from my professors, and I have to land in a platoon full of intellectuals."

"Why, what were you doing before coming here?"

"I was throwing away my father's money at the university" answered Vittorio. "But I really think the party's over now."

"Or else it's just beginning" answered Leonida. "It all depends what you want to do with your life."

During the first military drill in the courtyard of the Monte Paradiso barracks the wind was blowing so hard that the men couldn't stand at attention and the brutal gusts were almost tearing the feathers off their helmets. The Captain was observing from afar with his visor lowered over his forehead, his pants tucked inside his boots that he would whip regularly with his riding crop. He kept silent, letting the Second Lieutenants review each row of recruits. In the center of the quadrangle there was a

---

* Littoriali of culture: student competitions sponsored by the Fascist party to strengthen ideological commitment in the universities.

gun rack filled with rifles with mounted bayonets pointing
toward the sky.

From the other end, behind the deployed company, the
sound of marching was carried over by the relentless wind. It
became louder, and markedly aggressive. They were older officer
candidates from another company who were about to pin the
officer's gold stars on their shoulder boards. They were running
and singing: "Come come now, make 'em die, make 'em croak,
make 'em die, make 'em croak." They came in tight rows with
their fez tassels flying and appeared as if someone were pulling
the strings behind them, like puppets. They stamped their left
feet more aggressive as they marched closer to the new arrivals.
An order by the Second Lieutenants, just two words shouted
out, stopped the men instantly. The first four in line left the
group and went beyond the gun rack. The others lined up, and
ran toward the bayonets that were jutting up threateningly
toward the sky. A step up on the board, a death jump over the
bayonets, and on the other side their comrades poised to receive
them.

The young candidates looked at those proceedings in fear,
since their turn was sure to come soon after. The Captain made
an about-face without even looking at them and walked slowly
back to the barracks, decorated with a huge fascist symbol
adorning the wall like a sculpture. The second lieutenants then
handed over command of the company to the older instructor
candidates and followed the captain up the steps.

"Do you know why they are not speaking to you?" asked an
instructor with a Lombard accent. "Because you don't deserve it.
You're like insects to them, less than nothing. It's simply useless
to even waste any breath on you, until you can demonstrate that
you have become real soldiers."

The instructor went up to Leonida:

"Candidate, do you know what the letters ROC on your
papers stand for?"

"Yes!"

"Candidate, do you think you're on a battleship on top of the waves?"

"No!"

"Well, then as long as you are in the army you will kindly answer any question yes Sir! and no Sir! Only those ridiculous sailors say simply "Aye Aye Sir!"

"Yes Sir!"

"I can't hear you!"

"Yes sir!"

"I can't hear a fucking thing!"

"Yes Sir!"

"Louder!"

"Yes Sir!"

"So, now do you know what that word means?"

"Yes Sir, Reserve Officer Candidate."

"That's why you must die for, since you don't even know your own name."

Leonida looked at the instructor, with a puzzled expression but without the guts to contradict him.

"It really means "I used to have a home. Now I have a barracks." Don't you ever forget that, candidate. Forget that you ever were a civilian. You came to Pola to die and you will succeed without any problem. And make sure you don't make any other mistakes, unless you want to get yourself and your comrades in trouble. In the army if just one of you makes a mistake everyone else pays for it as well."

The other instructors ordered the platoon to fall in line and had the last ones marching bring over the bicycles. They were to be trained as cycling Bersaglieri, until the sores they developed on their buttocks would force them to go to the sick-bay.

Once all the candidates had their bikes, the leader of the older candidates announced:

"This, along with your side arm, is your life. Take care of her as you would your fiancée! You should even sleep with her, because if she breaks you'll be left to face the enemy alone on your feet. Is that clear?"

"Yes sir!"

"Good. Dismissed!"

Vittorio took his bicycle toward the stairs leading up to the entrance of the barracks but the instructor stopped him.

"Where do you think you're going?"

"Sir, you dismissed us and told us to go to the barracks."

The older instructor turned around impatiently. Then he faced Vittorio: "Candidate, you would probably prefer that I walk you to the elevator?"

"No Sir!"

"Do you see the ropes that are hanging from the eaves of the barracks in front of your windows?"

"Yes Sir!"

"What do think they are there for?"

"To climb up, Sir."

"And what are the twine on the bikes for then?"

"Perhaps to carry it on our back and climb up the ropes?"

"You will find the answer, but you had better make it snappy!"

***

To learn how to stay perfectly still while the tracks of a tank roll over you, and then jump up on the turret from the rear and lob a hand grenade inside, helps you become "harder dick heads" - as the older instructor candidates liked to say. But the entire barracks longed for the days when they would be off-duty and on leave.

"Did you see the new duty officer?" asked Antonello to his fellow soldiers.

"No" answered Leonida "who is he?"

"He's a cavalry officer who was transferred here out of his unit. No one knows the reason why. He must have done something wrong. The Bersaglieri officers make sure he always gets to put on duty, and he takes his revenge himself on us candidates."

"How do you mean?"

"When you want to go on leave he asks you questions about the stanzas and mottos of the cavalry. He says "Savoia", and you must answer "Savoye bonnes nouvelles." If you don't know the motto he yanks you back into the barracks."

Vittorio reacted impetuously: "On the collar of my jacket I wear the crimson flames, and I don't give a damn about that dandified horse soldier. He can study the stanzas and mottos of the cavalry by himself all he wants."

"Fine" interrupted Antonello, "and how will you get to go on leave?"

"There's a spot on the wall around the barracks" answered Vittorio, "from where you can jump, if the Bersagliere on guard duty looks the other way and helps you out. This evening I'm going out that way. Then we'll meet at the usual café in the via Decia."

Pola was a town full of stimulating energy, similar to when an orchestra intones the closing waltz at the end of a party. Vittorio entered the café wearing his cape, even though it was soiled after he jumped over the wall. Antonello was waiting for him at the counter that was decorated like one of the Habsburg royal palaces. His uniform was as freshly pressed as a farmer's suit attending high mass.

"Did you see that girl, alone at the back of the room?" asked Vittorio.

"Not bad at all" said Antonello.

"Looks like she'd like some company."

"I see, so I'm supposed to hook up with her then?"

"Antonello, you're the poet, you always manage to find the right thing to say, so you go! Then I'll show up to help."

The young lady was really hoping to find some company, even though the available men were always those braggarts from the Bersaglieri on leave for the night. So she settled for Antonello who bowed deferentially and asked her name.

"Pleased to meet you, I'm Catherine."

"Nice, a Greek name. Greece is a great country. I am Antonello, officer candidate, and I am from Rome. This is my colleague Vittorio, from Puglia."

"How is that possible" she stares at Vittorio, "a southern Italian with curly blond hair and blue eyes? You're so tall and pale you look more like a local German from these parts than a southerner."

"What they say is" answered Vittorio with pride, "that my ancestors came to Puglia with the Swabian emperors. They liked the south, they married local women and never left. We have Swabian blood in our veins and in the family everybody is tall, fair haired with blue eyes.

"Like us up here, mixed with Slavs and Germans. So how long do you expect to stay in Pola?"

"We like it up north, right Antonello?"

"Just like a verse from D'Annunzio, right."

"What are you talking about?" - Catherine asked aggressively. "Why do you always sing that song then? The one you sing in the barracks? Engineer, engineer from Pola, put more oil, put more oil in the engine rods, because we are fed up with Pola and want to go back home."

"No, it has nothing to do with it" answered Vittorio defensively, "it's only a joke for the recruits. Granted, that everyone is far better off at home. But this land is Italian: we took it back with our blood and we will not let it be taken away by anyone."

"Maybe" answered Catherine skeptically as she adjusted her hair on her forehead, "what I know is that my family grew up under the Austrians, I lived under the Duce and tomorrow my children, if I ever have any, will grow up under who knows who. And what about you, Bersaglieri, will you still be here when we will need you?"

At the end of 1939, a few months after that evening on the via Decia in Pola, Vittorio, Antonello and Leonida all received the gold stars as Second Lieutenants.

"So this intellectual's platoon" said Vittorio in jest, "has become a real soldier's platoon, made up of tough military men."

The machinist from Pola had really oiled up the machines as the boys shook hands for the last time. Vittorio was off to Bolzano and the 7th Bersaglieri regiment, for the swearing in and his first assignment. Then off to Pinerolo, just below the mountains that form the border between Italy and France.

4.

For someone who grew up in Puglia, the coastline of Albania looks exactly like home. Those are the lands across the sea that you can almost make out in nice weather. "Poor guys, they are much worse off than we are." Alberto said to himself, as he looked at the still dark line of the rocky shores far in the distance that were the objective of his mission just before dawn. He didn't know why the poet Horace came to mind: "Those who cross the sea change the sky above them but not their soul."

As he had told his father, he was off the cruiser Zara and was now on board the battleship Cavour, the pride of Italy's battle fleet. He also got promoted faster than he expected: he was now a lieutenant, and with the new symbol of his rank on his shoulder boards he was now getting closer to one of the moments that a soldier can never forget for his entire life. At four in the morning on April 7, 1939 Alberto's ship headed the column that was about to land in the harbor at Valona.

Following the Anschluss with Austria and then the takeover of the Sudetenland in 1938, in March 1939 Hitler grabbed Bohemia. He did so without warning Mussolini or at least by telling him as little as possible. When the Duce received the

Führer's derisive "announcement" of his latest conquest he was beside himself: "Hitler told us to stay put for two years but in the meantime he starts the Danzig affair. He wants the city back into his enlarged Reich." After his misleading success at Munich, Mussolini was running the risk of looking like an artless amateur. Actually he was really in danger of losing ground, since his German colleague was taking all the territory he wanted and greatly increasing his influence in the Balkans. The Italian Empire was actually only rhetoric. So he then remembered that his son in law, the foreign minister Galeazzo Ciano, had an old hobby horse idea regarding Albania.

When Ciano attended the wedding of King Zogu he became convinced that Tirana was really a very good deal: thousands of hungry Italians could work there on the farms or building roads and bridges, creating a military base to serve as a balance to the Anglo-French presence in Greece. Besides, it was rumored that there was oil, or something of the sort, in those harsh mountains.

The country was already a virtual Italian protectorate for obvious geographic reasons, but on March 25, 1939 Rome attempted to make Albania's submission official. It sent an annexation proposal that Zogu didn't even deign to answer. So on April 2 it was followed by an ultimatum: the Albanian government had until April 6 to accept Italy's demands. On the 5th the executive branch and parliament both refused to even consider the ultimatum, while the population took to the streets asking for weapons to defend its homeland. So, at 4 a.m. on April 7, Alberto was on the deck of the Cavour observing the coastline that he was about to attack a few minutes later. He had already fired his first shot and had offered the traditional dinner to his fellow officers. But it's a far cry to be shooting at fixed targets during an exercise and to target human beings who might very well die as a result. And then who knows, those shepherds already sick with malaria might still have a few hidden weapons after all, and tonight some of our men may not be writing letters home telling about the excitement of battle.

Just ahead of him was a young sailor who was part of the landing forces, carrying a heavy machine gun as big as both his arms. He had been looking at Alberto for some time until he gathered the courage to say: "Afraid, Lieutenant?"

"And you?"

"Yes. Of course. Maybe these guys will shoot back instead of bringing us flowers."

"What's your name?"

"Sailor Arturo Solustri, sir. From Civitavecchia."

"Very good, Sailor Solustri. Be sure to follow orders and your commanding officers, and use that machine gun properly. You'll see, you will make it out of all this."

Alberto's orders were clear but they were not that simple: to make sure that the communications between the forward units and the commanders were functioning. This meant he must land ahead of everyone else with a field telephone in his hand instead of a rifle. General Guzzoni, who was in charge of the landing forces, trusted him but the smallest mistake on Alberto's part could very well be fatal for many of his fellow soldiers.

When his dinghy reached the port of Valona it was still dark and everything looked quiet ashore. According to the information he received and exchanged, some 20,000 Bersaglieri, infantry and militia troops were about to undertake the same mission at Durazzo, San Giovanni di Medua and Saranda.

He had thought about this moment thousands of times. The fear when you actually see the enemy getting ready to kill you for the first time, and you must be ready to kill to survive. Those were the thoughts that were on his mind, rather than victory. He had replayed the images of battle scores of times in his mind, but at this precise moment those scenes simply refused to appear anymore. He was on a landing barge, sailing closer to the Albanian coast that looked just like Italy. Stung by the cold of that dawn, he was having trouble making the connection between what he was actually seeing and what he had imagined when he was at the Academy. Except for that first artillery shell that seemed intended specifically for him, but that instead whistled over the heads of his men to explode far off at sea. Alberto grabbed the transmitter and signaled his commanding officer: "The defenses have started to fire at us." Then he gave the coordinates.

The Italian support ships began shelling the coast to wipe out the defenses before the landings. Several dozen airplanes all along the Albanian coastline were also bombing their targets. Local defenses didn't fire back, as if those initial shots that missed the target were only some show of pride rather than a strategy. In any case Tirana's army had been created by advisors sent from Rome, who had told King Zogu that the air force was actually useless as were anti-aircraft guns and heavy artillery pieces.

Alberto followed the battalion commander and disembarked, as the men were told which streets to take. The orders were to occupy the town as fast as possible and also move to take a few key points inland. At the same time the column that had landed at Durazzo was moving toward Tirana to conclude the operation without delay. Sailor Solustri was following Alberto with his machine gun at the ready to cover the flank, exposed to the buildings overlooking the harbor that were all encrusted with sea salt.

As soon as Alberto's men came within range, the first shots broke the silence. The surprise was far greater than any damage, nevertheless the entire platoon hit the ground and Solustri placed the bipod securely. The bursts of the Italian machine gun filled the void left by the Albanian rifles: there were few enemy troops and perhaps they were taking turns reloading. The commander ordered to keep on advancing while other units were coming ashore. Alberto was right behind the scouts: his

mission was not to fight but to maintain communications, and to
do so you have to be with the units that are in the vanguard.
Sailor Solustri was walking next to him, as if the lieutenant provided some kind of lucky shield or perhaps simply because he
looked like someone who knew what he was doing.

The rest of the men around them didn't appear to be too
well organized. Some carried only very light weapons, others had
no firearms at all. Arturo could hear from Alberto's receiver that
there were problems in the harbor, because the water's depth
had not been properly measured and the ships were running the
risk of getting stuck.

Solustri kept advancing with the scout units while keeping an
eye on the Lieutenant. They had gone too far out in front
because at the water's edge something had stopped the landings
and the rearguard units were no longer catching up to the vanguard fast enough. When Arturo stopped and looked behind, he
understood that the entire platoon including Alberto were
isolated. From a building in front the Albanians kept on firing.
Behind them nothing was moving. The Lieutenant was on the
field telephone keeping a low voice so the men couldn't hear.
When he looked up he didn't seem happy: "We will hold our
positions right here. We must wait. Solustri, put the machine gun
there and keep it pointed at the enemy."

Arturo had already understood and was directing his fire
straight at the house. Both Italians and Albanians then began
shooting as if to signal their existence. A bullet strafed a sailor's
leg as he tried to take cover near Solustri, who for the first time
saw blood staining the uniform of a fellow soldier. He reloaded
and kept on shooting while the wounded man cursed. "Must we
get killed by these Albanians who keep on shooting wildly? Why
can't those jerks behind us find their way?", he thought, as he
kept looking at Alberto. The Lieutenant remained silent as he
waited for signals that were not coming through.

The shooting from the building that had pinned them down stopped suddenly. Solustri reloaded and fired but there was no response. Alberto spoke on the phone raising his voice, then he looked at Arturo and gave him a signal. The sailor got on his elbows and pushed his weapon forward to get a better line of fire. The rest of the squad followed him, jumping forward as prescribed in the field manual. The men on the right flank stood up and ran a few meters forward, covered by machine gunfire. Then it was their turn to stop and start shooting, while Solustri and the left flank kept on running, led by Alberto. Machine gun bursts again covered the group on the right that finally reached the wall surrounding the house where they were out of the line of Albanian fire. The closest soldiers extracted hand grenades from their kits, pulled the latches and threw them over. The left wing took advantage of the explosions to launch their assault, with Arturo hand carrying the machine gun and shooting without stopping.

Solustri was the first to enter:

"Lieutenant, there's no one left in there."

Alberto came closer, while making sure of his cover as well as that of the other men.

"The machine gun fire made them run away." Said Arturo. Alberto called the commander again, trying not to show his impatience. Right in front of him was the bullet-riddled body of a dead Albanian, just under the open window.

In less than 48 hours Italian troops had Tirana under control. Alberto read the official report of the losses during the landings: 11 killed and 42 wounded at Durazzo, where there was a stronger defense since that bridgehead opened the road to the capital; one killed and 10 wounded at Saranda; little or nothing at Valona. The Albanian army preferred to fall back and was forced to do so, when faced with the power of the Fascist regime that was following in the footsteps of Hitler's successful aggressions. King Zogu fled to Greece with his wife and their small child named Leka. The Duce proposed that the Kingdom of Albania be annexed to Italy thereby keeping a semblance of independence that didn't even exist on paper. On April 15 the country's most prominent citizens traveled to Rome to meet Mussolini, and offered the new crown to King Emmanuel III the next day.

A few months later Alberto received a message from the ministry of the navy:

"The Cross for War Merit is hereby awarded to Lieutenant Commissioner Alberto Conte." The justification signed by the minister read: "While commanding a platoon during a landing operation under heavy fire and in charge of communications, he maintained telephone connections while moving at the head of the dock at the entrance of Valona, following the scout units and battalion command during its movements and attacks. Albania, April 1939, Year XVII of the Fascist era."

In his diary Alberto made an entry:

"The Albanian operation was nothing but a glorified landing test, coordinated with a few rounds fired at the coastline. We will find out the truth when we will face the supreme challenge of war with the strongest enemy in the world, the British."

5.

From the balcony of the Palazzo Venezia the Duce had announced that the time "for irrevocable decisions" was at hand. On June 19, 1940 Vittorio, following his orders, was to reach "the territory in a state of declared war" on the border with France. His unit of bicycle riders was now a motorcycle battalion, and he suffered frostbite on the soles of his feet from riding in the Alps of Piedmont, because he was already wearing summer shoes.

He read his orders several times, before reporting to the headquarters of the 7th Regiment of Bersaglieri to receive final instructions. Those four lines, in their cold bureaucratic jargon, meant that things were now very serious. War was no longer a game for young boys in snappy "Balilla" uniforms with toy muskets, or even the dizzying rhetoric of the jump through the circle of fire at the officer's candidate's course at Pola. From now on it was shoot to kill, and death was unfortunately also a part of it. Wasn't that what you wanted, to prove your valor to yourself and to everyone else? Wasn't that what Italy needed, to prove itself to the world?

Capt. Giovanni Comel, who was in command of the company, shook hands with his officers and handed out the first assignments: "Lieutenant Conte, starting now this soldier will be your orderly."

Vittorio turned around and couldn't avoid being surprised:

"Vito! What the hell are you doing here?" Capt. Comel commented: "I see that you know each other."

Vittorio smiled like a young boy:

"This is Vito, the farmer who tills the land next to the country house belonging to my family down in Puglia. We call that area "The Crusts", because you need to be stubborn and ready to sweat like a mule from the Tavoliere to grow anything to eat from that earth."

"Hello Lieutenant", Vito saluted with pride and stood at attention, with his hands knotty like the roots of trees at his side. He was making an effort to look soldierly and not be too familiar with that young officer who had just received his commission, whom he had known when he was still wetting his shorts.

"And how did you wind up here?" asked Vittorio.

"By train, lieutenant. I'd never traveled in one in my entire life. The King sent me a postcard telling me to leave and I did."

"Are you all right? Everything ok?"

"No complaints, Lieutenant. After all, we are at least guaranteed to have three meals a day."

"You're not afraid of the cold on those mountains?"

"I prefer the sunshine. But I didn't have that much to wear at home as well. They even gave me a helmet with feathers."

Vittorio put his hand on Vito's shoulder and smiled.

"Well, it looks like we'll be spending lots of time together."

"Just like at home, Lieutenant. And we also get to see the world. And then, as you know, running and marching don't bother me at all."

"But, Vito, you know that we're going off to war?"

"That's the way it goes, lieutenant. Like my father, and my grandfather before him."

Until the day before the orders were to wait. Mussolini declared war on France on June 10 just to buy himself a seat at the peace negotiations, once the expected victory was achieved. Before issuing orders to the army to advance, knowing that his forces were unprepared, he was waiting for Hitler's troops to advance into the Ardennes, the blitzkrieg of operation "Fall Gelb" that would take the Nazis all the way to Paris. On June 21, just as the French appeared to be crumbling without even having been fired upon by the Italians, the Duce decided to cross the border and attack toward the French Riviera and Val d'Isère. The city of Nice and the lands of the upper Savoy that Napoleon III had robbed in exchange for helping Italy against Austria during the wars of independence were territories that were to be restored to Italy.

Vittorio led his motorcycle unit around the winding roads under the Monte Rosa, but the main opposition came because of an unseasonable snow fall rather than from enemy fire. Somewhere though Italian soldiers had started to die, because in spite of the fact that the French were already on their knees, General Olry's three divisions were opening fire and blocking the entrance to the valleys. For anyone wanting to fight it was a race against time. If you remained too far to the rear you might miss out, and not discover whether fear is stronger than arrogance once the bullets start flying around.

Vito, with his helmet fastened under his chin, looked around both surprised but also finding it familiar. His father had described those high and beautiful mountains, where he would reminisce about the nights he had spent on the Pasubio or the Grappa Mountains during the First World War. But he was thinking of the poor peasants like those numb infantrymen marching toward the front, or coming back wounded after the first clashes with the French. They were the same faces he had seen by the hundreds, since he had been born: whether in the Tavoliere or the Alps, the people who must work for a living all looked the same.

After two days of fighting, with many casualties and great difficulty, Italian soldiers managed to take Fort Traversette on the Little Saint Bernard Mountain, overtaking the defense lines and opening the road to Val d'Isère. Captain Comel's orders were clear: tomorrow, June 24, will be Vittorio's unit's turn.

It was hard to get any sleep, either out of fear or excitement. The cold and the artillery fire in the background didn't help either.

At dawn the unit with the equipment and weapons was ready. Vittorio was expecting fear in his stomach, but he only found recklessness, as he shaved using the rear view mirror of his motorcycle as though he were preparing for a roll call in the barracks at Pola.

Then he saw Vito running toward him, holding his helmet with one hand and the other on his chest.

"Lieutenant, Sir, this message came in for you from headquarters. They said it was urgent and to run it to you."

He handed a letter to Vittorio who read it out loud:

"Armistice! France has surrendered."

6.

In the spring the Gulf of Naples is always a magnificent sight. But now there was a war going on. Vittorio was back in the city of his alma mater in uniform, as he looked down the streets for the night spots he had haunted just a few years before. It was a happy and mindless good time, paid for by his father Luigi regularly, since he signed the checks and mailed in money orders.

After the French campaign Vittorio attended the paratrooper's course, to be prepared if besides fighting on motorcycles and motorized troop transports it became necessary to jump out of airplanes. But he had been reassigned back to the 7th Regiment Bersaglieri because things were going wrong in North Africa. Following Marshal Graziani's initial advance into Egypt, the British launched a counter offensive. They captured all of Cyrenaica including the fortress of Tobruk, that had been built by Fascist Italy between the two world wars. Now the "Desert Rats" were even threatening Tripoli and Mussolini was running the risk of handing the Axis its first strategic defeat in the Mediterranean. Hitler understood the problem and dispatched his best soldier, General Erwin Rommel. Vito's father must have spit on the ground when he was given the news, because it was

Rommel, then a young officer, who managed to create a breach in the Italian lines at Caporetto during World War I. Those bad memories aside, his presence allowed some hope that the Afrika Korps might turn the tables in the Arab lands that were part of the Italian Empire.

Rommel and his panzers were already in Libya when Vittorio arrived in Naples on March 31, 1941. His orders were to join the 7th Bersaglieri and embark on the Royal Ship *Marco Polo*. The destination was North Africa.

Vito had returned home on leave, so when he saw Vittorio at the pier he attempted to bring him back to Lucera, at least in thought:

"Lieutenant, I bring you the greetings of the notary Luigi, baroness Annita, your brothers and sisters. Maria, Elena, Clara and Ester asked me to give you this."

"Thank you Vito." answered Vittorio, as he unfurled an officer's *sache* that was so shiny it could only be used for the march into Cairo.

"I, on the other hand - said the orderly - have brought you this."

Vittorio put his hand in the envelope and laughed,

"And what do expect me to do with this thing?"

"Just like I do Lieutenant, you hang it on the belt loops of your pants."

"A red ivory horn? You want me to run around Africa with an officer's blue sache embroidered by my sisters and your twisted horn?"

"It has even been blessed, Lieutenant. I took it to the parish priest before leaving and asked him for the sign of the cross. It won't cost you anything, believe me!"

Vittorio hooked the horn to his belt loop and walked up the gangway to the *Marco Polo*. On the pier it was like Easter Sunday, with little children all decked out to the nines running after one another and waving at their fathers. The wives and fiancées of the soldiers were standing together, dressed with understated elegance, and the mothers had their cheeks streaked with tears.

Captain Comel, who had assigned Vito to be Vittorio's orderly at the Monte Rosa, saluted and went aboard a different ship in the same convoy to North Africa.

"Lieutenant Conte, this time I seriously doubt that we will be stopped by an armistice." They shook hands and made an appointment in Tripoli.

The advantage of being a veteran is that each one knows what to do. As the *Marco Polo* sailed out of the harbor Colonel Duranti, the commanding officer of the 7th Regiment, assembled the officers on deck. He didn't have much to say because everyone knew what to expect.

"We are going to take back Libya and win the war in Africa. Look at the Italian coastline now that we are about to sail around it, because the only way for us to come back will be through Alexandria and Cairo."

Then Duranti reminded them that they were Bersaglieri:

"The Germans of the Afrika Korps have already landed a few days ago. We must run, overtake them and stay ahead, because the land we are about to liberate belongs to the Italian Empire."

After a full day at sea the view of the Italian peninsula slowly disappeared, as the convoy that included the *Marco Polo* sailed south. Vittorio found the Colonel looking out into the horizon with his binoculars.

"Is what they are saying true, Sir?"

"It's true, Lieutenant Conte. Now all we can do is wait and hope for the best. Just like pheasants when the hunting season begins."

Beyond the horizon, what bothered Duranti most was the island of Malta. Geography dictated that it should be Italian but those rocks were occupied by the British. From the beginning it was obvious that it had to be taken, so that the convoys could sail back and forth with their supplies to Tripoli. But there was no time, no opportunity or even perhaps the will to undertake such an operation. Now, as the ships were beginning to pass through, they watched and prayed they would make it, because once they entered that sea lane there was nothing else they could do.

The alarm sounded off at midday, on April 1. Vito could hear it as he tidied up his bunk below deck in steerage and he ran up to the bridge to look for Vittorio.

"Vito, this is it!"

"What do you mean, Lieutenant?"

"The British are attacking us out of Malta. Distribute life vests to all the men in the unit."

"And not the rifles?"

"They'd only be in the way. If we must fire any shots the escort ships will do that."

"Nothing we can do at all then, sir?"

"That horn you gave me in Naples, is it really blessed?"

Vito looked down and ran off to get the life vests for himself and Vittorio, as he moved the men in the unit along. He returned to the bridge where the other squads were assembling. Scores of soldiers were suddenly at the mercy of events, when someone cried out:

"Torpedo in the water!"

Those close to the railing looked over. At first it wasn't easy to make anything out, but then you could see the splashes on the surface coming quickly toward the ship. The convoy maneuvered by opening up, with the ships moving to the side. The *Marco Polo* went through the motions to avoid being hit. There were long minutes of terror and helplessness on deck.

The path of the British torpedo then formed an arc. It moved to the side and missed by a wide angle, as it disappeared into the sea. Vito felt his hand gripping the horn as tight as he could.

"Torpedo in the water!" the same voice cried once more.

The Bersaglieri looked stunned. Months of training on bicycles, motorcycles, troop transports; all those hours of target practice with rifles, machine guns, hand grenades, to then die in a tin can a few miles off the coast of Sicily, just seemed too ironic.

"Jesus!" cried an officer near Vittorio. The second torpedo was easier to spot, since it was closer and more threatening. It skimmed through the water with the mindless determination of an unstoppable weapon. The convoy continued its counter measures, to get as far away as possible. On deck the men could only look on, most of them didn't even have the strength to curse.

The torpedo veered once again taking a complicated path and appeared about to strafe the hull of the *Marco Polo,* barely avoiding it. But this didn't give the Bersaglieri any relief. It moved directly and precisely toward the ship that was closest. The soldiers were forced to watch the cruel explosion that sent a tower of water jutting up in the air. Screams and flames could be heard on board, as comrades and friends they had known for months or days dropped into the sea. The wounded ship slowed down, listed and quickly keeled over. The only possible feeling was one of powerlessness. To witness death without having any way of defending yourself, not even the satisfaction of holding your head high and reacting.

The escort ships were in charge of the rescue, so there wasn't even the comfort of being able to help one's comrades. It would have been the alibi to justify your survival, before experiencing the confused pleasure of being still alive and on your way to Libya. Colonel Duranti lowered his binoculars and turned to his officers who were all silent.

"Only one loss. It's better than the other times."

***

Tripoli, the white bride of the Mediterranean, was both fascinatingly exotic and something of an imperial mirage for the soldiers arriving from Italy's provinces. In early spring it was already hot and attractive with the sounds, the temptations and the pungent odors of the souk, just beneath the red castle of Assai-al-Hamra overlooking the sea. On the right side of the harbor, beyond the palm trees, Vittorio and Vito looked with curiosity at the minarets of the oldest mosques of Othman Pasha, Draghut, Karamanli and Gurgi, and heard the rhythmic calls of the Muezzhins for the faithful to come to prayer. They saw the smaller shape of Sidi Abdul Wahab, the mosque that Mussolini wanted to knock down to give an unobstructed view of the Roman arch of Marcus Aurelius. On the left they were attracted to the lights of the Piazza Italia, the Corso Sicilia and the Via Torino, the elegant colonial streets that created the feeling of being in a truly Italian town erected on the African landscape.

Those who arrived with the *Marco Polo* convoy had no time to play tourist however, as their ships were being moored to the pier. It was April 2, 1941 and Rommel had just reoccupied Agedabia. Soon his panzers would split into three columns to reach Benghazi, El Mechili and Bir Tengeder, to cut the enemy's retreat back into Egypt. The British army of Sir Archibald Wavell seemed to only want to run away: if the Bersaglieri really intended to fly the Italian flag at the head of the counter offensive, they had to hurry and get up front.

Colonel Duranti ordered a series of forced marches and the 7th Regiment immediately took the Via Balbia on the coast, heading east to catch up on the one thousand kilometers that separated them from the front lines. The trucks rolled through Misurata and Sirte, that prior to Rommel's arrival were the last line of defense in front of Tripoli. Then there were El Nofilia, the marshes of El Aghelia and Marsa el Brega.

Beyond the coastline that was cultivated with olive trees, the Arabs watched the column with their usual indifference, unable to understand why their bald land was the theater of such harsh warfare. Vito saw them looking on and also wondered what he was doing in those fields, that were assuredly much harder and far less generous than the ones he was used to breaking his back on back in Puglia.

The nights were freezing and the days stifling with heat. As soon as they drifted away from the trail, the soldiers quickly learned about the first April "ghibli", the hot desert wind that mixes the sky and the land as it whips up the red sand into a frenzy.

Duranti's wishes became reality near El Mechili, where the Colonel finally saw Rommel's ghost. The *Desert Fox* had a plan to trap General Rimington's armored brigade, advancing toward Derna in the hope of opening a path to Tobruk. The Bersaglieri were useful at night when the exhausted British troops tried to rest near a wadi, one of those dried up riverbeds where the water flows only when it rains.

While waiting for Duranti to return from a meeting with German officers, Vittorio walked past the Afrika Korps panzers. If he hadn't seen it with his own eyes he wouldn't have believed it. Next to the massive tanks there were Volkswagen cars camouflaged to look like panzers. Every piece of equipment had branches tied to its sides, covering it all the way to the ground.

"When they start moving they'll look like twice their number, seen at a distance." said Vittorio to Vito.

The orderly answered with a sly twist:

"They are playing at confusing the enemy Lieutenant, Sir. That also serves a purpose."

Duranti assembled his officers behind a truck and handed out his orders for the attack. Vittorio's unit along with that of another officer would move around the wadi where, according to German spies, a British column was planning to stop. They were to attack from the rear at night. It would be pitch black around the dry riverbed and they would have to move in suddenly when a signal was given, and kill as many enemy soldiers as possible. They were not to follow those who fled since German units would be waiting for them further ahead.

There would be a tactical smoke signal. At war, if you happen to be hooked on nicotine, you'd never hold a cigarette so that turns it into a tiny glowing light. The tip must be cupped in your hand allowing it only to create a kind of vague afterglow. Once both units were in position the commanding officers would have a tactical smoke, serving as the signal for the attack to begin.

Vittorio's men slid across the banks of the wadi eluding all the sentries. At night even a tiny mound will make you invisible, if you know how to take advantage of it.

Very few men remained at the British camp and they were not expecting to stay there very long. Many of them were sleeping in their fatigues as soldiers need to at war, where you have to learn how to snooze with your head on the handle of an artillery piece inside a Matilda tank. Perhaps it was the fatigue, the disappointment of the retreat and the mistaken assessment of the distance separating them from the enemy. However it was certainly a major error that went against the rule book, because a tank that wasn't moving was a dead tank, as they teach you on the first day of training.

Once the entire unit was within the range of fire and the machine gun was set up on the ground, Vittorio extracted his cigarette from his pocket. Smoking had always been a pleasure, who could tell whether it could be once again. Vito tugged at him: a British sentry was coming closer to the edge of the wadi. The Bersaglieri on the other side of the bank extracted their bayonets from the scabbards to use them as daggers. The sentry came closer first looking up at the sky, then around for a moment, and then turned back toward his area without paying attention. From the other side of the wadi, where the second unit was in position, came the glow of the other tactical cigarette. Vittorio drew on his cigarette as well and the silence of the night was suddenly cracked by a series of explosions.

It was practically impossible to see anything. The machine guns were triangulating their fire to cover the space occupied by the enemy and the hand grenades were raining on the guards. You could hear screaming from the British camp where those who were awake and not yet hit were attempting to respond. The others started the engines of their trucks to move away from the ambush by the Italians, only to fall into the second one prepared by the waiting Germans. The tracers lit up the sky and besides the exploding hand grenades provided the only light to shine intermittently on the camp. The deafening noise was enough to frighten the men into pulling the trigger hysterically until it would jam.

Someone fell near Vittorio but there was no time for him to find out. The British were taken by surprise and attempted to escape: the men had to scramble beyond the protection of the wadi to finish off all those who were unable to flee. Vittorio jumped out, since there was no time to organize the assault waves. The men were firing on shadows they saw move in the darkness, hoping they were not hitting their own Bersaglieri who had moved ahead too fast. They were shooting instinctively out of anger and fear.

Two British trucks had been left behind: perhaps they had a broken track or had been hit by anti-tank rockets. The Bersaglieri bit off the latches on their hand grenades and threw them into the turrets - then hit the ground to avoid being hit by the shrapnel themselves.

Finally Vittorio saw his counterpart from the other unit a few dozen meters away, they had managed to close the circle around the British camp that no longer existed. Those who had not been hit had managed to fall into the trap set by Rommel's units that were waiting further ahead. The two commanding officers summoned their men.

Vito was looking at the Lieutenant to see whether the fighting was over.

"He was too close to miss," said Vittorio. The orderly walked next to him in silence. "Vito, I saw that English soldier die. I could see him even in the dark."

* * *

The days outside Tobruk were tedious and oppressively hot. There was nothing to do until the patrol and the daily firefight, and the sun created as much tension as the hours on guard duty.

After the offensive began at the beginning of April, Rommel sent his units beyond the border with Egypt to Sollum and the Halfaya Pass. He ordered the Italians - before they were placed under the overall command of Marshal Ettore Bastico, whom the German would tease by calling him "Bombastico" - to lay siege around the fortress that was still being held by the British and acted much like a tumor in the stomach.

Tobruk was on a tiny peninsula on the sea surrounded by high ground, an ideal location to receive supplies. The Italians had fortified Tobruk after the First World War as one of the key fortresses of the Empire in Libya.

Beyond the walls now under Axis control, were airfields like that of Acroma. The farthest defense perimeter, known as the red line, was some fifty kilometers long running east to west along the small mountains that surrounded the town. Barbed wire, machine gun nests, some observation points like Ras-el-Medam, that the soldiers called "Hill 209" and was the highest elevation of the area. Three or four kilometers inward, closer to the port, was the second line of defense known as the blue line. The area was flat but four forts: Parrone, Arienti, Solaro and Pilastrino threatened those who tried to come too close. The machine gun nests were dug into the rocky desert surface close to one another. Trenches made of reinforced concrete dotted the line with passageways, underground bunkers and anti-tank positions. Beyond this system stood the fortified city with some 36,000 British, Australian and Polish soldiers; 120 tanks and 76 artillery pieces, under the overall command of General Leslie Morshead. These were the "Desert Rats", as both Germans and Italians referred to them disparagingly once they had been encircled.

Vittorio's platoon was deployed in front of Fort Pilastrino. During the day, under a blinding sun that prevented him even from breathing, he was looking straight into the eyes of the Englishmen who were defending the city. The patrols from both sides came out at night and sometimes ran into one another, by mistake and at other times on purpose. Every night they would shoot at each other and some men would die without making any progress either way, not even a centimeter's worth. The rations were meager and disheartening, consisting mostly of biscuits and canned beef, and they spent the rest of the time hunting for lice that always managed to burrow their way into one's hair and clothing. Water was limited to half a liter a day and only for drinking, not to be used for washing. One morning the sky opened up to an unseasonable storm that rained out both British and Italians in their foxholes. The British waved a white flag and Vittorio went with Vito to meet them.

"They're requesting a 24-hour truce to dry their clothes," said the Lieutenant to his orderly. Vito nodded:

"Yes, it's like when it rains on the harvest and you try to save it from the hail stones."

Vittorio, who had flunked economics in college but had studied English, shook hands with his British opponent with his reddish hair, who appeared to have just graduated from the Royal Military College at Sandhurst. It was the first and only

official truce during the siege of Tobruk, even though neither
Bastico, Rommel nor Wavell knew anything about it.

The boredom ended in early June when Colonel Duranti
summoned Vittorio:

"In the middle of May" - explained the commanding officer
- "The British tried to throw us off with operation Brevity and
they failed. The Germans are convinced they will try again and
have decided to reinforce the defense on the border with Egypt.
You will move with your platoon to Fort Capuzzo."

It took a lot of imagination to think that a transfer inside
four walls in the middle of the desert was good news. Fort
Capuzzo was on the line that went from Halfaya Pass and
Sollum to Bardia and Tobruk. If the British decided to attack
that was the path they would take.

Seen from afar the fort looks rather ominous, like a medieval
castle. There's even a tiny church inside built like a hut made of
bricks. Vito thought it was like being in the country in Puglia, in
front of the walls of the "Cruste." Since there were very few
Generals and Colonels that would visit, you could walk around
in shorts and a tee shirt and smoke a cigarette.

"You're at home everywhere you go, aren't you?" said
Vittorio teasing his orderly.

"I learned to take things as they come, Lieutenant."

"All right but be careful not to let the vipers bite you - the
ones with horns."

"Why horns, Sir?"

"Do you think they have horns because they are unfaithful,
as we use to say in Italy?"

"I don't know, but as far as I can tell, all vipers are horned
bastards to be feared."

"You're right – said Vittorio laughing - . But around here the
vipers are known to have horns because they really have two
small horns on their head. Be careful, because they are extremely
deadly."

Vittorio looked across the Egyptian desert with his binoculars but couldn't see all the way out at sea, where the convoy named "Tiger" had already reached Alexandria. It delivered 238 tanks, among them the brand new Crusaders, as well as fresh orders signed by Winston Churchill. The prime minister was becoming impatient: the siege of Tobruk must be broken.

On the evening of June 14 Vito was on guard duty at the Fort that was already shrouded in the twilight. However the dust he could see rising in the distance hadn't been there during the previous sunsets. It also looked different from the sandstorms kicked up during the day by the wind - that started and died down like ghosts in the trenches. The sound it made was not that of the usual 'ghibli' wind.

He ran to warn Vittorio:

"Over there, Lieutenant."

It didn't take long to figure out once he looked through his binoculars:

"Duranti was correct. The Brits are trying once again."

Wavell had begun operation "Battleaxe", mostly to keep Churchill happy more than any other military consideration. But all Vittorio knew was that the dust in the air and the noise of the Matilda and Crusader tanks on the move were coming his way. He ordered the anti-tank 47/32 pieces to aim at the line leading up to the Fort. But once the tanks came in that close it would already be too late to stop them. Something had to be done long before they reached that point.

"Vito, take five men with all the grenades and explosive bottles you can find. Tell the artillery men to fire only when I give the order. And send a messenger to the rear to warn the Germans."

Ten minutes later Vittorio, Vito and five other Bersaglieri moved away from the Fort into the desert. There was a path the tanks had to take in order to attack Fort Capuzzo. You couldn't see it from the Fort itself and it was therefore out of artillery range. The British would feel safe up to that point. Vittorio took cover and waited just below the road the Matildas and Crusaders had to take.

The first and second tank in the column went ahead with their turrets turned to sweep the desert at a 180-degree angle. Vittorio remembered his training at Pola. He knew that the pilots were blind when you got up close to the turrets, a few meters away, because they couldn't see what was going on under their tank. The Crusader was advancing slowly with its hatch still open, its tracks crushing the rocks as the earth shook under its weight. The metallic howling of the engine filled the air like a physical presence that shakes the lungs and makes it hard to breathe.

Once the tank was five meters away, Vittorio rolled over onto the road, and placed himself in between the tanks' tracks so the Crusader would keep rolling above him. It was a matter of endless seconds. Then he climbed up on the engine from the rear and dropped a grenade down the hatch before jumping off. The explosion echoed inside the turret. The other Bersaglieri threw their incendiary bombs at the second tank forcing it to stop. The fire inside the tank drew the soldiers out and they were cut down by Italian gunfire.

The rest of the column saw the ambush from a few hundred meters' distance and stopped, allowing Vittorio's squad enough time to scramble back to the Fort. The tanks moved forming a line as though they were about to attack. But they also lost the protection afforded by the terrain they were using as a cover against shelling by the 47/32 artillery pieces. Vittorio gave the order to open fire. The anti-tank guns were too weak but occasionally they could do the job. With a bit of luck they could even dent the thick armor of the slow moving Matildas, or at least make enough noise to scare them off. The British column hesitated, slowed down and then stopped to move back to safety and then regroup.

Capuzzo was taken the next day like Halfaya and Sollum. But when Wavell's tanks arrived their losses were far superior to what Churchill expected and they found that the Fort was empty. The action taken the day before gave Vittorio enough time to fall back, allowing the Germans to stage their own attack. Wavell advanced again until the evening of the 15th but on the following dawn Rommel began his counter attack with the 15th Panzer Division. On June 17 Capuzzo and Halfaya were again in German hands and Churchill was signing orders to replace General Wavell with General Claude Auchinleck, the British army commander in India. Rommel asked to review the Italian units that had taken part in the defense with proposals for medals to all those who distinguished themselves.

Vito had tucked his shirt back into his canvas trousers and stood at attention next to his Lieutenant. The Desert Fox arrived standing up in his command car and jumped off. He walked past the assembled troops. An interpreter approached but the General stopped him with his hand. He looked at the men and said in Italian: "The German soldier has amazed the world. The Bersaglieri have amazed the German soldier." Vito couldn't help notice the red horn that was hanging from Vittorio's trousers for good luck. It was broken.

7.

"But this is precisely what we find incomprehensible: how is it possible that we didn't think of improving our harbor defenses?" Alberto continued to ask himself the same question and couldn't come up with an answer, as he walked along the pier at Taranto.

In early March 1941 his brother Federico, who had attended the military school at Acqui to be an officer candidate, came to visit while on leave. He arrived to celebrate Alberto's promotion to captain and tried to cheer him up by teasing:

"Your career is moving faster than Marcello Petacci's. Are you sure you don't have one of the Fascist leaders' wife as a girl-friend?" "Shut up" answered Alberto, "don't even mention that draft dodger's name. He pretends to play doctor on board ship, but since he is the brother of the Duce's lover the only thing the ship's captain can think of is to make sure that nothing should happen to Marcello. If he is on a ship it's as if it were going on a cruise rather than into battle."

"No, Alberto, keep quiet" interrupted Federico, "I don't think you should say such things, not in public at least."

Alberto had been promoted to captain and assigned to Supermarina, the navy's central command in Rome. A special mission took him to Taranto.

"Do you realize what happened here?" he suddenly asked his brother.

"I did hear something" said Federico.

"Well, I'm preparing a report for the high command. Have you any idea how important the base at Taranto is to Italy?"

"Very important."

"More than that. It is our key naval base in the eastern Mediterranean. From here we can control access to the Adriatic, the coasts of Greece and Yugoslavia and even take back Malta, freeing the routes for the convoys to Libya."

Federico agreed.

"The British understood this long ago, so much so in fact that in 1935 Admiral Lyster had prepared plans to attack our fleet inside the port of Taranto using torpedo planes. We had the same weapons but simply decided not to develop them further."

"So?" asked Federico.

"Well, immediately following the declaration of war Admiral Andrew Cunningham, now in overall command of the Mediterranean fleet, thought Lyster's strategy was a good one. He revived the old plans and modified them with an innovative idea that was guaranteed to humiliate us."

"What do you mean?"

"The plan was to take the aircraft carriers *Illustrious* and *Eagle* followed by battleships, cruisers and destroyers, up to one hundred miles off our coastline. Then attack without any opposition as if he were on a holiday cruise. We found out and guess what the Admirals decided? They sent a patrol into the Sicilian channel and concentrated the bulk of the fleet at Taranto: the battleships *Andrea Doria, Caio Duilio, Cavour, Giulio Cesare, Littorio, Vittorio Veneto* and the heavy cruisers *Zara, Pola, Trento, Trieste, Fiume* etc."

Federico was shaking his head: "A trap we manufactured ourselves."

"Precisely. You know what Cunningham said, when his reconnaissance forces informed him of the Italian moves?"

"I can just imagine."

"He said: 'all the pheasants are in their nest.'"

Alberto kept on walking and said:

"To think that the carrier *Eagle* was unable to stay with the convoy because it had engine trouble. Yet the admiral was so confident that he kept on going ahead anyway with half his strength."

"And how had we prepared our defenses?" asked Federico.

"As usual, meaning, poorly. We were supposed to have about ninety "balloons" in the air to prevent planes from flying in low over the port, but two thirds had been torn away by the high winds and not replaced. The ships were supposed to be protected by anti-torpedo netting but we only had half the required quantity."

"Why is that?"

"Because of that animal of Undersecretary Cavagnari…"

"Quiet, are you crazy? Why do you talk that way?"

"That animal of an Undersecretary that Mussolini had named to lead the navy only knew how to promote himself. He spent millions of lire building ships of doubtful usefulness, only to have them cruise for show in the Gulf of Naples. But he didn't invest a cent in radio locators, telemetric devices, infrared electronic machines for night fighting and other necessary accessories to compete against the British, simply because you couldn't see them and he would therefore not be able to boast about them. Without even mentioning the issue of aircraft carriers: the Duce says that Italy is one giant aircraft carrier and all the Admirals kept silent. Not one of them had the guts to open his mouth and tell him that we can't bomb Alexandria in Egypt using Calabria as a battleship."

"So how did the attack take place?" asked Federico.

"The only way it could. At eight thirty in the evening on November 11, 1940 the first wave of Swordfish torpedo planes took off from the *Illustrious*. By eleven they were flying over Taranto and had managed to sink the *Cavour*. The second wave came at eleven thirty to finish the job and hit the *Caio Duilio*, the *Littorio* and so forth. It was a real pheasant shoot. Half of our fleet was knocked out in ninety minutes."

"Incredible."

"Cunningham dubbed it "Operation: Judgement Day", the judgement day of poor Italian planning." Finally Alberto lowered his voice when he saw a sailor looking at him from the pier.

"Good evening, Lieutenant. Oh, I am sorry, I hadn't noticed your new rank in the darkness, sir."

"Sailor Solustri, what are you doing in Taranto?"

"I am on the cruiser *Zara* Captain. We have been here a few days."

"Well, how about that! The *Zara* was the first ship I was assigned to right after graduating from the academy."

"It's a great ship, Captain."

Alberto nodded and pointed to the person next to him.

"Solustri, this is my brother Federico. He is also an officer and just switched from the Army to the Navy."

"You have chosen correctly, sir. I'm very honored to meet you. Sailor Arturo Solustri."

Federico shook hands while Alberto explained: "He was with me in Albania when we landed. A very brave man."

"Thank you, Captain. But I shall leave you with your brother now. Excuse my interruption and congratulations on your promotion."

"Thank you Solustri. And be careful with my *Zara*."

* * *

On March 28, 1941 Alberto was still on duty at the base in
Taranto. He would stand for twenty four hours straight, just like
all his other colleagues around him. Three days before the Italian
navy had started its most ambitious mission since the war began:
to cut off the British convoys that were sailing from Egypt to
supply their troops in Greece, that were still putting up a tough
resistance against the Germans. Admiral Raeder, the commander
in chief of the German Navy, had requested as much to Admiral
Riccardi, his Italian counterpart, when they met in February at
Merano. And once again Mussolini was unable to say no to
Hitler.

At noon Alberto was at the command center while in Rome
the naval chief of staff and Admirals Campioni, Fioravanzo,
Ferreri and de Courten were reviewing the situation.

Riccardi began his review.

"So, this is what we know up to now. Admiral Iachino, in
overall command, left Naples on the 26th on the battleship
Vittorio Veneto. From Messina sailed the 3rd division under
Admiral Sansonetti; from Brindisi the 6th with the *Duca degli
Abruzzi* led by Rear Admiral Legnani; and out of Taranto the 1st
with cruisers *Zara*, *Pola* and *Fiume* under Admiral Cattaneo. Their
mission was to move toward Crete to intercept and sink British
supply convoys on their way to Greece. German intelligence
informed us with certainty that Admiral Cunningham had only
one battleship left at Alexandria, since the Luftwaffe claims to
have sunk two of them. Admiral Campioni, please take over."

Riccardi let his colleague in charge of operations continue
the briefing:

"At 12:25 on the 27th the *Trieste* signaled to Iachino the
presence of a British reconnaissance vessel, the *Sunderland,* that
had spotted our fleet moving ahead. We nevertheless kept on
course but found no British convoys sailing toward Greece. This
morning at 07:55 the cruisers *Trieste*, *Trento* and *Bolzano* made
contact with four enemy ships near Gaudo. At 08:12 they

opened fire but didn't sink the ships. They were in pursuit for about one hour and then changed course in the expectation of luring them toward Iachino's ships. At 10:55 the *Vittorio Veneto* spotted the British ships and opened fire but the enemy cruiser got away. Shortly after the *Vittorio Veneto* came under fire from British torpedo planes and Iachino decided to change course."

Campioni stopped briefly and concluded:

"Right now the situation stands as follows. Our units are on their way back to their bases. There were no British supply convoys in the area they were patrolling. The presence of enemy ships has been signaled but we do not know exactly their size and location. Your instructions are to remain in constant contact with us and the units at sea to prepare for their return and defend the port of Taranto."

Alberto looked at his colleagues in silence as he waited for the connection to the admirals at Supermarina to end without any other comments. Once it was clear that Rome was no longer on the air, Admiral Tosi, the commanding officer, spoke for everyone:

"What they have just told us is that we fell into a trap. A trap of our own making. The largest naval squadron since the beginning of the war reached Crete without finding what it was looking for. On the other hand the British managed to find us, so now Cunningham is hunting us down."

Tosi looked at his officers for a moment, to give them enough time to digest the bad news and see how they reacted. Then he went on:

"Unfortunately that's not the end of it. Iachino turned around because he knows that he has no air cover and therefore as we speak he is completely exposed to enemy attack. As if that were not enough, we also don't know the exact strength of the British since no air reconnaissance was able to corroborate the Luftwaffe claim of sinking two battleships. The enemy appears on the other hand to be perfectly well informed about our course."

Tosi concluded with his orders:

"From now on all leave is suspended. Prepare the base for defensive measures and maintain open lines to Rome and the units at sea. I want to know about any developments immediately."

The news didn't take long to arrive: at around 15:30 hours Alberto knocked on the admiral's door.

"Captain Conte, what do you have?"

Alberto handed over a sheet of paper.

"We received this dispatch. The *Vittorio Veneto* was again under enemy attack by torpedo planes and bombers at 15:09 hours. As yet we have no information on the extent of the damage."

"Thank you." The Admiral left his desk and went over to the radio room.

At 17:30 hours a new message came in:

"The left outer propeller of the *Vittorio Veneto* was hit in the 15:09 attack and took in 4000 tons of water. At first the ship had to stop but at 16:42 it managed to move again. Maximum speed is reduced to 19 knots."

Tosi read the dispatch and covered his forehead with his hand:

"From now on it's going to be a rat hunt. Cunningham knows that Iachino is wounded and he won't let go until he manages to take him." No one was breathing in the command room. Fatigue and tension had drained the strength away from the officers to voice any comments. They could only wait. Around 20:30 hours the hunt came to an end and Alberto read the dispatch he was hoping to avoid:

"Between 19:36 and 19:50 hours a very brutal attack by torpedo planes hit the cruiser *Pola*. The ship has stopped in the area off Cape Matapan."

Tosi first called Supermarina in Rome, then tried to contact Iachino at sea. Afterwards he called in the officers for a report:

"The worse has happened. The *Vittorio Veneto* is almost safe but *Pola* is adrift. Iachino ordered Admiral Cattaneo to change course to go help the ship with the cruisers *Zara* and *Fiume* and the destroyers Alfieri, *Gioberti, Carducci* and *Oriani.* Supermarina is silent and therefore agrees. Perhaps they have better intelligence on Cunnigham's position than we have. May God help them." May God help the *Zara* - thought Alberto - that was now forced to sail toward the enemy in the dark to save the *Pola.* He remembered sailor Salustri and all his other friends on board with whom he had shared his first posting.

"Sir" said Alberto addressing Tosi, "Are you sure this is the best option? I was on duty on the *Zara* when I started out. It's a beautiful ship but it has no radar and the crew has very little experience with night combat."

"Captain Conte, you are an optimist. Our crews don't know how to fight in the dark: that's all there is to it. Our only hope is that the British are also unable to do so."

The minutes slipped by turning into a painfully long wait. Supermarina remained silent like the radio and the other instruments. The only certainty was that the *Vittorio Veneto* was on its way back to Italy. Everything else was up for grabs, a matter of pure luck.

It was almost 23:00 hours when the command center received its first communication in hours: "Units under attack off Cape Matapan." That was all.

"What does this mean?" asked Tosi out loud.

"Which units were attacked by whom?"

Supermarina responded that the situation was not clear. Iachino could see the glow of explosions where he had sent Cattaneo to retrieve the *Pola,* but he was unable to make contact with the crew on board to find out what was happening.

Silence, waiting and anxiety gripped the command center at Taranto. No one had the courage to make any comments or speculate, because the officers were reluctant to say out loud what everyone was logically thinking.

At dawn a new message came in, but it was in English, directly from Cunningham this time. The British admiral said he was leaving the area of battle around Cape Matapan because of attacks from German planes. He confirmed that he had taken all the Italian survivors he could on board but that many were still in the water. So before leaving he was sending their coordinates to Supermarina. Riccardi answered that the hospital ship *Gradisca* was already on its way and thanked him.

On the evening of March 29 Admiral Tosi called in his officers who were all completely exhausted, for a final report.

"Gentlemen, at this time I don't know whether to tell you that the pain for the loss of our colleagues and friends is greater than the shame at the way we behaved. Matapan is the Italian navy's Caporetto at sea." Alberto came closer to the table where the map was unfolded as the admiral recounted the last news he had received:

"Somehow Cunningham knew what was going on. He left Alexandria as early as the 27th, leaving a night club by the back door to avoid being recognized. The Luftwaffe made some very big mistakes. The British ships had either not been sunk or had been replaced. In any case Cunningham had the battleships *Warspite*, *Valiant* and *Barham* besides the aircraft carrier *Formidable*. Clearly Iachino was not sailing toward supply convoys at all, because they had already been interrupted. Without his knowledge he was heading toward an extremely powerful battle fleet."

Tosi stopped as the officers kept silent and then went on. "It was already too late when we decided to change course, since we had no air cover, while Cunningham had his planes ready on the deck of the *Formidable* plus those on the bases in Crete and in

Greece. The British hit the *Vittorio Veneto* from the air since they knew it was faster than their ships and that was the only way to stop it. But instead of stopping the battleship they crippled the *Pola*. In the meantime Supermarina found out about an enemy fleet at sea but had the wrong information as to its size and distance. Then Iachino sent Cattaneo to bring back the *Pola* without knowing that he was dispatching him to go straight to Cunningham."

Alberto shook his head, and kept silent like his colleagues. The admiral went on.

"Around 22:20 hours on the 28th, when we received the message of the attack, the cruisers *Zara* and *Fiume* had just arrived alongside the *Pola*. However the British were also on location, around 3000 meters away. Since we had no radar we couldn't see them, while they knew everything about us. They turned on the projectors for night fighting and began firing. They were basically doing target practice. Lobbing shells over 1000 kilos each, they sank the *Zara*, the *Fiume* and the destroyers *Alfieri* and *Carducci*. Cunningham finished the job by sinking the *Pola*. The results are still temporary but there may have been some 2303 dead Italian sailors: 782 on the *Zara*; 813 on the *Fiume*; 328 on the *Pola*; 211 on the *Alfieri* and 169 on the *Carducci*. Admiral Cattaneo was also among the dead."

Alberto hit the back of the armchair with his hand. Tosi called him to order:

"Supermarina is aware that those men were your friends and colleagues. Specially those who sailed from Taranto with whom you were on duty. They know you have been through some terrible moments during these last three days. Therefore Admiral Riccardi wishes to speak to you. He is connected from Rome."

The voice of the navy's chief of staff came across filling the silence of the room:

"Italy thanks you for your work and your sacrifice. Tell your men that those who gave their lives were heroes who went down fighting to the end. It was only chance that defeated them, not the lack of valor. But we will know how to avenge them."

Tosi saluted and thanked Riccardi. Once the line with Rome was silent however the admiral added: "Perhaps it wasn't just bad luck that defeated us. Perhaps there is also a traitor, since it was rather odd that Cunningham knew about all our movements with such accuracy. If there was a British spy I guarantee you that we will find him and that he will pay."

8.

"The Federal Secretary has been informed by the Command of a Bersaglieri Regiment in North Africa about the excellent behavior in combat by Second Lieutenant of the Reserves Vittorio Conte, son of Luigi, our fellow citizen and among the most active organizers of the G.I.L.* The Commander underscores that Conte, in charge of a platoon, full of enthusiasm and energy in the course of a violent enemy attack consisting of infantry and tanks, regardless of danger, with energetic and rapid fire was able to concentrate enough pressure on the enemy to force him to end his attempt to encircle the position held by the company. Because of his action Conte has been proposed for the medal for Military Valor.

As we are reminded once again how our young people behave, thanks to the education they have received in the new Fascist atmosphere, as they face the challenges and greatest dangers for the Homeland's imperial greatness, we send to the family of our brave comrade our fraternal and proud congratulations."

---

* GIL stood for Gioventù Italiana del Littorio was the Fascist party's university student movement.

That was published on page 2 of the fortnightly bulletin *Il Littorio* of Lucera, issued by the Fasces of combat on September 1, 1941. Luigi, the notary, placed his round rimmed glasses on his desk, folded the clipping and put it back in the drawer to be sure he would not lose it. He never expected to read news of his children in the local newspaper and was unsure whether to share in the pride of those printed words or be fearful and worried instead.

"They are your sons" said the Baroness Annita, as she could sense her husband's preoccupation. "Yes, but I have trouble coping with certain things" answered Luigi.

"What do you mean?"

"Vittorio is impulsive and aggressive, this we already knew. Until a short time ago he was only really interested in chasing skirts. He didn't like to study and perhaps he found the identity he has been seeking in the Fascist rhetoric, in the myth of the homeland, the adventure of war. But Alberto?"

"Alberto what about him…?" asked his wife.

"I don't know. He was always the reflective type, a detached intellectual, I would say. Why did he insist on wearing a uniform when he could have done anything he wanted?"

"What do you think?"

"He was always interested in politics. But why would he have the same kind of motivations as Vittorio?"

***

Vito was sitting on his feathered helmet in his foxhole facing Fort Pilastrino. Those were strange days, filled with the boredom of waiting that was interrupted only by sporadic firefights with the enemy. Tobruk was not falling and yet the German Italian siege was not allowing its prey to live in peace. Rommel was not mounting attacks into Egypt and the British were not-counter attacking. General Auchinleck, the new commander, "Auk" as his men called him, didn't think he was ready.

Vittorio looked at his orderly who was extracting some old pieces of paper from his crumpled jacket and decided to tease him:

"Are you writing to your fiancée?"

"If I only knew how lieutenant! I can't read or write and neither can she. Like two deaf mutes who start screaming."

"So what is that stuff?"

"A picture. At least I can look at her."

Vittorio looked at it and asked:

"Homesick?"

"No, Lieutenant. Well, a little bit, yes. Right now I'd feel better with her rather than under this sun that's broiling my brains."

"Do you think you should have such thoughts while you're at war?"

"Lieutenant, I have those thoughts precisely because I'm at war. If they kill us tomorrow at least today I can look at my fiancée's picture."

Vittorio smiled:

"Don't you ever feel like having some fun? Like those exotic girls under the veils that we saw at Tripoli."

"What does exotic mean?"

"Different, Vito...special."

"I think my fiancée is special. We've been together since we were fifteen, without our parents knowing it. Don't you think that's special?"

"You're just as headstrong as a mule!"

"I was born among the mules, lieutenant. And you?"

"Me, what?"

"I mean the fiancée, not the mules."

"Well..."

"I know there are rumors going around the village..."

"What kind of rumors?"

"That you're having a good time. How do they say in Naples, at the university? A womanizer, right?"

"Some womanizer, Vito. In the middle of the desert?"

"So where is your fiancée's picture?"

"What does that have to do with it? Not everyone is as lucky as you are."

"True Lieutenant, very true."

"So, do you want to write her a letter or not?"

"How would I do that?"

"I'll write it for you. Then the parish priest will read it to her."

"Yes, Lieutenant, …thank you."

"Come here. Tell me: what do you want to tell her?"

* * *

The boredom of waiting and the peace and quiet all came to an end on November 18, 1941. "Auk" had received the reinforcements he was expecting and decided to please Churchill by beginning the hunt for the Desert Fox.

Operation "Crusader", as the British general decided to call it, began with tanks crossing the barbed wire fences between Egypt and Libya in the direction of Sidi Rezegh and Bir el Gobi. The objective was to break the siege of Tobruk and if possible throw Rommel back into the sea. The problem was that at the same time Rommel was also planning to put "Auk" back on a ship and was in the process of preparing his offensive for the end of the month. So a surreal kind of battle began, with divisions running after one another to attack behind the enemy's back and getting confused in the dust of their tracks. The confusion was so great that at times Vittorio's platoon was moving like a billiard ball running after changes at the front in the desert. Sidi Omar, Halfaya, El Duda: forward and back according to the decisions of the commander in chief of the Afrika Korps.

On December 7 Rommel decided that perhaps the best way to win was in effect to run away, forcing the enemy to run after him in a crazy race, that would tire him out by drawing the supply lines longer and opening up his flank for the coming counter offensive. For the first time in eight months the Desert Fox was ready to give up on the siege of Tobruk.

Someone had to provide cover for the retreat. Vittorio's platoon was given the task of defending Acroma, where one of the airfields was located in the outskirts of town. The Germans were slipping away in a strategic retreat while the British were in hot pursuit seconded by the "Tobruk Rats", who could at last leave their hiding place. Vittorio and his men were to remain isolated in the middle. The orders were to resist, slow down the British advance and possibly survive as a thorn in the enemy's rear.

"Someone has to do it" - said the lieutenant as he handed the men their orders - "But remember that what we do may decide who will control Cyrenaica a few months from now. And then at last get us ready for the push into Egypt."

The Bersaglieri agreed and began preparing the fortified position using sandbags, foxholes dug into the rocky surface and machine guns dug into the ground. They were to expect attacks coming from all directions.

RAF planes were beginning to sweep across the front since the German Stukas had abandoned the sky as they were anticipating the return of the British. Clusters of bombs were followed by long machine gun blasts. Then came the units of the 11th Hussars, the Australians, the Polish infantrymen from the Carpathian Mountains and finally the British Crusader tanks. Vito was wearing his helmet low over his forehead, while bullets rained like a hail storm over the harvest. Vittorio was handling a machine gun heated by firing and dried up by the dust. He opened a can of lubricating oil and cursed out loud: "Lemon juice! Those stevedore bastards at the port of Naples stole the oil to sell it on the black market and filled our cans with lemon juice."

Vito pulled his helmet down even lower and said nothing. Vittorio went on shooting: "Traitors, we are here to die while they boycott us."

By December 12 Rommel had almost succeeded. He was running from Ain-el-Gazala to Agedabia, in spite of the objections of the Italian commanding officers who didn't want to abandon Cyrenaica, even though the immediate objective was to run away from the enemy to return in force later on.

Vittorio's platoon was cut in half but was still able to hold on for one week. That was one whole week without sleep, with water being nothing more than a memory, and under constant British fire. One morning Vittorio finally fell asleep on a pile of bombs. Vito came to wake him up:

"Lieutenant, please excuse me sir, but all you need here is half a cigarette to blow yourself up, sky high!"

The RAF was back at night because "Auk" was tired of waiting around: he was to follow the Desert Fox rather than waste time with these bums. The earth around the stronghold was shaking amid the explosions and the noise was so intense that it covered the machine gun.

At first Vittorio didn't understand. He felt a sharp hot flash behind his ear but it had happened before. Then he saw the Bersaglieri screaming but he couldn't hear them. He tried to move his arm to take aim but felt as if his limbs were responding in slow motion. He was observing his own movements as though he were removed from his body and felt a muffled blast all around him.

Angered by his loss of orientation he decided to shake it off by running to another position of the stronghold. But his legs tangled him up and refused to follow the decisions of his mind.

He had trouble deciding how he was to walk, then he staggered and finally fell.

"Lieutenant!" Vito cried out as he went up to him: "Lieutenant, Lieutenant!" he kept on yelling. Vittorio saw him but failed to understand. Vito ran his hand behind Vittorio's head and showed him how it was covered with blood. "Lieutenant, you're wounded!"

Vittorio saw the bloodied hand of his orderly, felt the pain and pushed him away.

"Get out of here Vito! They are going to kill us all. Go, get out!"

"Lieutenant, you're wounded. Let me take a look where."

Vittorio felt that he was losing consciousness but kept on yelling:

"Vito, for God's sake, it's an order! Go away!"

9.

"The admirals are saying that they want to find the traitor of Matapan and have him shot. Do you understand?"

Alberto was in his office at the Ministry of the Navy where he had returned after the bloodbath off the coast of Greece. His brother Federico was sitting in front of his desk; since his switch from the army to the navy Federico had also been assigned to the Ministry. Together they shared a house at 58 Lungotevere Flaminio.

"Wouldn't they just open an inquiry?" asked Federico.

"Certainly, if there were reasons to do so."

"What do you mean?"

"I was there, Federico. I had also been on board one of the ships that had been sunk; I knew their strong and weak points perfectly well. I also know how the operation had been prepared and I followed the battle from the operational headquarters at Taranto by the minute."

"So then what happened?"

Alberto came closer to his brother and lowered his voice to a whisper:

"If there is one traitor in this whole massacre it is Super-marina itself. The admirals are the traitors because before the war they didn't give our units the instruments we needed and the necessary training. Then they sent the ships off to the four winds with plans that were improvised, only because they were unable to say no to the Duce."

Federico stared at him in disbelief:

"How can you prove such an accusation? What I mean is that I agree it's possible that we were not prepared to undertake an operation like the one off Cape Matapan. Fine. But to then say that the admirals sent their ships off to the slaughter knowingly, is something altogether different."

"It all depends on the communications that took place that night. If there were proof that Supermarina knew about the threat, then it behaved criminally. If the admirals gave their orders in good faith, then they had to be incompetent. I can't tell which is worse."

Federico answered without hesitation

"Incompetence is not honorable for the commanders, but it is still far better than criminal intent."

"Of course, but then you agree with the point I'm trying to make."

"Meaning?"

Alberto leaned over toward his brother:

"The only way to start an inquiry regarding the traitor of Cape Matapan is to say that the culprit is a ghost, thereby avoiding an investigation and having to admit to true responsibility. But this way we'll never fix our mistakes and shortcomings and next time there will be another massacre."

"I understand."

"No Federico, unfortunately you can't understand. There's more to it but we'll talk about that some other time."

* * *

Admiral Malceri summoned Alberto to his office. When he walked in he showed him a short document. It read: "Safe conduct for Captain of the Royal Navy Conte, Alberto." Inside there was an identity head shot of Alberto in civilian clothes, wearing his gray pin striped suit with a vest, and a conservative tie. Description: 1,73 meters, regular build, light brown hair, blue eyes, fair complexion, clean shaven, small scar on the chin." On the second page, under two rubber stamps of the Royal Navy High Command, the detail of his mission was spelled out:

"Captain Conte is being sent on a mission to Athens."

Once Alberto had read the instructions, Malceri asked: "Captain, do you know what this is all about?"

"I think I do."

The admiral took him by the arm:

"No, no way. Look, let's stop playing around. I've known you since you were a cadet at the Naval Academy. You were one of my best students and in fact you have advanced faster than any of your fellow officers in the Navy. But this time there's more than just a promotion at stake."

Alberto looked at Malceri.

"I don't understand."

"You understand perfectly well, but since I must be as clear as possible, I will tell you."

"Please."

"Captain Conte, you know that Admiral Iachino is convinced that someone informed the British before the battle of Cape Matapan?"

"Yes, everyone knows that."

"Good. Then you also know that the high command at Supermarina want to start an inquiry since discovering a traitor would in many ways...lighten their responsibility."

"Obviously."

"If this is all clear captain, then you should know that your department is the number one suspect." Aberto stared at the frozen expression on Malceri's face.

"You have heard me correctly Captain, and you probably already knew it."

"Admiral, the *Zara* was my first assignment on board ship. During the night of the battle I was at Taranto and I lost fellow sailors who were brothers to me."

"I know, I was the one to assigned you on that ship. However you are one of the people that are being scrutinized. You are thought of as a potential culprit because you were in the best position to pass along information and also due to your mastery of English. And then, quite frankly, your ideas are no secret to anyone."

"What do you mean?"

"Captain Conte, you have always had a mind of your own. I can attest to that since I was correcting your papers at the Academy. This helped you in your career but also aroused some jealousy among your fellow officers. Some people believe that someone with your disposition could be inclined to create surprises."

"Admiral, please forgive me if I ask. It's only because of the respect and confidence I have in you. Am I being investigated?"

"Well, that's where the document I gave you comes into play."

"Why do you want me to go to Greece?"

"Because that's where the solution to the problem may be."

"Can you be more specific?"

"Captain Conte, you have understood correctly that I'm not one of those who is suspicious of you. Had that not been the case I wouldn't have summoned you to my office and wouldn't have spoken as freely, in a way that some of my colleagues would think of as treason. Therefore I must ask you for your absolute discretion."

"It is in both our interests Admiral."

"Good. This safe conduct could be your last opportunity. The only way to get out of trouble, if I were in your shoes, would be to find out the truth before you get stuck with an accusation."

"How do I do that?"

"Greece is now under Axis control so we have a better opportunity to find out what really happened at Cape Matapan. Your official cover is a mission to verify our supply routes to Athens. Once you reach the city one of our men will pick you up and take you to our agent. All you have to do is meet with him and listen to what he has to say. Let's hope it will be enough to stave off the accusations."

Alberto used the trip to the Brindisi air station as an opportunity to organize his thoughts:

"The admirals sent my comrades to their death and now, to cover up their mistakes, they are seeking to sling mud at me and who knows how many others."

Something was shattered. His loyalty to Italy wasn't in doubt, since the homeland was only an involuntary spectator of the tragedy. Yet his superiors, and the regime itself, had become ruthless adversaries ready to sacrifice anything to preserve their narrow interests. There were no good intentions toward the country behind the plot. The only possible move was to find the mistakes and correct them to avoid them from recurring once again. But that kind of sensible position was not even being considered. The only thing they were thinking about was how to save their armchairs. If along the way someone was to lose his life, so what: he was expendable in any case.

He went through the checkpoints at Brindisi quickly and the flight to Athens took about one hour. Arriving in the Greek capital under German military control the safe conduct from the high command worked wonders. It was like an order that couldn't be discussed.

"You are here on official business?" asked the guard checking his travel documents. "Yes" answered Alberto, who was dressed in civilian clothes as shown in his identity photograph. There were no further questions. The captain remembered his high school studies and his love of classical literature. He felt like running up to the Acropolis to spend a whole day amid the ruins of the Parthenon but the car was waiting to drive him to Piraeus for the inspection of supply convoys.

Once inside the car the driver handed him a sealed envelope with his orders. But inside he only found a slip of paper with a dinner date in a restaurant at the Plaka, a maze of busy streets in downtown Athens. Malceri's contact likes the night life, thought Alberto. According to his instructions he would recognize him from the light blue color of his breast pocket handkerchief. But the informer would be the one to recognize him since he had seen his photograph.

After the first inspection at Piraeus, Alberto agreed to finish the following day and asked the driver to take him to the most obvious place for any foreigner to visit in Athens. He tipped the driver and entered the Plaka area on foot.

The restaurant was a few hundred meters away and the short walk helped him relax and feel like an ordinary traveler. It was not a small place. As soon as Alberto took off his rain coat a tall man with reddish hair came up to him with a smile as though he were meeting an old friend.

"Good evening, Mr. Conte" said his host in almost perfect English. The handkerchief seemed to be the right one.

"Good evening, it's a pleasure to meet you" answered Alberto.

"My pleasure, shall we take a table?"

"Please lead the way."

The host went on making small talk while the waiter handed out the menus.

"I always loved this city, even though our Lord Elgin had torn it apart. Do you know the history?"

Alberto nodded.

"The marble statues that Lord Elgin took from the Parthenon back to London in the nineteenth century."

"Yes but don't think that all British subjects were pleased about that. Do you know who protested the loudest?"

"No I don't."

"Lord Byron. He even wrote some poisonous lines about Lord Elgin's robbery."

"I must remember to read them."

"And do you know which is the oddest coincidence?"

"No, but please tell me" answered Alberto, who by now was feeling confused.

"When the marble statues were shipped off to London part of the cargo sank off Cape Matapan. It would take two full years and quite a bit of money before Lord Elgin could salvage all the lost pieces. To rethread history requires a lot of patience and determination."

The waiter walked away and Alberto, even more disoriented, simply nodded politely.

"Of course."

"For example" continued his host, "did you ever hear about Enigma - the German machine to encrypt secret messages?"

"That's intelligence department information," Answered Alberto reacting with surprise.

"So, you must know that you Italians also use it and are convinced that it is very secure."

"That's what you say."

"You also know that it is being used by the smallest cargo ships that have machines on board to decrypt information in code."

"Go on."

"This means that all it would take was to capture an Italian or German ship in the Mediterranean, and get on board quickly enough knowing what to look for, to find the key to the Enigma machine."

"It makes sense."

"Or that a very clever mathematician could solve the conundrum in a lab situation."

"That's more difficult, but possible."

"Good, did you ever hear about Ultra?"

"Maybe."

"Then you should know that that would be the place to look, if you want to find your traitor. Should such a person even exist."

"How should I look?"

"It seems to me that you have already started."

Alberto nodded and his host went on.

"Now listen to me carefully. In a few seconds I will get up to go to the bathroom. You will call the waiter to order dinner for two, with different kinds of plates. Don't wait for me to start eating. I will not be back."

10.

Vittorio was having difficulty opening his eyes. Before the images, before the senses, there came a sharp pain starting from the ear and running back up into the brain. Vittorio turned instinctively in his bed to shift his weight to the part of his head that was less painful. Then his eyelids allowed the sunlight to filter through. There were the muffled sounds of footsteps and a few moans. The smell of alcohol disinfectant made him noxious but forced him to wake up.

A few moments later, as Vittorio attempted to open his eyes, things were getting better. At first he couldn't see clearly, then he saw the shadow of a person coming closer.

"Lieutenant, are you all right? Lieutenant at least you opened your eyes, that's good."

"Vito?"

"Vito Lieutenant. Vito. That's good."

"Where are we?"

"In the hospital at Camp Geneifa."

"Geneifa? Isn't that in Egypt?"

"That's what they told me Lieutenant, we are in Egypt."

"But there aren't any Italian camps at Geneifa."

"No sir."

"So?"

"Thank God you're alive still, that's what matters."

Vittorio moved his head and felt another sharp pain. He was grinding his teeth but remained silent.

"Be strong lieutenant. We're prisoners of the British but we are alive."

"What happened?"

"They attacked our stronghold at Acroma with many troops while the air force was dumping bombs on us from the sky. Not just fireworks at the village fair. One bomb exploded a few meters from you and a piece of shrapnel hit you in the head behind the ear. You lost quite a bit of blood and there's a hole big enough to accommodate your finger. But you were very lucky; had it gone deeper and touched the brain, I wouldn't be here now telling you this story."

"And you? What are you doing here?"

"The British captured me with you."

Vittorio shook his head:

"You are as stubborn as the mules. That's what you are!"

"I already told you lieutenant, I was brought up with the mules."

The prisoner of war camps built by the British on the Bitter Lakes area, just north of Suez, were the crossroads of the absurd that only a war could create. On one end, surrounded by a barbed wire fence, were the tents of captured German and Italian soldiers. It was all over for them and they could only watch the rest of the game from a bench on the sidelines. On the other side were the barracks of the Australians, arriving at the port of Suez on their way to kill the Italians and Germans who were still fighting in the desert. The POWs and the free soldiers looked at each other hurling insults and even crossing paths at the fountain, where a small amount of drinking water was available twice a day.

Soon Vittorio was once again able to stand on his own two feet. He could walk on the sun baked gravel outside the hospital tent while he was blinded by the unobstructed light of the desert. He was walking behind barbed wire for the first time, knowing that he couldn't go when he pleased. He was alive, all right, but no better than a caged animal. The guards had dressed him up in khakis, just like the British Army, and his shirt had a blue marking sewn into it to identify the prisoners.

"It's not so bad here, lieutenant. Or at least, no worse than in Libya."

Vittorio didn't answer.

"Lieutenant, you could have died."

Another silence.

"Lieutenant, in your lifetime you have never had to bow your head. When I was a farm worker, I couldn't do as I pleased. Yet we manage to survive just the same."

Vittorio was walking and didn't respond, so Vito just followed him.

On the other side of the barbed wire fence an Australian soldier called out to them.

"Hey Dago! I am talking to you, Dago!"

It was their way of humiliating the Italians, just like calling a peasant from the Puglie region "terrone", or an Italian immigrant in Brooklyn a Mafioso.

The Australians were free to go to Cairo on leave or swim in the Bitter Lake, to get rid of the sand that was sticking to their skin because of the perspiration.

"They drink all the English tea they can get and even have beer." complained Vito. "But actually they are far worse off than we are because it could be the last drink they'll ever have."

"Hey Dago, come over here!" said the Australian. Vittorio kept walking away from the barbed wire fence but Vito went in closer.

"Look at this!" said the Australian. Vito didn't understand English but noticed how the Australian was waving the pages of a newspaper.

"Read this Dago. We're going into the desert now to end this war, so we can all go back home." Vito made a face but walked away from the fence with a copy of the paper.

"Lieutenant, he gave me this stuff. Can you understand what's written here?"

Vittorio opened up the crumpled pages:

"They are announcing the arrival of Australian troops in Africa. That's why they're so cocky!"

Then he saw another article on the same page:

"Down here they write how Rommel is on the offensive in Cyrenaica. He is said to have already recaptured Benghazi."

Vittorio's eyes were suddenly shining:

"Let me see the date of the paper. It's dated February 6, 1942, Vito, one week ago. We did the right thing in holding out at Acroma! The counterattack is on. The Germans will break through across the Egyptian border shortly. In a week or two they may even come here and free us."

Chow time was perhaps the moment of greatest humiliation for the POWs. A clump of sticky rice and a few pieces of boiled mutton and that was it. The British left the few meager pickings on a tray in the middle of the table, to see if the Italians would fight amongst themselves to grab an extra portion. They passed around a bucket filled with bitter tea, where the leaves were still floating, for something to drink. A hungry Air Force pilot put his cup on the surface of the tea to grab the leaves which he proceeded to chew. The quartermasters in charge of the camp looked at him and laughed.

Vittorio was refusing to eat the food and on the second day an officer summoned him.

"You don't like what's on our menu?" asked the officer, who remained seated at his desk.

Vittorio didn't answer.

"I understand you, I'd also avoid it. But you don't have to survive like that, you know."

The British officer opened his desk drawer and took out a pack of cigarettes.

"Do you smoke?"

Vittorio nodded but didn't take the offer.

"What I mean" said the British officer, "is that we can help one another. We need information: how big was your unit, what were your orders, why did Rommel abandon you at Acroma without putting up a fight. In exchange, I can make your life much more pleasant."

"Name, rank and serial number, according to the Geneva Convention: that's all you'll get out of me." Was Vittorio's only answer.

"Honorable, without a doubt," continued the British officer, as he took a cigarette from the pack on his desk. "However we also can use different methods."

For four days the officer would call Vittorio while the meals were being served, and the same script was repeated without any variations. On the fifth day he was awakened and taken straight from his bunk at dawn.

"I have done my best to help you, Lieutenant, but you either didn't understand or pretended not to. During the last few days you have actively engaged in spreading propaganda and false rumors among your colleagues, and tried to get them to escape."

Vittorio remained silent but his eyes indicated that he was very surprised.

"Don't give me that stupid look" said the Englishman, "because you know very well what I am talking about. I offered you a way out but you refused to take it. This forces us to use other methods."

The officer waved at the soldiers who were standing **on** guard and they took Vittorio by the arms into the courtyard. The sun was barely rising in the East and Vittorio noticed a unit lined up with their rifles at the ready.

The English officer came up with a rag in his hand.

"Do you wish to be blindfolded?"

Vittorio looked at the rag and the firing squad.

"Do you understand me? Do you wish to be blindfolded?"

"You can't do this, it would be a war crime. The Geneva Convention allows me to give only my name, rank and serial number."

"Geneva is far away and you tried to organize an escape from this camp."

"It's not true and you know you are lying."

"Out of compassion, I'll have you tied with a chain and blindfolded."

The officer waved again and the soldiers dragged Vittorio toward the wall of the courtyard. He reacted and they hit him in the stomach. He was tied and blindfolded and he heard the orders being given to the unit lined up behind him.

"Ready!"

He lifted his head, trying to see from under the blindfold.

"Aim!"

The air he was breathing brought all the smells of the desert into his lungs. He thought of his home, the land of the "Cruste," and his mother's look, when he announced her that he would be going into the Army.

"There is one final opportunity, lieutenant" said the officer, "one last possibility to collaborate and save your life."

Vittorio remained silent, as he caressed his mother in his thoughts. The rifles of the firing squad were still aimed at his chest.

"Untie him," ordered the officer, as he walked nervously back toward his office.

* * *

On March 1 at dawn outside the tents at Geneifa there were no soldiers of the Afrika Corps, as Vittorio was hoping. Only the same freckled face quartermaster, ordering everyone to fall in line. And he was in a big hurry.

"Form the line. Get on with it!"

There was no baggage to take, besides the few things they had when they were captured in Libya, so that the camp was empty very quickly.

"Where are they taking us Lieutenant?" asked Vito, fearing he would lose the personal peace he was now accustomed to, under the control of International Red Cross inspectors.

"I don't know" answered a worried Vittorio.

"I even heard they dragged someone in front of a firing squad."

"They did that to me as well, but it was only a trick to get some information on our unit, if ever I had any. No, this must be a different story."

The prisoners in a long column started to kick up dust in the desert without marching in step. At the railroad station there was a long line of wooden railroad cars. Vito looked quizzically at Vittorio but the Lieutenant had no answers.

"Get on and settle in as best you can. This will not be a long journey" said the quartermaster. A metallic screeching sound and the noise of the wooden axels straining told the prisoners that the train was moving. Then came the usual sandy landscape of rocks and sun, that threaded by for some thirty miles. And the usual flock of Arabs selling souvenirs, a sure sign they were close to a city, where people were traveling.

The Red Sea was a blinding deep blue and it cleared up the mystery. It was Suez, the door to who knows where. Several ships, both civilian and military, were moored to the pier. The quartermaster ordered the men to get off the train and lined them up in front of the ships according to some incomprehensible logic.

Vittorio and Vito got on the *Westerland,* and it was only when they were on deck that they began to understand something.

The captain explained the plan through the Maltese interpreter, collaborators who spoke Italian because they came from the island of Malta, just south of Sicily.

"In a few hours we will be sailing. You are going to India. The enlisted men will sleep in steerage and the officers will share the cabins. It will be a long trip and we expect all of you to collaborate fully. But quite frankly I don't think we will have any problems once we will be at sea. These are shark infested waters and I want you to believe me when I tell you that I am not joking."

There was nothing more to say, they could only go down the metal staircase and look for a bunk.

"India, Lieutenant? And where would that be?"

"On the other side of the world, Vito. That was the land Christopher Columbus was searching for when he discovered America instead."

"So they're not going to shoot us after all?"

"Not for the moment. The Red Cross is present on the pier at the port of Suez as well."

Vito settled in steerage that felt like a pot boiling on the fire. A bit more heat would have even made your thoughts evaporate, besides every drop of water that still lingered in your body. He took over a hammock hanging against the wall and managed to sleep in that odd position. He gagged at the smell of the bunk, that had been soiled by too many poor bastards that had used it before him, and the sweat from the guys above him that was dripping down. The alternative was to sprawl on the dirty metal floor among the darkened faces of the other prisoners who also hunkered down. The only shower was the trickle of sticky and cloudy salt water from the tiny showerheads above. To satisfy your bodily functions, or throw up because of the rough seas, you used the hole at the latrine that immediately became disgusting and smelly. As the ship forged ahead, water would regurgitate from the hole and spread feces all over the floor where the prisoners were lying down.

The Indian cooks made a surprise dish for the first meal: pasta. But they cooked it with sugar and milk, turning it into a sort of sweet glue.

"My God, Lieutenant, this food will really kill us," said Vito looking disgusted.

Vittorio was not eating at all because his thoughts were set on other things. Besides India, where were they going? Besides the war that was going on without him?

"It's really too bad" said Vito, "because it could have been good food. Better they should give us their other awful stuff and forget about attempting to cook pasta."

After a few boring days at sea, half way across the ship called at the port of Aden before entering the Indian Ocean.

The Maltese interpreters repeated to the prisoners as the anchor was dropping:

"We are stopping only for a few hours for technical reasons. Then we will be on our way to India. We reiterate what we told you before about the dangers of these waters. Don't try anything foolish."

The ship docked near two other vessels both flying a Red Cross flag under the broiling sun. Everything happened in a few seconds. Two Italian Navy officers suddenly jumped over the railing falling for a few meters, then splashing into the blue transparent water with thud. As soon as they emerged they began swimming furiously to the Red Cross ships that meant freedom, if they could reach them.

The other prisoners of war crowded at the railings to watch but the sentries didn't shoot. Strange. Instead of aiming at the two fugitives to try and kill them, their rifles were on the other prisoners so they wouldn't try to do the same. Dozens of eyes were looking and hoping in silence. The only sound came from the frenzied arms of the swimmers hitting the water as they got further away from the ship. But still the sentries didn't shoot.

The prisoners on the *Westerland* looked at the rifles of the soldiers on guard duty, then the Red Cross ships, then at the distance between the ships and the wakes that were moving ahead, becoming shorter. Then nothing more. The two wakes converged in white splashes that shot higher up, changed direction brutally and became dark red. Then they stopped. The guards lowered their rifles and returned to their usual posts. "That was a silly decision" said the commander to the silent prisoners. "Brave and noble, but still very silly."

* * *

If anyone arrived at Bombay in any other circumstances, you would notice the wet wooden boats the local fishermen use to go out to sea, the sacred cows strolling through the streets, the beggars who live on the sidewalks, the smell of fermentation of human waste under the tropical sun. But after two weeks as a prisoner on a ship, with dysentery on board and doubts about the following morning, Vito couldn't even distinguish the misery that was everywhere in India. It simply disappeared in the physical fatigue and the moral depression of those who were deprived of their freedom. Vito looked at the surrounding squalor and was amazed at the fact that he was no different. Indian soldiers wearing turbans looked at the Italians as they came ashore with identical curiosity. "Who are these fellows Lieutenant? Sarrasins?"

Bombay was characterized by the humid tropical air that smells of mildew. It was the heat of the season announcing the coming monsoons, it was the luxuriant palm trees and vegetation, and the elephants that were used as taxis in the streets.

There was a generalized indolence among the inhabitants who were supremely indifferent to everything, as if the British had power on earth, but only Indians knew what was truly important.

Vito looked around in amazement.

"My God, Lieutenant, if only we had such huge animals in the Tavoliere. What kind of animals are they?"

He was looking intently at the elephants that went by dragging lumber behind them. Vittorio was also looking at them with curiosity because up until then he'd only read about them in stories by Emilio Salgari.

A British Sergeant lined up the prisoners and marched them to the railroad platform in the main terminal, the nerve center of all of India. Vittorio followed orders as there was nothing else to do, but he knew he was walking on a tightrope. The man ahead of him was still the enemy and he had not lost his honor in the sand at Acroma. There was a tense feeling that any move, look, provocation or lack of respect could turn into a brawl. The British held the keys to survival, food, water and the destiny of a youth robbed by the captivity that could turn out to be endless. The only keys he had left were those of his dignity, without which everything else would become worthless.

The Sergeant came up to Vittorio:

"Rank?"

"Second Lieutenant."

Then he looked at Vito

"Rank?"

"Lieutenant, what the hell does he want?" asked Vito of Vittorio.

"He wants to know your rank."

"What rank?"

Vittorio turned to the sergeant and said in English.

"He's a private and my orderly."

The sergeant pointed Vittorio to one column and Vito to another one.

"What does this guy want, lieutenant? My orders are to follow you."

Vittorio tried to explain to the sergeant:

"He's my orderly, and we've been together since the war started."

The sergeant didn't move. Then he raised his lathi, the club used by local police, and showed Vito the line that went to a different train. Vito didn't move and the club started downwards toward his face. Vittorio grabbed the lathi still in the air, stopped it and came up to a few inches of the sergeant. The British sergeant blew his whistle and other guards came running, stopping Vittorio by grabbing his arms. "Lieutenant! Where are they taking him? Lieutenant!" Two guards with their clubs raised were on either side of Vito, pushing him to the other train while he looked back.

11.

"Ultra, it's obvious."
Admiral Malceri measured his office step by step, as he paced up and down. "I think that is the most credible possibility" he said looking at Alberto, who had just reported back on his trip to Athens.

The captain lifted his arms almost attempting to excuse himself.

"I was hoping to gather more information, but the contact disappeared after just a few minutes."

Malceri immediately said:

"Our contact did much more than I expected. Now I can just hope he can manage down in Greece."

"I don't understand."

"Well, Captain, we always suspected that the British knew about our moves. On too many occasions they showed only too clearly that they knew everything, even though they later tried very hard to cover their tracks."

"Meaning?"

"I'll give you one example. At Cape Matapan the initial alarm signal came at 12:25 on the 27th of March, when Admiral Iachino noticed that a Sunderland reconnaissance plane was flying over our ships. But if that were the time the British discovered our mission, why was Cunningham already on the move several hours before?"

"He obviously knew something."

"Precisely. The reconnaissance flight was only a diversion to lead us to believe that the fleet at sea had been discovered that way. Cunningham wanted to avoid any suspicion by hiding the true source of his information."

"And that would be?"

"Ultra, precisely as the contact in Athens confirmed. Have you ever heard anything about Ultra?"

Alberto nodded:

"I did hear something."

"It's the name of a British spying operation that is being ran out of Bletchley Park, just north of London. The purpose is to decrypt our coded messages. Now I am not certain that the Athens contact is correct in saying that the German Enigma system had been breached, or that at Cape Matapan communications between Italian units were using different instruments. But this is after all irrelevant."

"If we were being spied upon then everything is clear" commented Alberto.

"Precisely" said Malceri. "If the British knew everything, then we placed ourselves in a mousetrap. Ultra is therefore the real traitor."

"However" said Alberto, "this would allow the admirals to find an excuse to cover up their mistakes."

"Yes, in part. They will say that the intelligence services were fooled by the British and therefore condemned them to defeat. But that issue will be for future debate. Right now our most urgent objective is to avoid that you and a few other innocent parties don't end up in front of a firing squad."

Alberto didn't react or show any kind of emotion. He had already understood that this was the key problem.

Malceri went on:

"The investigation has not yet begun officially. Before they go ahead the admirals want to have in their hands all the elements they need to reach a quick sentence. It's a race against time, the fastest one will win."

"What should I do?"

"Keep working along these lines to find proof of the British intercepts. Once we find them we can plan ahead and reveal them, or set them aside and wait for their moves."

"Why not tell the truth right away?"

"To be sure we are not damaged by it in the process. Captain, these matters of honor in the military can drag on for a long time. Years go by and so do governments, but career military men remain at their posts and they never forget. The specialized units, the corps and the regiments forget even less, because they have been around for centuries. When someone puts his cards on the table in a game of this size he must have some assurance of being able to win the final hand. And I seriously doubt that the solution to Cape Matapan is around the corner."

"Please, pardon me admiral, but I'd like to ask you a question. Why have you decided to play this game in my favor?"

Malceri stopped pacing and looked straight at Alberto, "And why shouldn't I?"

***

"Any news of Vittorio?" Alberto asked Federico as he was getting his dress uniform ready in their house on Lugotevere Flaminio. He had been invited to a reception and Malceri insisted that he be present. "No news," answered Federico. "Since he was listed missing at Tobruk we have no information."

"Not even from the Red Cross?"

"No, they keep saying not to worry. In some cases months can go by before you get any news. But now it's been a whole year."

"So we must keep up hope. If he is a prisoner there are thousands of them in Africa and the British are in no hurry to allow them to communicate with their relatives."

"Maybe he wrote and the letter got lost?" injected Federico.

"Correct, or the Red Cross hasn't yet located him in the mix up of the camps," answered Alberto.

"I just don't know how I can placate our mother anymore."

"We must keep saying that this is only normal. We know how hundreds of soldiers are listed as missing for months and later reappeared in a hospital or a POW camp. We can't allow her and dad to lose hope."

"Absolutely. You should write home then, since they think you know more about this than I do."

Alberto nodded. Then he confided in his brother:

"My situation is also serious. Very serious."

Federico looked puzzled.

"A few admirals suspect that I or someone in my office gave the British our plans for the mission to Cape Matapan."

"What?" asked Federico.

"You heard right. They think that the British sank our ships because I or someone close to me was a spy."

"But how?"

"I can't give you any details right now."

Federico looked at his brother and was at a loss for words.

"I could ask you – said Alberto - to believe that I had nothing to do with all this because I am your brother and because you know the rules I live by. But there's a lot more going on behind the scenes."

Alberto went on:

"First of all the *Zara* was one of the ships that went under, the one I first served on. Had I been a spy I'd have been sending my own men to their death, the same fellows I ate, bunked and worked with for months."

Federico kept on listening in silence.

"Of course that's far from enough to prove my innocence. I could have had a personal interest that was so overwhelming, it would lead me to sacrifice the lives of those men. The truth is that the massacre at Matapan took place because of the incompetence of the admirals, just like the bombing of the port of Taranto. Now they are out to save themselves and are desperate to accuse a phantom traitor."

"Even so, how can you prove that they are wrong?"

"We are working on it. The absolute proof that the British didn't get their information from an Italian spy may actually exist. For the moment I need your help and your trust."

* * *

The reception took place in an ornate ballroom that had somehow managed to elude the wartime restrictions. Alberto saw Malceri in a group and went over to salute his commanding officer.

"Good evening, Admiral."

"Good evening, Captain Conte."

Malceri took Alberto by the arm into a corner where an Army officer was waiting alone for both of them.

"I asked you to make sure you came tonight because I wanted you to meet a friend," said the Admiral. Then, addressing the Army officer, he made the introductions:

"Colonel Montezemolo, this is Captain Conte."

"I am honored" said Alberto, as they shook hands.

Malceri went on:

"The Colonel and I have known one another for many years. We were colleagues when we were teaching at the School of Military Specialization in Turin. Besides a military career we also have many other things in common."

"If in times like these there could be anything besides a military career," joked Montezemolo.

Malceri took his leave.

"Excuse me, I must go and greet a guest."

As he stepped away, Montezemolo went on:

"The Admiral had very positive things to say about you."

"Thank you, sir."

"Especially during times like these in the armed forces we need capable people who are able to think for themselves."

"Absolutely," said Alberto, who was wondering about the motive for the meeting.

Then the Colonel asked:

"How do you see the war developing?"

"It is rather delicate at the moment."

"That is a very diplomatic answer. The truth is that since the end of 1942 nothing is going right: the defeats in North Africa, the retreat from Russia. Now the Americans are even pushing the Japanese back in the Pacific."

"Do you fear for the integrity of our borders?"

"Captain, we are soldiers and have sworn allegiance to the king and to Italy, even though the government may think otherwise. Our duty is always to look ahead to the country's future."

12.

The railroad car assigned to Vittorio was a lot worse than the one from Geneifa to Suez, with its wooden boards nailed across the windows to prevent a view of the surroundings. And yet, after they left, they saw something that erased even the hunger they were suffering from.

As it pulled out of Bombay, the train that carried the prisoners of war was on its way to New Delhi, and traveled through the last stretch of the desert of Rajastan. It was a different world of flashy and bright colors, turbans, temples with traditional Hindu effigies, and barefoot peasants tilling the earth. Vittorio saw the rhododendrons with flowers so red they reminded him of the sight of blood. The harsh smells unleashed by the warm humidity were brutally invasive, as if he were inhaling some kind of incense or a mysterious drug. With the other prisoners they managed to take off the wooden slats that prevented them from seeing the countryside. There were scores of vultures flying in a circle above little green hills. He wondered why, since he couldn't imagine that the birds of prey used to be the undertakers of the Parsi, India's ancient people that didn't cremate its dead but left them as a meal for the vultures.

In the evening Vittorio sat down in a corner. He didn't want to speak to anyone, nor did the others have the strength to do so either. He thought how Vito with his stubborn ways was bound to survive. He thought about his family that probably didn't even know whether he was dead or alive. Then he examined his own situation since he joined the Army and the motivations of the Fascist regime. Although it was all over for him, Italy was still at war, even in a stockade all the way off in India.

He noticed the confusion of New Delhi from the window grates, since the guards had nailed the boards back up. After a short stopover the convoy continued to travel north. The vegetation was suddenly even more luxuriant but it had lost its tropical colors. Long lines of eucalyptus trees and a few pine trees were making their first appearance. It became very cold, especially at night, and some smells of natural resins reminded him of the forests in the Alps.

When the train stopped once again, the railroad station bore the name of Dehradun.

"Consider yourselves lucky!" the British officer cried out, as the prisoners stepped off the train. "For the Indians this is a town to go to for a vacation."

The journey ended in the State of Uttaranchal, a few kilometers south of the Himalayan mountain chain. The Ganges originated near there. On the road connecting Dehradun to Delhi was Haridwar, a northern Varanasi where pilgrims came to bathe in the sacred waters that had just flowed from the mountains. This was before the remains of the cremated bodies were thrown in further downstream and ended up polluting the river.

Vittorio traveled the final part of the journey by truck. The prisoner of war camp was located just outside the town in a place called Prem Nagar, which means the city of love. It was on a higher ground and there were mango trees, and underneath he could see the rows of eucalyptus trees in the valley that was crossed by a river.

The prisoners were divided in groups. There were four camps: 21, 22, 23 and 24. Vittorio was assigned to the last one. The huts had a concrete base and a sloping wooden roof, which in theory was meant to allow the rain water to slide down during the rainy season that was about to begin. Each hut had a number just like each prisoner: Vittorio was now 177633 ME, which stood for Middle East, the location where he had been captured.

The camp commander assembled the new arrivals.

"You are now at Dehradun and you are lucky. This is a vacation spot south of the Himalayas, cool enough to avoid the worse diseases that would have broken you in Bombay. There are mostly officers in the wing that has been assigned to you, and the detaining power expects you to behave in accordance with your rank. For you the war is over, as it shall also soon be for Italy. Help each other make this prison camp experience tolerable. It is a privilege to be at Dehradun. I suggest that you not throw it away."

The Indian guards led the prisoners to their barracks. Vittorio entered his hut that was dark because the windows were low and tiny. He was given a straw bed called an angareb which was considered a luxury. He immediately heard someone coughing from the bunk just ahead of his.

"Welcome to Dehradun comrade" - said the man in a gravelly voice - "Did the camp commander also tell you the tale about the vacation spot? Then how do you account for this damned cough that hasn't allowed me to breathe for weeks now?"

Vittorio kept silent as he tidied up his few possessions on the angareb. The other prisoner turned in his bed and offered his hand.

"My pleasure, I'm Lieutenant Leonida…"

Vittorio swung around and interrupted him.

"This I cannot believe: Leonida!"

"Vittorio, damn it! These English bastards also managed to nab you as well."

Just like it was at Pola they were sharing the same room, only this time hope was lagging far behind them. Vittorio grabbed Leonida's hand. He sat up on the angareb but he stopped his friend from giving him a hug. "Hold off on the greetings until they tell me what this cough is all about. But please, tell me, how you wound up here?"

"Acroma" said Vittorio. "I was wounded during a bombing while the British were attempting to chase us out of Tobruk. I heard, however, that Rommel has already launched his counter offensive."

"Certainly. Don't you listen to the British or those cowards of Italians who cooperate with them. They may have grabbed us, but Italy will hold out."

"And you? What did you do after Officer's Candidate School at Pola?" asked Vittorio.

"North Africa, just like you. Only I was even dumber. They grabbed me on the Halfaya Pass in March 1941."

"That's incredible. At that same time I was boarding a ship bound for Tripoli. I had been in France first but we didn't even fire a shot."

"And what happened when you reached Libya?" asked Leonida.

"Rommel's Afrika Korps had just landed over there. Within a few days we retook all of Cirenaica and had thrown the British back into Egypt. The British counter attacked at the end of 1941 and I suffered a head wound. Rommel was retreating while he was expecting his reinforcements to arrive. Now he's back on the offensive."

"So, you see? How could we even know all this?" said Leonida, shaking his head as he continued to cough. Then he went on. "Here all the British want is to break our will. They want to convince us that Italy is through, that there's no way out.

They hope that we officers, those who wanted to fight, will give up. They try to be friendly but only to make you give in and betray fascism. As soon as you do that they treat you like dirt, as the usual Italian turncoat who sells himself for a pile of beans."

"Leonida, they can forget all that with me. I am and intend to remain a soldier at war."

* * *

The camp commander summoned Vittorio:

"Lieutenant Conte, you are fluent in English and French, correct?"

"Yes."

"Well then, let me introduce Monsieur Charles Huber. He is the international Red Cross delegate who is here to inspect our camp. He needs an interpreter and hopes you will collaborate."

"Collaborate?"

"Not with us, Lieutenant Conte. With the international Red Cross, a neutral organization that is here for the benefit of your colleagues in arms."

Huber shook Vittorio's hand.

"Nothing political. My job is exclusively humanitarian, above taking sides. By the way, have you ever written back home?"

"No."

"Then we could begin with that." Huber showed Vittorio a form letter. "Unfortunately censorship doesn't allow us to transmit actual letters. If you fill out this form you can at least inform your family about the condition you are in."

Vittorio marked the box that read: "I am well."

"Very good!" said Huber "We will send this to your parents to let them know that you are a prisoner of the British. They can then write back to you through us."

A few days later, after he had been accompanied by Vittorio through the barracks, Huber sat down to compile his report to Geneva.

"Camps 21, 22, 23 and 24. Each camp is divided in different wings with one person in charge. Numbers are: 921 officers, 12053 NCO's and soldiers, all of them are Italian Pow's. They are in barracks that measure 48.5 meters by 5.70 meters. In each hut there are 22 General officers, 35 to 38 Second Lieutenants and Captains, 53 to 70 NCO's and privates. There are leaks in the roofs and it rains inside. Each wing has 24 showers and toilets with open tubing. Many prisoners have been issued sweaters similar to those of the British soldiers but pants, shirts, undershirts and socks are insufficient. The sandals don't last very long. The food has improved since we complained that many prisoners coming from the Sudan had vitamin deficiencies. It is possible to find all kinds of fruit that can overcome and prevent scurvy and beri-beri. With the exception of camp 24 the space available for physical activity is very large. Religious services are handled by Italian chaplains. The prisoners have protested because the official text of the prayer has been altered as it was being read during mass. The delegate complained to British authorities at Smila, who assured him that original text would be reinstated." The prayer for the Duce was missing, which was the reason the prisoners complained.

Huber went on to describe for the Geneva office the most heated issue he had encountered:

"Patriotic activities by the POW's. The detainees view patriotic duties as an inherent right that they should be allowed to have. We transmit herewith the orders written in Italian and posted by the Detaining Power in the various camps:

Proclamation
Political Activities
1. Any party activities are forbidden in the camps.

2. The following are examples of such forbidden activities:
    a. Displaying the following emblems under any form:
        the fasces and the axes
        the swastika
        the Japanese Rising Sun
        the letters P.N.F.
        the flags of any pro-Axis country
        the effigies of Hitler and Mussolini
        the fascist motto "I don't give a damn"
    b. emblems bearing any of the images above are forbidden.
    c. manufacturing party cards, to keep, to sign, or to distribute such cards is forbidden, it is also forbidden to list party members and to compile black lists.
    d. To cry out political slogans including 'Duce, Duce A NOI; 'EIA EIA ALALA' is also forbidden
    e. The call 'AL DUCE' and the response 'EVVIVA' after the parades is forbidden from now on.
    f. To sing 'Giovinezza' is forbidden.
    g. To publish and distribute illegal bulletins is forbidden.

3. The following are allowed:
    a. The Savoy coat of arms and the motto FERT
    b. The keys of the Papacy
    c. Regimental coats of arms
    d. The cries VIVA L'ITALIA, VIVA L'IMPERO, VIVA IL RE, VIVA IL RE IMPERATORE

4   Saluting must be done in accordance with Italian military custom, therefore:
    a. The right hand should be lined up with the helmet when the head is covered
    b. Give the Fascist salute when the head is not covered.

These regulations were introduced in all British prisoner of war camps as of March 22, 1942. They have generated widespread discontent among the prisoners of war."

Italians however were constantly taking the initiative. As Huber wrote: "In the mess halls of most of the wings theaters have been set up. Various bands have been created. The delegate has provided the prisoners of camps 21 and 22 with musical instruments that were acquired in Bombay for 1000 Rupees." There was also some bad news in the reports reaching Geneva: "There are 350 sick men in the separate hospital of Camp 24. This is the list of the most serious diseases:

> Turberculosis 15
> Dissentery 36
> Other intestinal ailments 32
> Common diseases 45
> Ears, nose and throat 32
> Dermatological 5
> Mental illness 8

The surgical unit has 94 patients, among them five cases of appendicitis, cystitis, gastritis, hemorrhoids, varicocele, kidney colics, hernias and fractures.

There are 152 persons with eye ailments. There are also 550 prisoners with syphilis inside the camp that should be separated from the others.

The Italian doctors are requesting calcium and general vitamins for those afflicted with tuberculosis."

Dehradun may have been a vacation spot for Indians, but the prisoners were dying there. "Cemetery. The delegate has not yet visited it because the camp commander didn't give him the proper authorization. The delegate plans to check the graves of dead soldiers as soon as possible. The cemetery is located some 8 kilometers away but the exact geographic location remains secret. Information about the dead attached to the report was provided by the highest ranking officer at the hospital, Major Perrini of the medical corps."

Huber ended his letter warning Geneva that he was not at all satisfied with his inspections: "Camp 24 appeared to the delegate to be a punishment center. We heard complaints about far too frequent searches where private papers were confiscated as well as valuables, fountain pens etc. The prisoners and supervisors of the wings have denounced collective punishments: two hundred men were forced to stand for several hours in the sun under the threat of rifles and were then forced to run toward their barracks."

After the evening count, that was invented more to annoy the prisoners rather than control them, Vittorio went toward his wing. The angareb in front of his was empty.

"Your friend Leonida went to the hospital." said the supervisor.

"Was he feeling ill?" asked Vittorio.

"It was that usual cough. But he said not to worry. It must be those awful English cigarettes he's constantly smoking."

"How does it work here? Can I go and pay him a visit?"

"You have to ask. They may even let you go inside the hospital. But you'll see, Leonida will be back before you get your pass to go and visit him."

Vittorio lay down in his angareb. He slipped his hand in his shirt pocket to fish out one of the awful English cigarettes that he was also constantly smoking.

"I forgot" said the supervisor as he came up to his bunk. "Your friend asked me to give you this, just in case." He gave Vittorio the coat of arms of the 23rd Officer's Candidate School of Pola, the one the Bersaglieri would get printed with their own money to have the same amulet sewn on their uniform.

Some time later a new Red Cross delegate appeared, a Mr. Reist. The camp commander asked Vittorio to accompany him as he had done previously with Huber to help write a report. Reist wrote back to Geneva:

"This summer saw a very heavy monsoon with more rain than at any time during the last fifty years."

The new delegate was a well organized man who asked the British to be very specific once and for all about what they were feeding their own troops and what they were giving the prisoners. He then noted punctiliously:

"Daily rations in ounces. Bread: British troops 16, prisoners 16. Mutton: British 16, prisoners 8. Flour: British 4, prisoners 4. Milk: British half a liter, prisoners zero. Sugar: 2½ oz. for everyone. Kitchen Salt: half for everyone. Tea: British $\frac{5}{7}$ oz; prisoners $\frac{3}{7}$ oz. Vegetables: 8 for all. Potatoes: 10 for everyone. Onions: 6. Besides this, 35 cigarettes are distributed to each man."

Camp life was about to change. "It appears that the British authorities want to introduce compulsory labor. It will be necessary to prepare the prisoners psychologically for that decision."

Reist was amazed at how the POWs were set on finding anything that might remind them of home:

"In section 5 of camp 22 a prisoner has built a machine to make Italian pasta. This cylinder entirely made of wood allows you to spread the pasta and cut it to the desired width. The builder has been commissioned to assemble eight such machines for the officer's camp."

Even though they were eating home made tagliatelle in the Dehradun barracks, this was not enough to keep the prisoners quiet: "A number of escapes have taken place. Within five weeks 35 men have escaped through a tunnel they had been digging. But since the prisoners didn't know the basic Indian dialects, the attempts were bound to fail and the escapees were invariably caught."

Those who tried to leave had a terrible experience: "Every camp has a detention block of 12 cells." Isolation became a paradox, since a POW was thousands of kilometers away from the first real port where a serious attempt to escape could reasonably take place.

The saddest part of the report was in its conclusion: "22 men of that group died. The first ones were buried in the town's civilian cemetery, but now they have been assigned a special section just outside the camp. It is a large piece of land surrounded by a brick wall three meters high. At the entrance there are two rows of 10 and 4 graves made as little mounds of earth without flowers. Only one grave has a small wooden cross and a name carved on it." Next to the name is a badge that reads: 23rd Officer's Candidate School of Pola.

* * *

Vittorio was having trouble admitting it but he did cry when he found out that Leonida had been killed by tuberculosis. He hadn't cried like that since he was a little boy. At war death becomes a habit: it can be seen everywhere, you give it and receive it. Vittorio had killed and he had seen others die. But that was a different story. When you first sit next to a classmate in school maybe you imagine that you'll grow old together. If the desk is at the officer's candidate school you imagine that you may very well share some great adventures. When that thought is replaced by the blood that was shed in the desert it becomes something you can chalk up to the bad luck that is part of war. But to waste away in a hospital bed thousands of kilometers from home, when you are convinced all you have to do is wait to make it. To end up like that, flaking away little by little, hour after hour, only because you lack basic medicine, is too much to bear. You remember the days back at Pola, when everything seemed possible, and compare them to now, when you know your days as a prisoner are counted and you will never get back to Italy. You must cry to bear any of it.

* * *

One morning, at the end of July 1943, the British camp commander summoned all the officers: "Gentlemen, you should know that Mussolini has fallen. He was overthrown on the 25th of the month by the Fascist Grand Council. The King has accepted his resignation and has appointed Marshall Pietro Badoglio to head the new government."

"Bullshit!" yelled out a colonel.

"You shall soon find out that I am not joking. Italy in any case remains at war with Great Britain."

It was a stab in the back. The certainty that kept the prisoners going, the conviction that their war also continued in India because Italy continued to hang on, had evaporated in just four sentences.

Vittorio felt stunned. He heard his fellow officer's voices mumbling. This couldn't possibly be true, it was obviously British propaganda to break us. In any case we were still at war and Marshal Badoglio wouldn't abandon us.

That evening in front of the barracks cavalry Major Lardone came up to him.

"Lieutenant Conte, you were an interpreter during the visits of the Red Cross delegate, correct?"

"Yes, Major."

"Then I'd have to ask you a favor."

"Feel free to ask."

"I need you to speak for us to the camp commander."

"Certainly, what is the problem?" asked Vittorio.

"With a few fellow officers at this point in the war we were thinking of organizing a mass for all the British dead in the conflict."

Vittorio looked at him intently and answered:

"Certainly Major, but many Italians also died in the war. We could propose a general ceremony for all of those who died."

"I certainly understand. But at this time Italians don't amount to much."

A brief second went by. Without a single word, nor any change of expression, Vittorio suddenly punched the Major in the face. Before the staggering officer could figure out what had hit him, or before anyone could stop him, Vittorio punched him again with all the rage and strength he had repressed for those three years of absurdity. Once the British guards finally restrained him the Major was still unable to stand up on his own.

Vittorio was taken to the camp commander.

"Lieutenant, do you realize what you have done?"

Vittorio looked up:

"Yes."

"You have struck a superior officer. Do you know what this means?"

"I certainly do."

"You understand that the reasons behind your actions have no bearing on the necessary discipline of the camp?"

Vittorio remained silent.

"Lieutenant, I am forced to punish you. I will take the incident to the Italian military court and you will be transferred out of Dehradun."

"Do whatever you have to do."

The family together before the war.

Alberto in full dress uniform when he graduated from the Naval Academy.

Alberto in civilian clothes before the war.

Vittorio in the uniform of a
Bersagliere, 1940.

Alberto's first ship was the *Zara*.

France surrenders on June 24, 1940: Marshal Badoglio reads the terms of the armistice to the French delegation headed by General Huntziger.

British carrier *HMS Illustrious* and Fairey Swordfish torpedo plane that attacked the fleet at Taranto on November 11, 1940.

Italian battleship *Conte di Cavour* sunk at Taranto.

Bersaglieri motorcycle unit in 1940.

Italian troops in foxholes in the Libyan desert in 1940.

Vittorio was decorated for bravery for anti-tank actions like this one.

Bersaglieri preparing to attack in the sand dunes, 1941.

General Rommel and General Bastico in Libya, 1941.

Map of the British POW camps where Italian prisoners were held in India 1940-1947.

The POW camp was behind thick barbed wire at the foot of the Himalayas.

The entrance to the camp.

The Gurkhas, fierce British Indian troops were the camp guards.

On July 25, 1943 the King dismissed Mussolini and replaced him with Marshal Badoglio.

Once freed, Mussolini, here with Marshal Graziani, formed a new pro-German Fascist regime in northern Italy in the fall of 1943.

German paratroopers occupy Rome, September 10, 1943.

American POWs captured at Anzio are paraded by the Germans in Rome. February 1944.

Liberation of Rome, June 4, 1944.

General Mark Clark enters the Eternal City, June 4, 1944.

King Victor Emanuel III.

Marshal Pietro Badoglio.

13.

At 7:45 p.m. on September 8, 1943 Marshal Pietro Badoglio had just begun a radio broadcast. "The Italian government, having concluded that it is impossible to pursue the unequal struggle against overwhelming enemy power and in seeking to prevent further and even worse disasters to the nation, has requested an armistice to General Eisenhower, the commander in chief of the allied Anglo-American forces. The request has been granted. Consequently any hostile action against Anglo-American forces by Italian forces must cease everywhere. However Italian forces may react to potential attacks coming from any other party."

Alberto wasted no time reflecting on the news. He ran to the ministry where Federico was waiting for him. People were beginning to crowd the streets, happy that once and for all the war was finally over, or so they thought. But he knew that wouldn't be the case and hurried ahead.

The ministry looked like a sinking ship where a dramatic "every man for himself" had been announced. Before the call was issued that "everyone must go home", some people had even started hoarding pens and anything they could carry. In the uncertain future any kind of object could come in handy.

Once he found Federico, Alberto went straight to Malceri's office, where the door was open and the lights were on.

"Admiral, what is going on?"

"Good to see you Captain Conte. You heard the radio?"

"Yes, I did."

"It's been something of a surprise for us as well."

"You didn't know about the armistice?"

"We didn't know" answered the admiral "that it would be announced so quickly. The armistice was signed on September 3 by General Castellano at Cassibile. The agreement was that it would remain secret until the 10th or the 15th of September, so that we could prepare to properly defend Rome."

"And instead?"

"Instead, Eisenhower decided to go public sooner."

"Even Admiral de Courten was unaware?"

"The Navy chief of staff had some inkling on September 6 or 7, but only regarding what we were to do with our ships in the event of a Nazi attempt to seize them. Up until the 7th he was telling the German commanding General Kesselring that our fleet was ready for action against the Allies, as agreed some time before. The situation changed very quickly on the evening of the 7th when two American officers came secretly to Rome. They were to analyze the possibility of a paratrooper drop on the city and set up its defenses. Once they saw this was tactically impossible they told Badoglio that Eisenhower would announce the armistice on the following day."

"And what was Badoglio's reply?"

"He didn't say much. This morning the Armed Forces chief of staff, General Ambrosio, ordered that de Courten wait and that he prevent the fleet from sailing. Then a few hours ago, around 6:30 p.m., the King summoned the Crown council to the Quirinal Palace. It was only then that Badoglio informed everyone that the armistice had been signed. Someone suggested that we should disavow Eisenhower, even if it meant accusing the Marshal of the misunderstanding. But King Victor Emmanuel replied that we must honor our commitment."

"But the Nazis are just outside Rome! How can we possibly defend the crowds that are beginning to fill the streets to celebrate the end of the war?"

"For the moment a few Army officers will handle that situation, Colonel Montezemolo is among them. You remember him? I introduced you some time ago. We have a different task."

"Which one?"

"The second clause of the armistice is a demand that we take our ships and aircraft to locations designated by the Allied high command. There are scores of ships scattered in Italian ports that the Germans would want or would be happy to sink. We must save those units."

"So we hand them over to the Allies?" asked Alberto.

"On condition that they safeguard the honor of the flag. Otherwise there is a coded signal for them to be scuttled."

"What are our orders?"

"Admiral Sansonetti, deputy head of the high command, has already contacted Admiral Bergamini at La Spezia. He convinced him to set sail with his entire naval squadron to Malta rather than launching the planned attack on the Allied forces. We must follow that situation and send out orders to the other units. All the ships that are able to sail are requesting information and orders."

Alberto went to his desk, and by 3 a.m. on September 9 the first bit of encouraging news came in: Bergamini's squadron was ready to sail after hooking up with a few cruisers that came down from Genoa. These are the battleships *Roma*, *Vittorio Veneto*, and *Italia*, the cruisers *Eugenio di Savoia*, *Duca d'Aosta*, *Duca degli Abruzzi*, *Garibaldi*, *Montecuccoli* and *Regolo*, plus eight detroyers.

Malceri then explained:

"De Courten has obtained from the Allies that the ships will go to Sardinia rather than to Malta, so they will be in an Italian port at La Maddalena."

A few hours later there was less optimism:

"Admiral, we have secret informers telling us that La Maddalena is already under German control."

Malceri looked at the map:

"We must warn Bergamini right away. Where is he now?"

"Near the Bocche di Bonifacio."

"Let's hope it's not too late. Tell him to switch towards the island of Asinara."

"But where is Admiral de Courten?" Asked Alberto.

"With the King. That's all we know. Sansonetti is substituting for him here."

The night was spent waiting and then it began to dawn, just like the day of the massacre at Cape Matapan. There were no crowds of happy Romans outside. One could feel the tension because of the sounds of gunfire resonating from afar. By 3:30 p.m. a dispatch that cancelled any remaining hope came in.

"A group of 27 Luftwaffe Dornier bombers has located the squadron as it made its way off Sardinia." The anguish of Matapan was repeated once again, everyone was waiting helplessly.

By 4 p.m. there was a new message: "The battleship *Roma* is burning. The *Italia* has been slightly hit."

A few minutes later the news was confirmed:

"The *Roma* has sunk with Admiral Bergamini on board."

Malceri brought his hand to his forehead, as if to cross himself, but instead he held his head to hide his personal distress. Events rushed in one after the other, like as many punches.

"The destroyer *Di Noli* has been sunk by German artillery in front of the Bocche di Bonifacio, the *Vivaldi* blew up on a mine."

There was not even enough time to stop and honor their fallen comrades. The surviving fleet was attempting to save itself: they all wanted information, orders and channels to safety.

One more update: "The cruiser *Regolo* has been rescuing survivors from the *Roma* and is sailing towards the Balearic Islands with other units, into neutral Spanish waters. The *Pegaso* and the *Impetuoso* were damaged and have scuttled themselves."

Messages were coming in from every deck: "Also lost are the cruisers *Gorizia*, *Bolzano* and *Taranto*."

Malceri left his office and returned a few minutes later: "I spoke to the Army high command. They are fighting on the outskirts of Rome on the via Ostiense, the via Appia, Casilina, and Prenestina. The Nazis are massing their forces to enter the city and the Allies are too far away. The paratroopers Eisenhower had promised will not be coming and the units that landed at Salerno are out of range. If anyone wants to save his skin, this is the time to do so. Perhaps very shortly there will no longer be any opportunity to flee." After he spoke there was only silence in the room. Nobody moved.

Shortly after 9 a.m. on September 10 the Admiral came into the office with a piece of paper that he was holding as if it were some sacred relic.

"They were able to get through. The surviving ships of Bergamini's squadron were intercepted by British ships that are escorting them to Malta."

Perhaps the worse was over and the Germans could no longer attack the ships that had slipped away. Hours went by and new confirmation came through. "Even the *Doria* and *Duilio* battleships that were at Taranto have joined up with the rest of the fleet at Malta, with the cruisers *Cadorna*, *Pompeo* and *Scipione* and a destroyer." Then more news. "The *Cesare* has sailed out of Pola and reached Taranto and then Malta without an escort." Malceri was relieved and almost overjoyed when he read a message stating: "The entire Naval Academy sailed from Venice on the oceanliner *Saturnia* and arrived unscathed at Brindisi."

Aboard the cruiser *Hambledon* Eisenhower and Admiral Cunningham watched the surviving Italian fleet as sailed into Malta. "Glorious sight", whispered the American General in admiration. It wasn't clear whether it was glorious for him to behold, or for those who managed to elude Nazi revenge. The honor of the flag was respected in any case. Italian crews piloted the ships into the harbor with their weapons on board.

At the ministry Alberto was summing up a balance sheet and the losses were very heavy: eight destroyers, twenty two cruisers, ten submarines, nine frigates and two hundred fifteen smaller and auxiliary ships were lost, most of them scuttled. But there was still an Italian Navy ready for combat. Those who sought to destroy it at Matapan now wanted it on their side.

Malceri shook hands with the officers and men who had remained with him. What was left of the Navy was safely at Malta and even the King had managed to board a ship at Pescara and reach Brindisi. But Malceri and his men were behind enemy lines, since Rome was now under Kesselring's control.

"And now?" asked Alberto.

"In the last three days we managed to snatch the Italian Navy away from the Nazis. I think our choice is made." answered the Admiral.

* * *

"So you have decided" Federico told Alberto, while they were in the living room of the apartment overlooking the Lungotevere Flaminio.

His brother nodded:

"I met Colonel Montezemolo, the same one Admiral Malceri introduced me to some time ago. There was also a former lieutenant of the Bersaglieri called Antonello and Sandro, our next

door neighbor who was politically active. They fought at the
Porta San Paolo to try and stop the Nazis from entering Rome
right after the armistice. Now they are setting up a military and
civilian resistance network. Even Malceri has created an underground group with men from the Navy's Secret Information
Service."

"You must realize that you are putting your life at risk."

"Federico, you are correct, but we've already lost thousands
of lives and we know it's not over yet. Our brother Vittorio,
according to that Red Cross message, is a POW in India where
he will remain until this war is finally over. And then what would
we achieve by running away? Do you think that two naval
officers like you and I could easily cross the German lines? Do
you think that if we could reach the Castelli Romani or the
Abruzzi we would be safe at last? The Nazis would consider us
as traitors."

Federico nodded as Alberto went on.

"The first thing that impressed me when I arrived at the
ministry was that on the evening of September 8, you saw it too
since you were with me, our colleagues were running away with
anything they could stuff into their briefcases. While on our
ships our friends and comrades from the Academy, both officers
and men with whom we shared our meals and barracks for years,
were sending in desperate calls for help, for information, for
orders about what they should do to defend themselves. That's
not the way I am, Federico. We are not that way. I wouldn't have
the courage to look at myself in the mirror the following day."

Federico objected:

"Personal dignity is one thing, fine. But now it's a matter of
political choice that puts your life on the line."

"You are right again. You know that I was never swayed by
fascism, but that's not the only issue. We must also mention the
country's dignity. When I became a soldier I swore allegiance to
the King, which meant to Italy, not to any particular govern-

ment. It is true that now the people are very angry at Victor Emmanuel and Badoglio because they fled to the south, and they keep saying that we naval officers are all staunch monarchists. First of all that's simply not true, since there are quite a few colleagues who are sincerely democratic. Second: why does that matter? The legitimate Italian government, no matter what I think of the King and Badoglio, is in the south. It is certainly not the one that the Nazis have set up in the north, propping up Mussolini like a puppet just so they can have their way."

"I have no doubts on that score" answered Federico.

"Not just that. Have you looked out the window? Have you seen the command cars filled with Germans drive by as though they owned the place? What should we do now, simply ask them over for dinner?"

Federico looked out the window as darkness was beginning to fall, signaling the start of the curfew in the city. Alberto took a small briefcase.

"In any case, don't fool yourself into thinking that we'll avoid this just by sticking our heads in the sand. Either we will be able to kick them out, or they will kill all of us and rule over those remaining as slaves. Look at this." He gave Federico a short report.

"What is this?"

"It's a report by Father Romualdo Formato, the military chaplain of the Acqui artillery regiment, where you were an officer candidate. On September 8 he was in Greece."

"How did you come by this?" asked Federico.

"Don't worry about that. It's best that you shouldn't know. Anyway read it."

Federico took the typed pages on thin yellowing paper, that began with the title:

"Report on the events on the islands of Kefalonia and Corfu." Then he went on:

"Italian military authorities in the island of Kefalonia found out about the armistice between Italian and Anglo-American forces through evening radio announcements on September 8, 1943.

At that date the island was occupied by a few units of the Acqui Division based in Argostoli, the main town located on the island.

The units were the entire 17th Infantry Regiment, the 317th Infantry, a group of the 33rd Artillery Regiment, the 7th, 94th and 188th Artillery Group of the Army Corps, the 3rd Anti-aircraft 75/27 c.k., two companies of the 110th Battalion of Army Corps machine gunners, one Engineer Battalion, two companies of laborers, one company of field engineers, a photoelectric section, minor units of cannons of 70/15 and anti-aircraft machine gunners of 20 mm, the 44th Medical Unit with three field hospitals of which two are active (the 37th and the 527th) and another, the 581st, that had retreated, and finally the naval units that were in charge of the port and in control of naval movements, plus other minor air force units. In total about 12,000 men.

The western part of the peninsula called Liruri was under the control of German troops that had arrived recently with a small detachment of 6 tanks in the town of Argostoli. The German units amounted to 2000 men.

The armistice clauses ordered that the Italian Army, wherever it may be located, "end all hostile actions against the Anglo-American forces" and was to offer "armed resistance against anyone who dared to engage in violent acts against Italian troops."

During the early hours of the following day, September 9, a radio message from the headquarters of the XIth Army signed by General Vecchiarelli made it clear that his orders were to not join "the English or the Greek rebels and to continue friendly relations with the German units, except for necessary armed resistance from any quarter including the latter."

News of the armistice was instantly circulated, leading to joyful reactions among both Italian and German soldiers and mostly among the civilian population. One could hear shots being fired in celebration with rifles, pistols or hand grenades; Italian and German enlisted men were fraternizing and singing together arm in arm: people would embrace one another in the streets; the bells of many churches, especially around Argostoli and in the countryside, were ringing uninterruptedly.

Strong measures stopped the celebrations and the confusion when large units of German and Italian soldiers began to patrol the streets of the towns and the environs, quickly returning the situation to normal.

At the same time during the night orders issued by General Gandin, the military commander of the island of Kefalonia and of the ACQUI division, began the movement of various artillery and infantry units towards the outskirts and around Argostoli. These movements and those that took place during the days that followed were justified as cautionary to safeguard public order. No one however could avoid thinking that they were actually precautions due to the uncertainty of German reactions that could take place against us.

On September 9 General Gandin invited the commander of the German units, Colonel Barge, to lunch at the mess of the divisional headquarters. There was a genuinely cordial atmosphere between the two men. During the toast the German officer expressed his thoughts more or less as follows: "The Italian armistice signals the defeat of your unfortunate homeland. This is no fault of yours. You have sworn allegiance to your King; we have sworn allegiance to our Führer. In no other part of the world have German soldiers received as warm and fraternal welcome as by you on this island. The warm words that you, General, have addressed to our men in our language filled us with pride for the cause we are fighting for, and of love for our friend, Italy. We have been allies until today. Our soldiers felt brotherly kinship with your soldiers. But if an ugly star were to turn us into adversaries, we shall be chivalrous and fair. I lift my glass to wish you the best future for your homeland!"

Throughout September 9, that was full of news from Italy and Greece, the situation remained extremely confused. Rumors were rife that the Germans had violently taken over XIth Army headquarters and those of the 8th Army Corps in command of the ACQUI Division. The soldiers became excited when they heard of clashes taking place nearby on the Greek mainland between our forces and the Germans, who were guilty of violence against the Italians.

The sudden appearance of written and oral Greek propaganda increased the confusion. Thousands of leaflets were being distributed among the enlisted men encouraging them to liberate Italy from the Germans, since it had already freed itself from the fascists. "Italy and Greece" proclaimed the leaflets "the two most civilized nations in the world, cannot be enslaved to the barbarous Germany. The Greek brothers shall stand next to their Italian brothers in their sacred struggle for freedom and civilization. Long live one single Italy, free and independent!" The propaganda was being distributed out in the open. The commanders ordered to have the leaflets confiscated but took no action against those responsible, except for a few isolated instances.

During the early hours of September 10 a coded radio message from XIth Army headquarters suddenly ordered (contrary to the wording of the previous message) to surrender all weapons to the Germans without conditions. General Gandin decided that it had to be apocryphal and the corps commanders agreed as well. (It was known that the headquarters of the XIth Army and the VIIIth Corps and their code books had been taken by the Germans.) That document was therefore ignored as they waited for better and more accurate information. The divisional commanders tried but failed to contact the high command in Italy or in Greece for clear instructions.

On the morning of September 11 there was the General Communion of my artillery regiment soldiers of the 3rd Battery, for three fellow soldiers who had recently become the victims of an accident. The divisional commander, Colonel Mario Romagnoli, spoke asking that everyone remain calm, confident, disciplined and loyal in every way. He warned against the ulterior motives of local propaganda and ordered everyone to remain compact and disciplined, and obey the orders of their commanders. "We will wait for decisions by the commanders and whatever they are we shall follow them, in perfect discipline and for the benefit of our unfortunate homeland."

That same afternoon the General summoned all the chaplains present on the island to his headquarters. We all went over thinking that he wanted to encourage us to intensify our mission and keep the morale of the soldiers high in such dire circumstances, and we repeated to ourselves: "If the General can maintain cordial relations with the German units they should erect a monument to him in solid gold!"

We were totally unprepared for the sad surprise awaiting us and the kind of critical advice we were going to be asked to give. The General was very pale, standing in front of his desk. He began: "Before I speak to the Corps commanders I wanted to call the chaplains. You are priests, the ministers of God. I value your advice very much. You know the feelings of the enlisted man better than anyone and can be of great help right now. This is a tragic moment for me, since I am responsible for the lives of over 10,000 young men that can be placed at risk by the decisions I am about to take.

Let me read you the ultimatum I have just received a few hours ago from the German high command in Athens:

The communication asks the Acqui Division to decide one of the following points:

1. To continue fighting against the old enemy with the German Armed Forces.
2. Fight against the German Armed forces.
3. Hand over your weapons peacefully.

The general had a short comment.

1. First of all we must remember that we have sworn to God and to our homeland to be loyal to His Majesty, the King Emperor. I will not be the one to remind our priests that an oath is a serious and sacred act, whereby God himself is called as a witness of what we say and promise to do. The new legitimate government of the King signed an armistice with the old enemy. We therefore cannot take up arms against that enemy.

2. On the other hand why - without serious motives or provocation - should we turn our guns against a nation that was at our side as an ally for three years, fighting the same war, sharing our sacrifices and hoping for the same victory?

3. Peacefully lay down our weapons!...They have assured me that this only meant heavy weapons, that for the most part have been provided by the Germans themselves. But wouldn't this violate the spirit of the armistice and would we not then go against the loyalty oath we swore to the King Emperor? And then what would happen to our honor, the single most important thing to us soldiers, and to an unfortunate Army that remained glorious, as the Italian Army?

I must decide on one of these three points! Think about the fact that should an armed conflict take place against the Germans, we would at first have the upper hand on this island since we have the greater numbers and are stronger. But let us not forget that the island is surrounded by the sea and that behind us, on the Greek mainland, are over 300,000 Germans ready to come to the rescue with men and supplies. We have no hope of any help or supplies. Finally we don't have a single plane, while the Germans can attack the island with squads of "Stukas" and butcher us all without any opposition.

Finally, would our men put up a fight? Would they continue to resist even while they were being bombed from the air? Please think about these decisions since I have very little time left (it is 6 p.m. and the German commander wants my answer by 7 p.m.). Each one of you should give me his views without wasting time with questions or useless discussions. Tell me which of the three points you can suggest I choose in good conscience, as a lesser evil."

Called upon to give advice of such a serious nature without having any time to be informed about the issue, nor being able to discuss it and debate among ourselves…we attempted to ask a few questions regarding the attitude the Germans might have toward the division and the way they would treat the men…But the General cut us off saying that he had no idea and requested once more that we give him our choice among the three points without further ado.

We all opted for point three, except for one of us.

The General thanked us and ended saying: "Pray to God so that he may assist me at such a grave hour for the Division that is so tragic for my conscience."

We then left and avoided speaking with the officers that were crowding the halls outside seeking information. As soon as we were outside we looked at each other dazed, as if we were in a dream. We decided to go nearby to the Institute of the Italian Nuns and stop to pray to Jesus of the Sacraments. Then we assembled in the main room and examined every angle at length. We agreed that all things considered, for us priests it was a duty to give the kind of advice that we had already offered to the General.

We immediately drafted a letter and sent it to him:

"General:

As soon as we left your office we went to church to request God's help and met once more in the main room of the Institute of Italian Nuns. We calmly examined and thought through what you described, and the opinions each one of us had in good conscience at such a grave moment.

In order to avoid a bloody battle that would be unequal and fateful against our former ally, and to remain loyal to the oath given to His Majesty the King Emperor - an oath that as you explained involves God himself as a witness - and finally in order to avoid useless bloodshed among brothers...then to lay down our arms peacefully.

Faced with the German ultimatum you, General, isolated and unable to communicate with the high command in Italy and in Greece to obtain specific orders, find yourself in the position of having to accept to make a difficult decision to avoid the useless supreme sacrifice of your officers and men.

We fully understand the extreme seriousness of your responsibility and the heavy burden that weighs on your shoulders. Now more than ever your chaplains are close to you. You may count on our devotion, our work and, most of all, our prayers. We ask God at this hour, at this time, to enlighten your spirit and provide comfort to your heart. May he always protect and bless you, General! And bless your family that is far away and your beloved Division.

Your Chaplains,
(Signed)
....
....
....

The General managed to delay his answer. He received the corps commanders. Later on he also saw Colonel Barge, the commander of the German garrison. In the meantime a few bombs went off and some rifle shots caused a panic among the population that went running for cover.

Some soldiers who returned from the island of Santa Maura had said that the garrison, after laying down their arms, hadn't been allowed to return to Italy but instead was marched off to concentration camps at Missolonghi. The thought of being treated as POWs and the news that the General had been handed a German ultimatum with less than honorable conditions made the officers and the men very nervous.

The following day, Sunday the 12th - I was saying mass - and was able to visit the batteries of my regiment. I could no longer recognize them. My artillery men who were usually in good spirits, well disciplined and quiet, suddenly appeared to be extremely agitated. The word was going around - among the rest of the troops as well - that the General intended to disarm the entire Division in a "cowardly" way when they were facing such a tiny number of Germans. The General was being called "pro-German," a "coward," a "traitor" and worse even. In a state of extreme agitation, officers and artillery men were screaming that I must report back that they would not have surrendered their weapons to anyone, because "you fall on your weapons but you don't give them up."

The level of excitement was very high and spreading like wildfire. Suddenly at 11 a.m. they sounded the "alert" for every unit on the island. I was at one of the batteries. The commander gave the order to "man the guns"! It was welcomed with cries of joy by the men who began cursing the Germans and were ready to open fire. Fortunately it turned out to be a false alarm but it only made the soldiers even more aggressive since they were ready to fight. The General was working day and night to reach an honorable solution, and as the officers were coming and going to negotiate it was clear how difficult it was to reach an agreement. In the meantime the Greek population became very agitated. Many former Greek officers showed up at the headquarters of various units, asking for weapons and requesting to be considered for a fight against the Germans. They were sent away rather brutally. Elsewhere, especially in the smaller units, Greek men and women obtained weapons and lots of ammunition.

Suddenly arrived the news that in the Lixuri area the Germans, having numerical superiority and without waiting for the conclusion of the ongoing negotiations, had surrounded and forced two batteries of 100/17 and 105/28 to surrender. This information - which was true - upset the tense soldiers even more.

Incidents by then were rife and even more so since German reinforcements were arriving continuously at the German fort at Lixuri, using motor rafts and large transport planes. There was shooting and hand grenades were exploding following inflammatory and threatening statements. No officer could use conciliatory language to call for discipline and calm without being instantly accused of being a "traitor" or a "coward."

In the late afternoon the General summoned the war council to artillery headquarters. Brigadier General Grezzi, all the Colonels of the corps, the Royal Navy commander, the commander of the Royal Carabinieri and the corps of Engineers commander were all present. A hand grenade was thrown at the General's car as he traveled to that meeting, fortunately without doing any damage. A bit later a soldier was foolhardy enough to force the car to slow down while another enlisted man tore off the tricolor flag, yelling at the General that he was not worthy to fly it.

The night turned into a war vigil. A few grenades were thrown into the artillery men's mess hall as intimidation. The units were in open revolt. Maps and very important documents were being destroyed in the offices; inkwells were smashed and the ink spilled on the floor, writing paper was destroyed, tables were turned upside down and files torn apart...Some were getting ready to escape, or planning reprisals, punishment and revenge...

At dawn on the 13th two large German motor rafts tried to dock at the port of Argostoli. Suddenly there was very heavy artillery and rifle fire. The two rafts were hit, killing every soldier on board. The Germans fired back with artillery from the batteries at Argostoli and cannon at Lixuri. There were casualties, dead and wounded on both sides. The divisional commander was unable to enforce his cease fire orders. Some artillery commanders refused to obey them and other artillery positions moved without proper orders from points inside the island toward the town.

The shelling lasted for about one hour and a half while the small arms fire and hand grenades went on for about three hours. In the meantime a seaplane arrived from Athens with a German Colonel and an Italian Air Force Captain. It reached the island in the midst of heavy shelling and was forced to circle for a long time before it could land on the water. The discussion with these new officers calmed everyone's nerves. The divisional commander informed all units that an agreement had been reached, and that the Division would cede the island to the German garrison and would return to Italy with all its heavy and light weapons. Everyone was told to remain calm since "the honor of the Division and the Army remained unsullied."

Unfortunately the reprieve was to be short lived. Orders followed for the units to move to the area of Sami, where the Division was to assemble before boarding ship. During the night Division headquarters and all Italian military units found out that the German high command was refusing to load the heavy weapons on board for the time being along with the soldiers, because of the dearth of shipping. Those weapons would therefore be assembled at Sami and shipped as soon as possible.

Everyone viewed this new delay - rightly thought to be a specious excuse - as the beginning of a new trick and a fraud. During the night the artillery men of the two batteries taken by the Germans at Lixuri arrived. They told the other men that although they surrendered without fighting, once they were disarmed, they were kept facing a wall for half a day with German machine guns pointed at them. They had been mistreated and humiliated in front of the local population. These descriptions gave rise to universal hatred everywhere that became a series of open calls for revenge. Some units began refusing to obey the orders to transfer out. Commanders were calling to say that their men were refusing to move and were becoming increasingly threatening. Even the General, seeing that the agreement couldn't be enforced, was beginning to think about taking decisive action. Through a few officers his ideas were relayed to all the units. Meanwhile the General compiled a history of the negotiations up to that point for all the units.

A warlike mood spread quickly everywhere and by noon the entire Division was ready for any kind of action. On the same day, during the early morning hours, negotiations started once more after a German initiative and continued all day with increasing intensity. In the Italian units the officers and men were now fed up with all these changes and the unnerving uncertainty. Everywhere there were protests: "Enough negotiations: let's end the talks!" The rekindled excitement began growing in intensity as more Germans were seen arriving at Lixuri by sea and on heavy transport planes. One exasperated battery aimed its artillery pieces at the Divisional Command intending to blow it to pieces.

Another news item got the soldiers very excited. There was a rumor that suddenly made the rounds that at Corfu Italian soldiers had overrun the German stronghold despite their Air Force's involvement. Around 15:00 hours the sky quickly filled with German "Stukas" flying over the island and the area of

Argostoli, with a number of spectacular acrobatics. Italian anti-Aircraft batteries did not open fire. The German planes also avoided making any attacks or bombing the area. Those moves were meant as a serious and meaningful warning for us. During the night of the 14th to the 15th large supplies continued to be ferried in by ship and by air. At divisional headquarters there were so many unanimous complaints and protests that the General was forced to inform the German commander that any further arrival of a German seaplane to the island during the negotiations would be viewed as a hostile action. A few hours later, as a big German seaplane tried to disembark men and supplies in the bay of Lixuri, our batteries opened fire against it.

The seaplane took a direct hit and sank. This virtually opened the hostilities. After one more hour the sky was filled once more with German aircraft and the area instantly became an inferno of explosions, shooting, fire and destruction. These operations lasted from September 15 to 22 with a number of other clashes. On the evening of the first day of fighting the German garrison on Argostoli was bravely and effectively attacked by the 2nd Battalion of our 17th Infantry Regiment and forced into combat on the small peninsula of San Teodoro, on the hills called "Telegraphos".

Many motorboats and rafts came in from Lixuri to rescue the embattled garrison, but Italian artillery hit each one with well aimed fire setting them on fire and sinking them with many casualties and men overboard. By midnight the garrison was forced to surrender, which was granted at 2 a.m. We had taken many prisoners and captured large quantities of weapons, including the mechanized artillery pieces at Argostoli.

During the early hours the next morning bloody fighting resumed in the western part of the island against the units at the garrison of Lixuri and continued fiercely for the next few days. However the unequal nature of the harsh fighting quickly became obvious to everyone. Thanks to the continuous flow of supplies the German adversary had certainly overtaken our numbers and equipment. The sky remained filled with German aircraft that turned the island into a constantly erupting volcano. Italian infantry could not move freely. The soldiers were being mercilessly massacred and cut down by dive bombers and constant deadly machine gunning at very low altitude. Our artillery was unable to react because as soon as they were located they were destroyed. On the morning of the fourth day of fighting German planes blanketed the island with huge clouds of leaflets. I reproduce that text in its entirety:

COMRADES OF THE ITALIAN ARMY

Because of Badoglio's treachery Fascist Italy and National Socialist Germany were deserted in a cowardly way during their fateful struggle. The Badoglio Army in Greece has laid down its arms completely without bloodshed. Only the ACQUI Division under General Gandin, a follower of Badoglio, located in the islands of Kefalonia and Corfù and therefore isolated from the other territories, has rejected the peaceful offer to hand over its weapons and began fighting against his German and fascist comrades.

This struggle is totally hopeless. The Division is split in two, surrounded by water with no supplies and no hope of any kind of rescue coming from our enemies.

We, your German comrades, do not want this fight. We therefore invite you to lay down your weapons and give yourselves up to the German garrisons on the islands. Then for you, as well as for the other Italian comrades, the road back to your homeland shall be open. If however the current unreasonable resistance shall continue, you will all be crushed and annihilated in a few hours by overwhelming German forces that are now being assembled. Those who fall prisoner on that occasion shall not be able to return home.

Therefore Italian comrades, join the German ranks as soon as you receive this leaflet.

It is your only hope to save yourselves!

THE GERMAN COMMANDING GENERAL OF THE ARMY CORPS

The leaflets, instead of weakening or changing the soldier's feelings, exacerbated them even more and strengthened their will to resist to the end. The struggle continued even more violently in the next few days. However enemy aircraft was attacking the Italian units and destroying the batteries with many casualties, causing increasingly wide gaps with deadly and devastating accuracy. Not a single Italian aircraft was available to counter the massive German airpower while the anti-aircraft batteries were unable to fire effectively, and were forced to remain almost completely inactive.

Once events took such a tragic turn the situation appeared to become absolutely desperate. It was humanly impossible to continue fighting, German units were advancing everywhere. Surrender now appeared inevitable since the morning of the 21st, when a final desperate Italian attack was stopped in time by the enemy. However the General wanted to "play the final card" and resist until the 22nd, hoping for some kind of help coming from Italy which had been promised in no uncertain terms during radio communications, that had reached the island with the warmest congratulations from the Italian High Command.

Finally on September 22 at noon - having accepted the futility of any further resistance since the divisional command was completely surrounded by advancing German units - the General was forced to surrender. It was accepted without conditions in the early afternoon.

In all probability the Germans had prior orders to destroy the entire Division once the battle was over, or to decimate it in large numbers. In fact since the morning of the 21st, as Italian units began surrendering according to the rules of war, they were being almost totally killed. Officers were separated from the men and were murdered for the most part, while the soldiers were decimated in massive numbers. Even the 44th Medical Unit, whose men all wore Red Cross armbands, was isolated and totally annihilated after falling into German hands. Out of 90 men only about fifteen survived.

Against every international rule the decimation of our troops went on after the official surrender of Divisional Command, during the entire afternoon of the 22nd and all day on the 23rd. The surviving officers were captured and some were taken to the "Mussolini Barracks", others to the prisons. The divisional command, the General and the artillery Colonel all went to the apartment of the former naval commander. I was captured with that group.

On the morning of the 24th at about 7 a.m. the General suddenly left with a German officer. We were told to be ready at 7:30 a.m. We were all thinking that they were taking us to an interrogation. At 7:45 they called us out and told us to get into a few command cars. A German sentry, seeing me wearing my hassock and a Red Cross armband, wanted to prevent me from getting on board but an officer signaled that I was to go with the others. The way the trip was being organized indicated to me and to my companions of the tragic purpose of that mysterious journey. We were all very calm. The cars passed by the civilian hospital, the munitions dump, the last buildings…traveling behind the peninsula of Saint Theodore where we all knew very well that there was only…a rocky desert.

At that point there could be no further doubt!

The tragic convoy reached a lonely country house. We got off and stood against the wall that surrounded the house, as we saw the German soldiers turned toward us with their helmets on and their submachine guns leveled at us.

We clearly understood the situation.

Three times, either to delay a mass execution that I thought was about to take place, or to try to stop the awful massacre, I went up to a group of German NCOs who were in charge of the unit. I protested several times: "It is impossible that even the lowest level Second Lieutenant could have no other responsibility than to obey his commanding officers! It is contrary to all international rules that you should put us to death like this after your commander has officially agreed and accepted surrender and we have all been disarmed!"

I begged for everyone's sake that they give us at least some form of interrogation. I proclaimed everyone to be innocent and not deserving to be put to death. But - and this was done on purpose - there were no officers present and able to take responsibility. I was brutally taken back against the wall. I made one final attempt showing my hassock and the International Red Cross armband that I was wearing. The ironic answer I received was exactly as follows: "Well, to talk about the Red Cross when we are in the fifth year of war…!"

Then I returned to the group of officers and told them: "Friends and Brothers! You now know what's in store for us. We can only address ourselves to God and trust in His infinite compassion. We shall all ask Him together to forgive our sins and I - his minister - with the authority that He and His Church have given me in this tragic moment, shall give everyone the sacramental absolution. Let us accept death with serenity and as a holocaust of expiation for the mistakes we made during our lives. Our blood, because of the blood of Christ Crucified, will be for our soul the cleansing of purification. Let us be ready to appear with confidence in front of the throne of God, our Father and Creator!"

What followed was a moving scene that reminded me of the beginnings of Christianity when the martyrs, before being thrown to the wild animals in the amphitheater, would all assemble in prayer around the priest as he gave the benediction. All the men fell to their knees. Many lifted their hands to the sky. Others had a prayer book or rosary beads. Some were looking at a sacred image or a medal that they had around their necks. Many took the photographs of their loved ones out of their wallets and showed them to the men next to them. Slowly we all recited the act of sorrow, marking each word calmly. Then loudly I recited in the plural the entire Absolution as it is prescribed in the individual sacrament of penance.

Three platoons of eight men each. Two executioners were aiming at one man: one at the chest, the other at the head. Each body was also given the so called "coup de grâce" at the temple. Everyone was absolutely calm. Each one came to me before going in front of the firing squad to give me his wedding ring for his wife to have, or a gold chain, or his watch, or some other small memento. All of them gave me their wallets. All of them had me write down their family's address and a few dictated their last will or some very special errand for me to do for them.

Many who feared they couldn't succeed in giving me their things and were unable to move away from the wall, called me desperately to come to them. For a short time, in that awful death house, there was only one cry being repeated everywhere by hundreds and hundreds of voices: "Chaplain! Chaplain! Here! Here one minute!..."

I thought I was losing my sanity not knowing where to go first, as I ran like an automaton from one side to the other, along the tragic lineup of men about to die. I was being given objects and wrote notes while I offered to each one my Christian words of comfort. The Germans, who at first had sent me roughly back against the wall with the others, were now allowing me to go on.

The terrible martyrdom of those goodbyes went on for four hours, with interminable hugs and tearful kisses that wet our faces. Some men threw themselves to my feet and not satisfied with the collective absolution wanted to make an individual confession. Others grabbed my hassock as if they would never let go. Many grab and kiss my hands in a frenzy, covering them with tears and cold sweat.

Second Lieutenant La Terza said: "Chaplain, I cling to you so I can live a minute longer!" He was brutally torn away and thrown to his death. My beloved Colonel Romagnoli who was always such an adoring father to one of his daughters, a university student and Red Cross volunteer, told me solemnly as he gave me his gold watch: "Don Formato, you know my family's address. If you can get to Rome go and comfort my wife and bring her this wedding ring. The watch you'll give to my daughter instead, and you will tell her that she will always live in the sacred memory of her father. Goodbye Don Formato, and thank you for your work for the Regiment." After hugging and kissing me again, the unforgettable Colonel went to his death with his pipe stuck in his mouth!

Captain Montanari, who was a dear friend, had recently lost his mother and told me: "Don Formato, tell my dad that I died as a strong and good Christian!" Second Lieutenant Poma: "Don Formato, go see my dad and tell everyone not to cry too much, because I am dying with a clear conscience!" Lieutenant Bernardini, from Rome gave me two photos for his fiancée and told me with tears in his eyes: "Chaplain tell that poor girl that since we couldn't be together on this earth we shall meet again up there!..."

It is impossible to give a detailed description of the individual and heartbreaking scenes that tore open the soul during those four hours of collective martyrdom. I attempted to make several protests to save this or that officer, showing the cards that proved their membership in the Fascist Party or the Voluntary Militia. For a few others I argued that they were very old and had many children. It was rare that any of them were allowed to move away. Others were saved by the fact that they came from South Tyrol or Trieste and its environs. Finally around 1 p.m., when I thought I could see fatigue and fear in the dark circles around the eyes of a German officer, I went up to him and held out my hands, crying out more than asking, with tears streaming down my face: "Please at least save this last group! You have been shooting for four hours! Enough, enough! Save the last ones!" I was unable to continue as I sobbed uncontrollably. But perhaps my cries shocked the officer who was already under stress. Shortly after the NCO interpreter came up to me and patted me on the shoulder, whispering "Good, good! Now the officer will go and ask the German commander."

I felt that there was some hope and thought to ask the Virgin collectively to confirm. I approached the survivors, some of whom were crying, and said: "Friends! Keep your chin up! Let's recite three Hail Marys to the Virgin, so she may fulfill the last attempt I just made." We prayed the Mother of God with such fervor:

"Pray for us sinners!"

Half an hour later, after immense moral anguish and excruciating expectation, the officer returned to announce:

"THE GERMAN COMMAND WILL ALLOW THOSE PRESENT TO LIVE!"

I warmly shook the officer's hand and began sobbing uncontrollably once more. Then I witnessed a ghoulish scene that filled me with both terror and indignation besides pity: the enraged German soldiers, who were now free, were suddenly opening and scattering the luggage of those executed, behaving like wild hyenas, and ripping those belongings apart. Then they took the names of the survivors and made them sign a statement adhering to Germany's decision to "Free Italy from the Anglo-American invaders."

I asked to be allowed to properly bury my dear friends and the others who had died. It was useless! They promised, they gave us hope, they betrayed us and finally they took me back to town, where I was locked up like any other prisoner. They didn't allow me to even identify the bodies or make a list of the dead, so that I don't even know the exact number of those who were killed nor the name and address of many of them. I know that most of the bodies of the officers and the men were not buried in separate pits or even collectively. For several nights many fires could be seen against the sky on that island. The bodies were piled one on top of the other, doused with gasoline and burned for a very long time! We also found out later on that after the escape of two officers from a field hospital, the Germans in reprisal took all the officers in hospitals for whatever reason, be it illness or wounded in combat - some in critical condition - and shot them by firing squad.

All the objects given to me by the officers along with the wallets, family addresses, the various notes of the last will and testament and personal errands, were all kept in two leather bags and two nap sacks. Even that sacred inheritance for the families far away was taken from me with the promise that it would be returned. In spite of all my begging, I was unable to obtain anything more and was told later on that those belongings had all been sent to the Red Cross. However, after careful investigations with the help of Apostolic Delegation and the Athens Red Cross, it became clear that this wasn't true. Like everyone else, I was relieved of everything except for the light clothing we were wearing. Then we were left to starve and sleep on the bare floor for over one month, until they finally took us away.

We said good bye with a heavy heart to that island of martyrdom on the rainy morning of November 12! The island that still has the unburied bodies of so many of our dearest friends and saw the ashes of the others scattered by the wind!

During the ten days of tragedy at Kefalonia it is estimated that 4000 men and 500 officers were killed. And this was not to be the end of the tragic fate of the ACQUI Division.

All the 7000 survivors were held as prisoners and left almost to die of hunger, and thirst. Then they were loaded on a few ships to be taken to the continent in Greece. Two of those ships, the larger ones, went on to hit mine fields and exploded, killing almost all the prisoners on board, the poor sons of Italy!

> Signed Romualdo Formato
> Sacred Heart Missionary
> Military Chaplain
> 33rd Artillery Regiment ACQUI

Alberto told Federico to turn the page. There was a short additional note under the following title:

WHAT HAPPENED TO THE OFFICERS
OF THE ACQUI DIVISION
GARRISONED AT CORFU?

"To the report" - the additional text read - "on the very sad events at Kefalonia, I must add another painful note. The garrison on the island of Corfu - where there also were units of the ACQUI Division - attempted to resist the demands made by the German troops. A few contradictory rumors had filtered in regarding the events at Kefalonia.

On Corfu the resistance was short lived (from September 23 to 26). It appears that after the surrender, the German command shot only Colonel Lusignani, the military commander on the island and of the 18th Infantry Regiment, and his aide de camp, a Major. All the other officers who had been captured were later taken by boat to the Greek continent. But a tragic mystery surrounded their fate.

What happened on the high seas or after landing in Greece? No one was ever able to find out the truth.

When in mid-November I was passing through Missolonghi on my way to Athens, two soldiers managed to contact me and give me the first page - the one with personal data - of the officer's identification booklet belonging to Captain Carlo Bonali, the commander of anti-aircraft artillery in Corfù.

They also told me what had happened.

There were rumors that a few days after the officers who were on Corfu were taken on board ship to Igoumeniza, on continental Greece, the dead body of Captain Bonali washed ashore. He was part of that same group. The corpse, although bloated from exposure, was still recognizable along with his wounds. He was in his shirtsleeves wearing his officer's pants. His hands were bound behind his back and there were signs of many wounds (over twenty five) that were unmistakably identified as bayonet stabs.

A few Italians who managed to elude the German watch were able to extract from the back pocket of his pants (his side pockets were empty) the dead man's identification booklet. Fearful that the booklet might be seized by the Germans, they decided to tear off only the first inside page - the most important one - that provides all personal identification about the officer. Later they were able to give that page to other soldiers going to the mainland to try to give it to the Chaplain.

On November 15 those soldiers saw me in transit at Missolonghi and handed me the paper, which I still have in my possession. Other soldiers from Corfu that I was able to meet said that two other corpses of officers had been sewn into a canvas bag, that also washed up on shore in tatters. I was told that several other officers of the garrison at Corfù who arrived at Igumeniza had been killed behind the hospital, in the buildings of the former command post.

In spite of my research regarding the officers of the Corfu garrison, I was never able to obtain any information about their fate. A frightful question surfaced out of all this: what happened to all the Italian officers at Corfu?

Signed: R.F."

Federico looked up from those crumpled pages. Outside, the Lungotevere was now shrouded in darkness. One more night of curfew, enforced by the many Nazi patrols that were now in control of the city.

14.

The train stopped at the station of a small village called Pathankot. Vittorio got off with a group of prisoners under tight British escort. It was raining. They were taken into another railroad car with a narrow gauge that wound its way through valleys and up hills that became progressively higher and more treacherous. Rice paddies were being cultivated on the terraces and creeks had to be crossed on very shaky bridges hanging among the rocks. Dirty dark skinned children moved cows around by beating them with long sticks.

Once they reached their destination, they found out from a battered sign that it was called Nagrota. The prisoners were loaded into trucks waiting along the road. Vittorio was disoriented and in awe of the immense mountains he could see in the background. The road that the trucks were on stopped rather quickly as a huge rocky surface appeared after a bend. At close range you could make out many small houses lined up next to one another. Maybe they were barracks. They were built in any case according to a pattern that was very different from that of other Indian villages. The trucks were heading in that direction and, as they came closer, you could see the barbed wire surrounding the rocky surface under an imposing mountain. These were actually barracks made of dark wood covered with aluminum siding, as they appeared at a distance. Behind the enclosure there was a varied crowd of men dressed in odd pieces of uniform picked up by chance or out of need.

Once they were inside the gate Vittorio and the others got off. It was raining hard without any pauses, thereby freeing many malodorous vapors. Below there were a Maltese and an Italian, wearing what had once been a Colonel's uniform. He introduced himself as Nardozzi and said: "You are now at Yol. The mountains behind the rocky mound are the beginning of the Himalayas. North of us there are only mountain tops eight thousand meters high that separates us from Tibet and Afghanistan. To the south we are thousands of kilometers from the first port. We are divided into four camps: 25, 26, 27 and 28, each one is under the command of an Italian superior officer. Above us is the British General Laird, in overall charge. Now you will be assigned to a barracks and your colleagues will explain everything else. Just remember one thing however: we are still at war with the British. Even though Mussolini was removed as a result of betrayal, we remain the soldiers of the Empire founded by the fascist government. Let us demonstrate this by our bearing in the face of the enemy."

Now Vittorio felt as if he had truly reached the end of the road, that was called the Valley of Kangra, in the State of Himachal Pradesh. The snowcapped mountain tops he could see, with mount Nodrani in the forefront, were part of the Dhola Dhar chain. Beyond there were only the Himalayas, the roof of the world. In theory it is every prisoner of war's duty to attempt to escape but in this place the very word sounded grotesque. Vittorio was sent to camp 28 under Nardozzi's command. A Captain of the Alpini welcomed him to the barracks:

"Where did you say you arrived from?"

"Dehradun."

"No, I meant in Italy. Where are you from?"

"Puglia" answered Vittorio.

"There's another Pugliese here in our wing. Maybe you know each other."

"It's a big region. What's his name?"

"Vito. He spends his time growing his garden out there."

Vittorio looked down and smiled. He left his pack on his angareb and went outside. The orderly was bent over a pile of rocks, working on something green that you couldn't quite make out.

"I knew that at some point or other you would wind up with me once again!" said Vittorio.

Vito turned around in disbelief and then looked embarrassed. He stood at attention holding his dirty hands at his side.

"Lieutenant! Sir! My God!"

"How are you Vito?"

"Doing well, Sir. At least, as well as we can."

"Why are you standing at attention like a frozen fish?"

"Doing my duty, Sir!"

Vittorio gave him a pat on the back

"What happened to you after leaving the ship at Bombay?"

"They put me on a train to a location called Bhopal. A rotten place full of mosquitoes and malaria. Fortunately I didn't stay there too long. After a few months they shipped me up here. And you Lieutenant? Where are you coming from?"

"Dehradun."

"Why did they transfer you here?"

"I beat up a Cavalry Major. He told me that the Italians who died at war were worthless."

"Good man, Lieutenant! Had I been there, I would have beat him up as well."

"Before I was shipped up here they gave me 28 days in the brig - the calabush - punitive isolation cells in the camps."

"Bastards."

Vittorio shrugged his shoulders.

"But here there are only rocks, Vito. What the hell are you growing?"

"With some patience you can get things to grow even between the rocks. You should know, that it's exactly like at the "Cruste". This land is good, if you know how to handle it. These are some red peppers."

"How can you cook them without any oil?"

"Lieutenant, you have bad habits. Back home we would make olive oil for the masters, but as for ourselves we cooked with water. I even invented a recipe: I call it peppers Indian Style, which is without everything else! Let me know what you think when you taste it."

"I can imagine it, Vito."

" The fact is that at times here we are really famished. You have to help yourself."

"How is the camp organized?"

"We are on top of the world and the Indian sentries will shoot very fast. A few months ago they killed two Italian Captains. I think their names were Viale and Rossi. The British claim they were trying to escape. We said that they were just singing a patriotic song. The fact remains that they shot them and now they are at Camp 29."

"But aren't there only four camps?" asked Vittorio.

"Yes, excuse-me. Camp 29 in prison parlance is the cemetery. It's a few kilometers outside Yol. When they bury someone they even have an honor guard and fly the tricolor flag."

Vittorio changed the subject.

"Have they informed you that Mussolini has been ousted?"

"Yes, with loudspeakers. But we also have our own phantom radio to get real news from Italy. But don't tell anyone. It's a secret. These two twin brothers built it, I think their name was Biscarini. They found bits of aluminum, copper wire, valves that were smuggled in and somehow they managed to set it up. But it works. The British know that it exists and they are going crazy looking for it, but never manage to do so."

"Are all the other prisoners in tatters?"

"Lieutenant, what can I say? After two or even three years behind barbed wire your brain gets feverish. Some of them even got engaged to one another. Can you imagine such a thing, Lieutenant?"

Vittorio started teasing him.

"You just keep thinking about your fiancée back home."

"Don't you worry, Lieutenant. I think about her a lot. The poor thing even wrote back to me. Well, actually the parish priest wrote the letter for her, that when I return home it will not even be necessary to confess to my bad thoughts."

Vittorio laughed.

"But what I don't like - continued Vito - are the fanatical fascists. They go around making black lists of those who support Badoglio. They threaten that once Mussolini returns to Rome they will make them pay. They even beat a few guys up, by placing them under a piece of canvas and then kicking them. They call it the "cover." But what does it mean? We are here, on the other side of the world, trying to survive. And I have always managed to keep my chin up all by myself."

* * *

The Red Cross delegate Charles Huber who had been active in the hills of Dehradun also traveled up to the mountains at Yol, to report on all the camps of Group V that was under the jurisdiction of the British commander at Smila. The report he sent to Geneva with the help of Colonel Gambuzza described the tension and uncertainty, but also the desperate need to create a kind of surrogate of normal life.

"Camp population for 25, 26, 27 and 28 is 9163 Italian officers and 3495 non-commissioned officers and soldiers."

Just like at Dehradun but even worse, he was worried about illness.

"At the time of our visit 345 prisoners (262 officers and 83 non-commissioned officers and men) were in the hospital wards. The illnesses are as follows:

Gastrointestinal problems: 115

Chronic illness: 26

Surgery: 24

Tuberculosis: 25

Malaria: 86

Mental illness: 8

Veneral disease: 16

Ordinary illness (fevers): 22

According to Doctor Cirillo who specializes in such cases, there are 260 internees with syphilis in the Group V camps.

Malaria. In India September and October are the worse months for this illness. Last September there were 58 new recorded cases and 208 relapsed cases. In October we counted 28 new cases and 142 relapses.

Second Lieutenant Mario De Marchis, who specializes in such cases, thinks that the weather in this region is not conducive to the treatment of tuberculosis. If the patients cannot be repatriated he requests that they be immediately transferred to a sanatorium."

Those who are not sick try to forget that they are being held behind barbed wire:

"The medical officers in the hospital have repeatedly requested the authorization to go on excursions into the mountains. The group commander has promised to consider this request favorably."

Father Gallo of the order of White Friars of Carthage was in charge of spiritual assistance.

"The authorization to fly the Italian national flag during mass has been rescinded. Use of the flag is limited to military funerals with honors. We attended the funeral of Captain Montanaro, Antonio, Camp 26, Section 2 who died at the hospital during our visit. We feel we should allow our trusted representatives to visit the sick who are at risk of death and record their final wishes. For example before the death of Captain Montanaro we asked over the phone for such an authorization for Trambusti, Ivo who had also made such a request in a letter 30 hours before the prisoner's death, but the request was unsuccessful."

You died alone at the hospital at Yol.

The Geneva Convention compels the countries holding prisoners of war to guarantee to all the officers one third of their monthly pay, but Huber was not convinced that the British were being that generous:

"The salary of the Second Lieutenants and Lieutenants is not sufficient, when you consider that they must pay 4 rupees daily for the mess hall. A Lieutenant's salary: 170 rupees, mess hall 120 rupees, which leaves 50 rupees. Second Lieutenant's: 138 rupees, mess hall 120 rupees, which leaves 18 rupees." Enough to buy one piece of underwear per month, a bar of soap or any kind of cigarette, in the shop that had been set up near the rock formation. Yet, in spite of all these hardships, the Italian prisoners who had been forgotten at the foot of the Himalayas refused to accept their stultifying situation.

"An inquiry has been started to create university courses and find out which professors are ready to give courses.

Who are the prisoners wishing to pursue their learning in the camps?

The group commander assured us that he would assemble in a single section both professors and students, once the inquiry is completed. We hope this project can be realized quickly."

A few months later Huber would inform Geneva:

University courses are open in camp 26:

Section I: Economics

Section II: Law

Section III: Polytechnical Studies, Agronomy, Natural Science

Section IV: Humanities and Philosophy

About sixty professors are giving classes, and there are 1100 students attending 7 hours of classes per day."

In order to survive at Yol you would discuss Plato or perhaps Gentile. And they also had a band:

"Colonel Buselli, the senior officer at Camp 25, had trouble finding or making a drum set for a jazz band. We purchased one at Delhi - naturally using funds from the officers of the section - and shipped it to the Camp."

But on occasion you could forget that you were behind barbed wire. "Our confidential informers agree that since the prisoners can go outside for excursions, along the river bed of a creek in the mountains they were able to create a swimming pool of sorts, using some large boulders. In Section 2 of Camp 26 the detainees found ways to create two tennis courts, two bocce courts and two volleyball courts."

It was complicated for the prisoners to communicate with Italy: "In general the prisoners noticed that the mail has slowed down. Packages take three or sometimes even six to eight months to arrive. Letters take between three and five months."

Yet Vittorio did receive something from his mother, once the Red Cross informed the family that he was still alive. Little pieces of torrone from Puglia, which was baroness Annita's specialty, arrived with the added unwelcome presence of big white worms as thick as spaghetti, that had grown fat over the months of the transoceanic trip. He wrote back on the tiny card with a few lines that were censored by the British: "Dearest Mother, I hope this letter finds you in excellent health and in good spirits. I feel well. Your thoughts made me very happy because they reminded me of the warmth of our home. When you can, please try to send me my university textbooks, the ones I failed to study in Naples that made Dad so unhappy. I hug everyone in the family and send you and my sisters an affectionate kiss."

Vito was busy removing the worms, throwing them beyond the earth of the little gardens, and he tasted the pieces of torrone: "Don't make that face Lieutenant. They are good! Your mother knows what she's doing."

Vittorio didn't want to have any and his orderly scolded him: "But why not? Where do you think the slice of bread and the soy sausages you eat at the mess come from? Can't you taste the sawdust? And those red lentils that sicken you every day, don't you know they are floating among worms?"

Vito was making an effort to create the appearance of a normal life. He had built a fetish for everything he didn't have and invented a solution to every problem, even malaria. As Huber wrote in his report to Geneva, the mosquitos were biting at Yol as well. There were nets over the angareb but too often they were not effective in stopping the insects. The doctors then gave the prisoners quinine as a remedy: the British would drink it with gin and tonic, but the Italians must swallow it in the form of a very bitter powder. Vito found a solution: in exchange for rudimentary drinking glasses, that he made by cutting with a string glass bottles stolen from the mess, he would obtain Clementine oranges from the Indian merchants. He would sprinkle the quinine over the slices and swallow it, as if it were very bitter orange marmalade: "Try it Lieutenant. It's good for you and it almost tastes good."

Using the same barter method he decided to help Lido Saltamartini, a Second Lieutenant and expert photographer, who was convinced that he could build a camera and take pictures of the camp right under the nose of the British. Lido had managed to smuggle some film and a tiny magnifying glass used by stamp collectors. Vito found a metal box of Waltham's cigarettes and some tin from a container of McLeans toothpaste. A military chaplain lent him a candle. With such instruments, God only knows how, Lido really managed to create a very small camera. He took tiny pictures by hiding it inside his pants and then rolling up the film in cigarettes after removing the tobacco. He then gave the remaining tobacco to Vito, who divided it with Vittorio by rolling it in toilet paper.

To get some additional energy the orderly reproduced the still that he had seen in the room of the Captain of the Alpini in camp 28. It distilled dried fruits and made grappa. He managed to sell the liquor under the table to the British quartermasters, who were all avid drinkers and couldn't figure out why it had such a bitter taste, that the orderly created by adding in the bottles tiny pieces of leather taken from a broken shoe.

The only missing person Vito couldn't replace was his fiancée. He didn't care to imitate the other men that had cut out photos of pin-ups from banned magazines, in order to fire up their erotic fantasies by placing them over their angareb. On some nights, though, he would go to sleep feeling so lonely and unhappy that he felt like crying.

***

There had to be a good reason to assemble all the prisoners at Yol under the loudspeakers. On the morning of September 9, 1943 one of the Maltese looking satisfied issued the orders to Vittorio's unit to go to the main assembly area. "Bad news, what else could it be?" commented Vito.

As the voice with its raspy sounds began, it announced what they were all expecting or fearing, since they were already politically split in two. Badoglio's communiqué announcing the armistice was read first, and then it was explained that those on one side of the barbed wire fence were to become the friends and allies of those on the other side.

Vittorio felt a sharp pain, just as he had when he was wounded in the head by the shrapnel from the bomb. He looked at the self-satisfied Maltese and couldn't see himself simply returning to the barracks and shaking hands. To have kept a stiff upper back would have been totally useless. The days he had spent in the brig were for nothing. To have listened to the radio in hiding to hear the banned bulletins, and find ways to nurture the will to resist, was all in vain and almost pathetic. To even try to redeem his country's honor by showing that Italians can be soldiers to the end was all simply grotesque, if they were now to turn into the obedient comrades of those who just two minutes before were the enemy. Why did it only take two minutes and why had everything changed? Perhaps because of that voice coming from the loud speakers, from a place that was far too removed to understand what it meant to defend one's dignity as a prisoner? Even the hunt for an extra piece of bread, to keep your body moving and keep alive the hope of being able to escape someday, became the empty wish of a little boy incapable of understanding the world of adults.

Vittorio returned to the barracks feeling empty but far more worried than sad. Actually he felt betrayed. It reminded him when, under the bombing at Tobruk, he found lemonade instead of oil to lubricate the weapons. A few hours later he understood that something had already changed. Colonel Nardozzi summoned the officers of camp 28 for a speech. He declared that at last it had happened, that Italy had finally made the right choice and was finally rejoining the group of civilized nations where it belonged. This time Vittorio didn't throw any punches because they wouldn't have been enough to vent the anger.

A few days later all the expectations created by the armistice came to an end. The suspicious stares at the mess hall, at the club where they played cards, or in the showers where they lined up to wash with the freezing mountain water, had to give way to a clear choice. The Colonel, in agreement with the British commanders, wanted to find out which side each prisoner was on. Their opinion on the armistice could no longer remain a private matter, since they had to find out who was ready to collaborate and perhaps even to fight on side of the new ally.

"Vito, we must discuss something important." said Vittorio

"Absolutely, Lieutenant."

"The Colonel will call us in one by one, to find out what our thoughts are regarding the armistice and what we intend to do."

"Yes, Sir."

"This will determine what will happen to each one of us. If we are sent back home, you can be with your fiancée, otherwise you'll have to continue to survive right here, at Yol. There are even rumors that those who refuse to collaborate might end up in Russian prison camps."

"I understand Lieutenant."

"On this issue now there are no more Lieutenants and soldiers. It's each one for himself. Understood?"

"What does that mean?"

"Vito, I am immensely grateful for all that you have done for me. As long as I live I will never forget your ugly mug when I opened my eyes and first saw it at the hospital at Geneifa. But here, and now, we must decide our own lives, each one of us, alone. It's not just about the war, where you had to swear and obey, and if you got shot it was included as part of your duty. Here each one must choose quietly what he's going to do. Once you go into that room there will be no ranks anymore. Only you, your conscience and what you want to do with your life. Got it?"

"Certainly Lieutenant, I understand."

Once Vittorio walked into the Colonel's office, with the British present on either side of the desk looking at him, things happened very quickly. He didn't read the form they pushed at him and didn't even pick it up, or looked at it.

"So, Lieutenant Conte, what do you intend to do?"

Vittorio stood at attention, looking straight ahead. He lifted his right arm in a rigid fascist salute, then brought it down and remained at attention. He then made the most military about face he could manage, in that humiliating semi-uniform he was wearing, and marched out turning his back on the Colonel.

When he returned to the barracks, Vittorio found Vito sitting on his angareb. Vito got up and asked:

"So, Lieutenant, how did it go?"

"I gave the fascist salute."

Vito's face twisted in a thoughtful grimace.

Vittorio explained,

"You know that I was not at all a fascist. In the village I was a 'Balilla' and attended the rallies, but I never took the party card. I was not a black shirt."

"Just like everybody else. I understand."

"Yes, but that's is not the excuse I am seeking. I volunteered for the war and know my responsibilities. The issue here is not whether we were fascist or not. This is a question of one's dignity, or whether you don't give a damn about anything just to grab an extra scrap of bread."

Vito was still standing rigidly, listening in silence as Vittorio went on:

"These are the people who tried to kill me in Africa. What has changed since then? They are the ones who made my friend Leonida die of tuberculosis at Dehradun. The ones who locked me up in the isolation cell because I beat up a Major who was insulting the Italian soldiers who had died in combat. They treat me like some dog they want to tame by throwing me a bone every day. So now I am expected to shake hands with them just because Badoglio says so from who knows where? Or following the orders of the King who screwed Mussolini and then ran away? I refused to give up when we were being bombed, and I should do so now for an extra helping of soup or a few days less detention?"

Vito remained silent.

"And then there is the matter of national honor. Since I was born I have been hearing that the world despises us because we are known to switch partners, because we are not trustworthy, because we betray our allies and we are always eager to kneel in front of the winners. It's not an issue of being fascist or anti-fascist, Vito, but whether or not we are serious people or just a bunch of poor bastards. We decided to go to war and when it was declared it appeared that every Italian wanted exactly that. We lost? That's too bad. Now we must accept the consequences to the bitter end and not bend over to avoid them. We must finally end a war on the same side we started it."

Vito looked embarrassed by the diatribe.

Vittorio asked him,

"Excuse-me, I'm on my soap box. And you?"

"Lieutenant, they handed me a piece of paper I couldn't even read. I put it back on the table."

"But, don't you realize what that means? Don't you want to go back home?"

"Lieutenant, I don't understand politics. I didn't when I was drafted and now even less. The postcard that I received from the King was read to me by the boss. But I can do some things on my own. If you are a man, you can tell it when they are trying to make you forget that."

15.

"This order has already been carried out." Alberto was reading the Stefani Agency dispatch, published by the newspapers on March 25, 1944 as soon as the curfew allowed the printers to resume working in the afternoon. Alberto actually no longer existed. He was going by a different identity, a false name and another address selected by the Military Resistance Front, once he went underground. Federico followed him and created a hiding place in the attic covered by a trap door, where he would go and hide when they felt that something was happening in the street. He also would find some black bread with vegetables that they would have at night when they became totally famished.

"Why are you making that face?" he asked Alberto.

"Read this."

Federico looked at the paper,

"Which order was carried out?"

"Reprisals" said Alberto. "Two days ago the partisans placed a bomb in via Rasella while a unit connected to the SS was marching past. Thirty soldiers were killed and the Nazis decided they would shoot ten Italians for every dead German. Here it says they already carried out the order. They didn't even have the guts to blackmail the city, and demand that those responsible be handed over."

"Are you involved?"

"Federico, you know the story. It's best for everyone that we don't talk."

"Did you know who they were?"

"Who?"

"Those responsible."

"I really don't. We are soldiers fighting an enemy who has occupied our country. The others are partisans. Sometimes we work together. We exchange weapons, explosives and information. We help those who want to join the new Army and escape to the south. But I know nothing about via Rasella, I'm serious."

"So why did you make that face?"

"The Nazis are said to have killed over three hundred people. If they used the excuse of via Rasella to eliminate their enemies, I'm afraid I know who may have fallen in the trap."

"Who do you mean?"

"In January, after the Allied landings at Anzio, someone informed on them. They arrested several leaders of the secret Military Front: Colonel Montezemolo, Colonel Frignani, other friends and colleagues. If they picked the hostages among political prisoners, those men would have been at the top of the list. Poor guys."

Alberto took the newspaper to find other details in the short paragraph.

"But perhaps it's better that it happened this way."

"What do you mean?" asked Federico.

"It's best that it be over for them."

"Have you gone crazy?"

"You can't understand."

"What is it I can't understand?"

"We found out what they were doing to them in the prison at the via Tasso."

"What do you mean?"

"You have no idea. If you got beaten up until you fainted you were lucky. They say they ripped out Montezemolo's teeth one by one, and since he still refused to talk they also tore out his fingernails and toenails."

"Maybe these are just stories."

"I don't think so. Anyway, he didn't talk, because I am still here."

Federico then commented.

"Perhaps the authors of the via Rasella bombing, who are in the Resistance as civilian partisans, wanted to get rid of the military leaders. They knew the Germans would take their revenge on you and your men."

"That sounds much too complicated. Three hundred victims are far too many for such a goal. There weren't that many officers being held as prisoners in the via Tasso, and civilian partisans were running the risk that the Nazis would end up killing their own comrades."

"What about the inquiry into Cape Matapan? I meant to ask you what happened to that?"

"It was an investigation instigated by the fascists inside the ministry, since they accused the Navy of being monarchist and therefore willing to betray. But those seeking to scapegoat me have other things to worry about now."

"What will you do?"

"Try to understand what's going on, first of all. Then we will have to take action."

***

The meeting was in the first confessional booth, along the left side in a parish in the center of the Eternal City. It was easy to locate and an excellent cover: it was still legal to confess one's sins in a Rome dominated by the Nazis. The priest pushed back the curtain and whispered.

"How long has it been since your last confession, my son?"

"Much too long, Don Ferdinando" said Alberto.

The priest answered.

"I knew Don Pietro Pappagallo since we were together in the seminary. He was a meek, and generous man, who was a far better person than I will ever be. I still can't believe that they killed him like a stray dog. To shoot him in the head in a cave, with his hands tied behind his back. Where did they find the courage to do such a thing?"

Alberto remained quiet and the silence of the church suddenly filled the confessional. Then the priest went on: "Be advised that I seek no revenge: Don Pietro would never forgive me. But justice he certainly would accept. There is no peace without justice."

"I agree."

"Good. Your contact is waiting in the Rectory. She is a Jewish girl but keep that to yourself. When you get up, light a candle in front of the image of the Virgin and say a few prayers, if you still know them. In ten minutes go to the far end of the church behind the altar, as if you were coming to make an offering. On the left you will find the door to the Rectory."

"Thank you Father"–said Alberto, while crossing himself as he rose from the confessional.

He followed the instructions of the priest, more out of his desire to do so than out of caution. He stopped to listen to the peaceful silence, that seemed almost unreal after four years of war, and the incense that permeated the church brought back the familiar smells of a distant childhood. The little door to the rectory opened on a narrow hallway, leading to the room where the priests would dress in their ceremonial gowns. There in a corner Alberto saw a woman dressed in black.

"How should I call you?" he asked as he went toward her.

"Dinah" she answered.

The black clothes of a mourner were a decoy and she probably used them for precisely that reason. She had to be a student no more than twenty years old, but her self assured manner struck Alberto even though she sounded very young.

"You are aware of what we need, correct?"

"Certainly. Otherwise I wouldn't have wasted your time" answered the girl.

"The information must be as detailed as possible. We have been aware of a few names for quite some time, naturally. But now we need more specific reports. We want addresses, phone numbers and daily habits."

"Certainly, that's very clear," Dinah agreed.

"We need information we can use to protect ourselves but also to take action. To get back at them, if you know what I mean?"

"I see. We think we can help."

"Who is the one doing the thinking?"

"There are other people in our cell who are very well informed. The Nazis think they are loyal."

"You are very young," commented Alberto. Dinah smiled and didn't answer.

"I am asking this to be sure that you are aware of the kind of risks you're taking."

She nodded and Alberto went on.

"The Germans shoot people like me on the spot, if they catch them. To them we are worse than the partisans. We are soldiers who have broken our oath, turncoats, traitors to the homeland. And this goes for anyone helping us as well. Do you understand?"

Dinah replied.

"The Nazis don't view any of us as human beings. They would kill me anyway, even if I weren't talking to you."

Alberto felt he couldn't look at her straight in the eyes, something that had not happened to him in years.

"Our next meeting will be set up through the same contact as today. He will let you know when and where."

* * *

There was another matter that had to be taken care of. Michele Coppola was a former Air Force volunteer who had lost an arm during the war, and requested to be admitted into the Navy's secret front. Malceri trusted him and agreed. Coppola was assigned to Rome's main telephone exchange to spy on the Gestapo's moves and uncover the phone numbers it was tapping. It was a necessary security move to find out whether the Nazis had discovered the location where the resistance was hiding.

A few days later however the new agent brought in some strange information: the Gestapo itself had contacted him, asking whether he would work for the Germans through an Italian collaborator named Bianconi, who was a recruiter. Malceri, still trusting him, gave him permission to become a double agent:

"Infiltrate and find out what they are up to."

Now Coppola was asking to meet with Alberto urgently and arranged to meet in a safe house in Parioli.

"What's going on?"

"There are very important things happening and I must know how I should act."

Alberto had Coppola explain.

"When I agreed to work for the Gestapo they introduced me to Major Aars, who runs a school for saboteurs. They teach you how to handle explosives and are holding training exercises in a field near the Magliana."

"Very interesting. What are their plans?"

"After the Allies landed at Anzio they took me to the office of Colonel Kappler, who heads the SS in Rome. He told me that should they be forced to evacuate the city, they wouldn't go peacefully. Then he revealed that the Germans were preparing a large offensive to the south to throw the Anglo-Americans back into the sea."

"We would need to find out more about that."

"To help the offensive they are planning to carry out attacks behind Allied lines. They are asking me to guide a unit of saboteurs that would attack the headquarters of Generals Clark and Alexander." Alberto looked amazed.

"You heard correctly: the allied leaders. This is the plan. In the next few days the Nazis will take me and three other men at Fossa Incastro, a small town south of Rome at the tip of the right flank of the German army. There we will receive explosives and a small boat to get around the front by sea. We will disembark at the mouth of the Moletta creek and move toward Selva di Nettuno, that is part of the territory now under Allied control. The headquarters are only a few hundred meters from that spot. Our mission is to place four large bombs timed to explode after thirty minutes."

"That's incredible. Do you know the date?"

"Not yet, but we were told to expect to leave in a few days. I was able to get away and let you know, but I won't have another opportunity to contact you. What should I do?"

Alberto thought for a moment, then went to the phone:

"It's too important for me to decide. I must alert my superiors."

Coppola placed his hand on the telephone and stopped him.

"I wouldn't, if I were you."

"Why?"

"There's a second important piece of news you should know: this phone number is now being tapped. Soon the Gestapo will give the address to the men of the X MAS that will come here and arrest everybody. We must decide what to do now, and then abandon this place forever."

Alberto had no choice or time, to think things over.

"Then go and try to sabotage the mission. We will inform the Allies that you are about to arrive, so that when they arrest you they will know who you are. We will ask the BBC to transmit a signal to let us know that you are safe among them. The signal will include the sentence "Francesco and Franceschina have arrived." Tell the British to broadcast it on the radio."

* * *

Alberto didn't know whether to be more surprised or satisfied, when he saw Dinah once again. He trusted her and had her come to his new hiding place: a basement in the outskirts of Rome with three wooden chairs and a mattress on the floor. It was a huge risk for both of them to be there: he could be denounced and she could get caught with a wanted man. The danger linked them together.

"Excellent work. How did you manage it?"

"In this city each one uses his own methods and secrets," She answered with a smile.

Now that he could see her near the little window, he noticed that she was much younger than he thought, with two dark and deep eyes circled by fatigue that you couldn't miss noticing.

He read two typed reports that Dinah had given him on carbon copy paper. The first was a "List of secure persons," seven single spaced pages that had the first and last names, addresses and the history of 205 Nazi collaborators. Alberto began reading those that struck him as the most important ones.

"Number 7. Carbonella, Enzo. About 21, from Naples, usually dressed in a Militia uniform. At 20:30 hours last February 2 he received 200,000 lire for helping in the arrest of the last 10 persons shot from the De Simone Group, from whom they expected to reveal the name of Montezemolo, who in fact was caught shortly after. Via dei Sediari 8, apt. 6 telephone 61205. With him also operate: Scotto, Rudi about 24 and with him a woman–nicknamed Vespa --who lives with him at Carbonella's in via dei Sediari. Enrichello, scars on his left ear, fat, short, is from northern Italy. Erina, short, fat from Naples, lives at the Continental hotel. A man named Radocchia who lives near San Giovanni, he is a poorly dressed young man with extremely protruding eyes. He led to the arrest of German and Italian deserters.

Also in contact with Carbonella are: Parisi, Emilio father's name Michele. Castellemmare 14/10/1911. Cook at the hotel Urbe. Alvino, former paratrooper sergeant, hotel Urbe. Rapa, di Monteporzio; Clerici, Vittorio and Clerici, Felice both agents of SIM."

It was incredible. Precisely what he was looking for: the people who had betrayed Montezemolo. Alberto went on reading the list that turned out to be a goldmine. All the information and the clues he was seeking were there: "Number 53. Mrs. Alvino via G.B. De Rossi 14, suspected of having denounced colonel Frignani." And then "Number 71. Di Thun, an Austrian count, age 90, wears monocle, works for the SS. Changes hotel every 50 days. Took part in the arrest of Colonel Montezemolo." And more: "Number 199, Belletti, Amleto son of Luigi 18-06-1909, industrialist. In close contact with the Germans whom he treats to copious dinners. Socializes with officers who are part of General Maelzer's staff at the Hotel Excelsior, to whom he denounced Colonel Montezemolo."

This was information useful for someone's defense but also to attack. In any case this was exactly what he had requested. Others were just a collection of miserable little stories: "Number 96. Countess San Severino. Organizer of prostitutes and spies. She operates in the area of the Piazza in Lucina. Extremely dangerous."

Also some horror stories: "Numbers 128 and 129, Marini and De Mauro. Part of the SS office in the via Tasso used for first grade interrogations. Number 136, tank soldier La Noia. Very dangerous. Was an informer of the police and is now working for the Germans. It appears that he is a confidant of Lt. Colonel of the SS Kappler. Koch, Pietro; Cenini, maiden name Tamara is married to Koch; Selmi, Achille; Castellani, Mario; De Sanctis, Renzo; Comotti, Elsa; Cirilli, Bruno; Brilli, Franco; Zaccagnini, Livio; Santi, Nestore, all work under orders of Police Commissioner Caruso and carry out important tasks. They almost all are living at the Bernini Hotel where there is a Republican Police cell."

Alberto was surprised when he reached number 179. "Actors Nunzio Filogamo; Stucchi, Pierino; Candiani, Carlo; Barlini, Vanda; Bettoja, Lillj. Artists, and Nazi collaborators. Hotel Excelsior."

He asked Dinah:

"How is it possible, these people too?"

"Trust us." she answered.

Then he took the second list entitled "List of suspects." Five pages with 140 names. At number 15 he read: "Evola, Giulio, writer."

Alberto folded the two reports placing them into a file. A sign of approval to Dinah became a caress on the head.

"What do you think you'll do with them?" she asked.

"The Germans are criminals, but these Italians have sold out other Italians. They are responsible for the murder of people like you and me, for some sordid reward from those who are occupying the country. We will catch them, Dinah. But if it is not us, it will be the partisans or the justice of the new Italian state, once it will be born. We will go and pick them up, one by one."

16.

"The desired separation between fascists and monarchists is now effective." wrote the Red Cross delegate Charles Huber back to Geneva. "The British have created a special camp for the fascists. It is camp number 25 and its commander is Consul Riccardo Gambrosier."

At Yol just as in Rome. The misery behind the barbed wire made no difference after the September 8, 1943 armistice: "The breaking in two of Italy is being replicated inside the prison camps and creates a host of complex and confusing problems," continued Charles Huber in his report.

Those poor devils behind the barbed wire even managed to surprise Huber with their insistence on placing their principles ahead of their own survival: "Consul Gambrosier gave us 500 Rupees in the name of the fascists in Camp 25. This is to thank us for the humanitarian work of the International Committee of the Red Cross and in particular our efficient work in separating the camps." Perhaps those poor devil fascists didn't get enough to eat, but they still managed to collect money to thank the people who separated them from the followers of Badoglio.

It also explains the paragraph entitled Discipline: "Whenever you find fascists and monarchists together, as is the case in a few camps, there is an excessive amount of intolerance. British military authorities themselves were placed in a difficult situation, when they saw 1800 soldiers arrive from the camps in Group I and assigned them as orderlies to monarchist officers. Those prisoners came from the "Special Camp" where the members of the fascist Militia and other men with fascist leanings were being held, and were furious at having been sent among the monarchists. A mutiny of sorts took place. They all refused to work for the monarchist officers and it resulted in a form of collective punishment. They were given hard labor duty: moving rocks under the close watch of the sentries. Then, in accordance with British regulations, they were given only bread and water for three days. The fascist officers, all those in Camp 25, refused to eat for one day as sign of protest for that punishment."

The disagreements could turn violent: "When we visited the detention centers we found 18 officers, of whom 8 were sentenced to prison and forced labor for 18 months, because they had wounded other officers."

The main worry of the British was not to prevent escapes, that were practically impossible at the foot of the Himalayas, but to stop the clashes between fascists and the followers of Badoglio: "Colonel Aizzi was seriously wounded during a political dispute. Now he is in the hospital with a fractured shoulder that will require four months of care. Those responsible were not identified or punished."

Vito was also forced to eat only bread and water, since he sided with the soldiers who refused to work for the monarchist officers. When he returned to Camp 25 his fellow detainees cheered him as if he had conquered Tobruk on his own.

"Lieutenant, they made me laugh. Moving rocks and eating bread and water? But that was my daily routine back home in

Puglia. They were seriously mistaken, if they thought they would break my back."

Vittorio walked back with the orderly to the barracks where he lived, surrounded by vegetables plants struggling to emerge and survive.

"I heard some bad news from Camp 28, though."

"Oh?" asked Vittorio

"Do you remember the Captain of the Alpini? The one who was distilling grappa in the hut where we met?"

"I do."

"They found him hanging by the neck in the showers."

"When?"

"A week ago. He managed to get a hold of some rope and hanged himself from one of the beams in the ceiling during the night. A soldier ran into the body on his way to the bathroom. It was dark and he didn't even see him hanging there."

Vittorio lowered his eyes and looked at his shoes. He saw the desert pants of his makeshift uniform, also a fetish of the discipline that the "25s" kept hanging on to at all costs.

"Why did it happen?"

"Who knows?" answered Vito. "His despair at having lost everything. The anguish of not knowing which side to take in this sordid life."

Camp 25 was run like a real barracks as much as that was possible. To set themselves apart, the prisoners referred to each other as the "twenty-fivers" among themselves. They went every morning to raise the colors, marching in step and screaming out all the fascist songs they had learned when they were still dreaming of fighting for the Duce and the Empire. They obeyed their superior officers, used the "voi" form, gave the fascist salute and tried to keep their patched up clothing in good repair, to make them look like real uniforms. To defeat boredom, that was an enemy even more vicious than the British, the twenty-fivers created a number of tournaments: chess, concerts, boxing bouts and fencing, with foils made out of bamboo. One of them, the sculptor Enzo Benedetto, even had an art show that he produced. Soccer matches were held between three teams: Ardita, Audace and Ardente; tennis tournaments, volleyball and basketball. They always kept the pathways of the camp clean, created vegetable gardens among the rocks and raised rabbits, that they would use to barter with the Indian suppliers. Vittorio had chickens roaming around and used their eggs to mix in with tagliatelle, whenever Vito managed to find some flour in the supplies. At the gates of section 2B they even created a wooden machine to make spaghetti to order, and a few of the more commercially minded took advantage to open up restaurants and cafés in the camp. But above all, the rebels of the "25" despised the "defeatists" at the other camps, who relayed the most disastrous news from the front to destroy their morale. It was a matter of pride and mental hygiene. To refuse to give up and give in: to the enemy, to the followers of Badoglio, to the British sentries, to India, to fate.

"I like it here because we're not living in a mess." said Vito inside the barracks. He tried to set it up like a house, using a sheet as a wall dividing his area from the other angarebs close by. Every time the earthquakes made it fall off—and they were as frequent as the monsoons --he would put it all back the way it was before.

"In the other camps the men are destroyed." said the orderly. And Vittorio replied:

"When you have no reasons to resist, a POW camp turns into an asylum. How can you explain that we are still behind barbed wire if the British are now supposedly our allies?"

"Well, I don't know much about philosophy, but I agree that's a good point. Think about the fact that in other camps, to find some kind of pleasure, have even created little theaters. Not so bad to be on the stage. But then there are men playing the role of women as though they really were divas. It must have gone to their heads, as well as to those who were drooling over them."

Yet in camp 28 they managed to organize a very nice concert that Huber recounted for Geneva: an orchestra and a quartet of string instruments. The first part included Abraham *Victoria and her hussar*; Tchaikovsky *Chant sans paroles*; Leoncavallo the prologue to *Pagliacci* with Lieutenant Carrara as the baritone; Porter's *Rosalie* and Brahms *Op 51*. After a five minute intermission Verdi *Aida* and *Il Trovatore*; Rubinstein *Melody in F*; Kalman *Play Gypsy* from Maritza; Mascagni *The Dream* from William Ratcliff and Weber's overture of *Der Freischutz*.

"As we had already pointed out" wrote the Red Cross delegate "in the various camps there are orchestras with very talented musicians. We attended a magnificent concert, the program of which we have enclosed, and congratulated the conductor for the perfect execution."

Perfect until the end, when to salute the audience of Italian prisoners they had to sing *God save the King*, the anthem of the former enemies.

* * *

There was no talk of going back home, at least for most of the prisoners. Even those who requested to fight with the allies to free Italy of the Nazis stayed in limbo at Yol. At the most the British allowed those willing to cooperate to keep an eye on their colleagues who were not convinced that they had really lost the war.

Vito was walking up and down, in front of the guard house of the sentry at the farthest corner of Camp 25. The oriental face was intriguing, half hidden under his hat, but the way he remained absolutely immobile was amazing.

"These Indians are serious people. But why do they obey the British so perfectly?"

"Those are not Indians," answered Vittorio.

"No? Well, what are they then?"

"Gurkhas."

"What?"

"Nepalese soldiers. They were given the privilege of being part of the British Empire troops."

"Mercenaries?"

"Something like that. But they are such great warriors that London thought it was a good idea to grant them the privilege."

The sentry leveled his rifle and told them to halt. Vittorio waved that he understood and stopped.

"What language do they speak?" asked Vito.

"Their own, but also English."

"So then why don't you call him?"

"Because he'll shoot us. I don't get it, Vito: what the hell do you care about the Gurkha sentry?"

"I don't know, because I'm curious. We're here in the same boat. We could exchange a few words."

The next day, after digging up the vegetable garden, Vito again returned in front of the same guard house where he saw the Gurkha. He scratched his head that was covered with lice. By then the sentry had learned to recognize him and no longer called a halt, because he knew that the prisoner would not come too close. But he still held his rifle cocked and leveled ready to shoot at the chest.

When his replacement arrived, Vito lifted his arm and yelled out: "Hey, Gurkha!"

The sentry answered with a wave and kept on marching to his barracks.

"We said hello," Vito told Vittorio when they met.

"Who did you salute?"

"Gurkha and I."

"You really are obsessed. How did you talk to him, in Napalese?"

"I yelled at him and he waved back at me."

"He didn't shoot?"

"No. It was during the changing of the guard, he was on his way home. Next time why don't you come and talk to him in English?"

Once Vito got an idea into his head it was physically impossible to pry it out. But then there weren't that many things to do in the camp. A few days later therefore, Vittorio stood by his orderly to wait for the changing of the guard. Vito made the first move once again:

"Hey, Gurkha!" The sentry waved again and Vittorio said in English: "His name is Vito, he just wants to get to know you. What's your name?"

The Gurkha stopped: "Ram Bahadur Gurung."

"You are young, right?"

"Twenty." Vittorio was translating almost simultaneously.

"Where are you from?"

"Chilghari, a village close by, in the Kangra valley."

"Look at that knife lieutenant! Ask him about the knife." Vito interrupted.

"He likes your knife," Vittorio told the sentry.

"This? It's a Kukri, the Gurkha weapon. We use it for just about everything: from the kitchen all the way to killing people."

Vittorio translated for his orderly:

"He says he'll cut you up with that thing, if you want."

Vito smiled with self satisfaction:

"He called it Kukri? Nice. It looks like a sickle to me. But ask him if he likes these British?"

"I don't think that's an appropriate question to ask."

"Why not? Ask him if he enjoys obeying the British."

Vittorio addressed the Gurkha:

"Vito would like to know if you get along with the English."

"No," answered the sentry, who continued on his way to the guard house.

One week later at Camp 25 a strange rumor began to circulate: it appeared that the British were beginning to hand out permission to visit outside the camp. Walks in the mountains, just as Huber had mentioned in his Red Cross reports. Now that they were allies, no one was even thinking of escaping. They were all expecting to be sent home at any time. Even if someone tried, it would no longer be so damaging.

"Actually to go outside this cage wouldn't displease me at all. Just to get to know the rest of the world," said Vito when he heard the rumors.

"You'll have to stand in line and ask the British for an authorization. They are just waiting to humiliate us. And then I doubt if they will be that generous with us '25s.'"

The orderly put his hands in his pockets and kicked a stone: "But we could also find another solution."

Two days later Vito was again right under the Gurkha's guard house. He dragged Vittorio once again, who reluctantly came over to act as the interpreter. After the guard changed the orderly raised his hand,

"Ram, hey Ram! Over here, it's Vito."

The sentry was now used to him and came over.

"Lieutenant ask him, ask about the story of taking walks outside."

Vittorio started out,

"Vito heard about the other camps allowing prisoners to go out on furlough. He'd like to know if it's true."

"It certainly is," answered the Gurkha.

"So how do we get to do it?"

"You must make a request to the British command. If they trust you, they'll let you get out for a few hours. You can't go beyond a few kilometers and you'll be under escort."

"What's he saying?" asked Vito anxiously.

"We have to go to the British and beg for permission to go outside for a walk. Perhaps in exchange they will ask us to swear allegiance to Badoglio and His Britannic Majesty."

"Shit!" answered Vito with a gesture of impatience.

"What's happening?" asked the Gurkha.

"Nothing. He doesn't like licking the boots of the British. And I don't like to either." Answered Vittorio.

"I understand." said Ram.

Vittorio and Vito looked at each other puzzled.

"What do you understand?" the Lieutenant asked the sentry.

"I understand you not liking to lick the boots of the English."

"But aren't you part of their Empire?" asked Vittorio.

"I work for them because they conquered us. I'm loyal because it's my duty as a soldier. That's all."

"Almost like us then. If you could, you'd drive that Kukri into their chest."

"I'd also drive it into yours, if I could, because this is my house and you should leave us alone. Haven't you heard about Gandhi? The movements to free India?"

"We barely know what's going on in Italy from here."

"But I do respect what you are doing in this camp. Most of all, I respect the fact that you were able to lose with dignity and without bending."

"We didn't lose." answered Vittorio.

"Perhaps, but you are the one behind the barbed wire and you would like to know how to get out."

"Why, do you know a way?" asked the Lieutenant.

Ram looked around at the barracks of Camp 25, then he turned toward the mountains.

"What's he saying Lieutenant? Can you let me in on this or not?" asked Vito who was getting frustrated.

"Keep quiet. It seems that Ram can help us with your walks outside."

"Offer him a bottle of the grappa we distill secretly inside the huts."

Vittorio tried but Ram shook his head.

"No, Vito. He's a young man and doesn't like your potion with rotting leather in it."

The Gurkha didn't walk away, though.

"Is there anything we can do for you?" asked Vittorio. Ram looked at the sports field that the prisoners had built by leveling off the rocks. Then he said: "I saw you playing soccer among yourselves. It's fun isn't it?"

"Of course it's fun. We even have tournaments. It's the only distraction they allow us to have. Would you like to learn?"

Ram smiled and Vito got impatient.

"Damn it Lieutenant. What does he want?"

"He says he likes playing ball. If we teach him how to play, perhaps he'll help us go into the mountains without asking permission to the British." Then Vittorio told the Gurkha: "If you like it that much, we can teach you. But outside this barbed wire fence."

One week later the game was on. Ram managed to convince his commanding officer to slip in the names of Vito and Vittorio into the list of prisoners authorized to leave the camp without informing the British. But the responsibility was completely on his shoulders: he had to be their escort outside and make sure they came back before sundown. If they tried to escape he was to shoot them.

"We screwed them lieutenant!" said Vito happily, as he tied up his shabby looking marching shoes.

"You're the one who screwed them, you old donkey!"

"Two "twenty-fivers" out on furlough, if only the followers of Badoglio knew about this they'd have us shot by firing squad."

Vito and Vittorio joined the group of Indian suppliers lined up in front of the gate after they had unloaded their merchandise in the camp warehouse. Ram went ahead with his rifle on his shoulder and his hand on his Kukri, making the most martial looking face he possibly could. The authorization to go outside the camp had been doctored so well that it looked absolutely authentic. Actually it was real, because Ram used the correct forms when he wrote it.

It was hot and the sentry's mind was on other things, and then the walk always followed the same pattern with the Gurkha following the prisoners. The guard waved them past looking bored. As soon as they had passed the gate, Vito was having trouble preventing himself from running.

"By the Holy Virgin Lieutenant, I feel like running away."

"That's really smart, so Ram can shoot you in the back and then he'll also kill me. We didn't wind up in India to get ourselves hacked down while taking a walk."

One kilometer from the camp, when the guards could no longer see them, a group of little kids with knotty hair and in rags came up to them.

"I knew it Lieutenant."

"What?"

"These kids, they call them the little devils."

"What does that mean?"

"For a few rupees, something to eat or a rag, they'll do anything you want. Really anything." Vittorio turned around to look at Vito without asking any questions.

"Jesus Lieutenant, they have sure done a job on us."

Vito and Vittorio kept on walking for about one kilometer in silence as the Indian peasants looked at them. They passed small Hindu temples painted in bright colors, where the faithful had lined up their morning offerings in front of the images of Ganesh, Vishnu and Shiva.

"Look at the one with elephant's head, Lieutenant. He looks like the Duce when he's at the balcony of the Palazzo Venezia."

Vittorio elbowed his orderly who started to laugh. "But what I don't get is this thing with the cows. What's so special about them? Maybe I'm so hungry I could eat them up raw."

Ram came up to them and pointed to a deviation in the path going down to the river, where the prisoners that had gone out before them had built themselves a kind of natural swimming pool by piling up large rocks.

"If you want, this is where your colleagues go and bathe." Vittorio and Vito had not been in water for years, this river was cold and clear and ran down directly from the mountains of the Hymalayas.

Vito jumped in still wearing his pants and shoes.

"They had to be washed anyway, Lieutenant."

Vittorio did the back stroke holding his head high. In part because he feared drinking, after the stories about the ashes of the dead spread around the rivers, and also to keep the water off the wound he still suffered from since Acroma. He could hear less and less from that ear and wondered whether the inside parts were still healthy.

"I couldn't remember what it felt like" repeated Vito, as he hit the water and sprinkled it around. They dried themselves while sitting on a rock in the hot rising sunlight. Ram kept looking at them with his rifle on his shoulder. The gun was tied to his body with a small chain.

"Maybe we should teach him how to play soccer?" asked Vito.

Vittorio waved at the Gurkha who came over.

"You didn't bring the ball with you?"

Ram opened up his arms. Vittorio pointed to a group of women wearing traditional saris with bright colors, and he told the Gurkha to ask them to lend him a few rags. Vito got involved saying:

"Now, a little fun with one of those, I wouldn't mind. As you officers said in Libya: exotic, right?"

"But they don't wash. Don't you know that they smell of dung?"

"So? That's what I would smell in the stables where I was working, back home."

"All right, but then I'll write to your fiancée in my next letter" warned Vittorio.

"I knew it. That's what friends are for." complained Vito.

Ram came back with a few rags. Vittorio proceeded to fill them with straw and tied them tightly with a string.

"Good, so now Vito and I will show you how to play and pass the ball. Then you try."

Once Ram missed the ball a few times, Vito cried out:

"Good God! It's like teaching geometry to a mule!"

The Gurkha's rifle was unhooked from the bracelet and left against a tree. Vittorio noticed it: if he could run ten paces, he could grab it. And then do what? And go where? Ram understood what Vittorio was looking at and measured the distance with his eyes. He could see that if Vittorio started running just then, he would reach the gun before him. He stopped and pushed the ball, that was rolling up to him.

"Ram, damn it, the game is to kick the ball!" yelled Vito losing his patience. Vittorio was still looking at the gun, but then he went over to the ball made of rags tied together, moving away from the tree where the rifle was resting.

"OK Ram, don't pay attention to him. You're making progress. We'll teach you the rest next time, when you bring a real ball with you."

The Gurkha nodded. A faint smile that came to his lips seemed to express gratitude, for something that Vito didn't understand.

"Nothing to laugh about Ram. Even Vittorio Pozzo[*] will not be able to turn you into a soccer player."

---

[*] Vittorio Pozzo was a legendary Italian soccer coach of the 1930s and 40s.

The Gurkha grabbed his rifle, hooked the bracelet back on and showed them a path going uphill. After a half hour Vito and Vittorio were both out of breath. They went up around the Dhola Dhar mountain range and were close to Mount Nodrani, the highest peak that seemed so near. Ram went up quickly, going from one boulder to the next with the speed and lightness of someone accustomed to that exercise. But years of hunger and deprivations had weakened Vittorio's legs and lungs.

"Lieutenant, we can't stop now. We can't."

Vito was attempting to keep up with Ram while not letting Vittorio fall too far behind. The Gurkha looked back a few times, proud of himself and of the raw beauty of his mountains. They could see the snow higher up, not too far removed from where they were. Vito and Vittorio couldn't speak and struggled to save their breath for the steep climb. At every step they were convinced it would be their last, and that they would be forced to stop and swing back down. Yet every time they moved upward, they were encouraged to go on. One more step. And then another.

The mountain was high and the air suddenly began to thin out. They had less oxygen and with every extra step they were getting even less of it. Their lungs would inflate but didn't work as well, as they attempted to gulp down more air to prevent the choking sensation. You felt like whipping your chest, to stop your heart from beating in your temples and throat. But Ram just kept on going up, keeping his mouth closed. Vito and Vittorio followed, but their mouths were wide open and they were completely out of breath. When the Gurkha finally stopped they thought they were dreaming. They were feeling dizzy, with their heads deprived of oxygen and their bodies shaking.

Ram reached a small flat space and turned toward the two prisoners, with his right hand on his Kukri. They came up barely able to breathe. Only then did they turn in Ram's direction and were able to look down. The entire mountain chain of the

Himalayas suddenly unfolded majestically at their feet, just like the scenery in an immense theater appearing like magic when the curtain rises. The gleaming snow was blinding and confusing, and the mountains seemed to never end in a long succession of peaks and valleys that kept on moving upward.

Ram smiled when he saw the look of amazement on the prisoner's faces.

"Jesus. Never seen anything like this. It makes me want to really run away. To go back to being alive." said Vito.

Vittorio turned to the Gurkha:

"Vito says this scenery is so marvelous he feels like running away."

Ram tightened his hand on the rifle:

"If he tries to, I'll kill you both."

17.

The news Alberto was expecting for the past nine months reached him at 10:20 pm on June 4, 1944. It came on light blue paper, the color used only for the most important messages. The sheet was signed "Castamaggiore General Oddone. Phonogram by hand, extremely urgent." It came from the command center in Rome and was directed to the commands of the Royal Navy, Royal Air Force and Reserves."

The message was only one and one half lines long, but it was enough: "Allied troops have entered the city. Begin the operation immediately as planned."

Alberto felt like running into the streets to hug the people that were already outside to celebrate. Everyone was a bit numb because of the happiness they felt, still disbelieving that they had survived the hunger, the black market, the Allied bombings, the Germans and the most ferocious fascists, who were ready for the dead-end fight. He felt like walking through Rome's squares without the fear of a traitor ready to finger and sell him to the Gestapo at any moment. But the war kept grinding on and the time for celebrations wasn't yet at hand.

The "planned operation" General Oddone was referring to was one of the main reasons that Colonel Montezemolo and others of the Military Front stayed behind the German lines. The operation was in the works for many months, to make sure that the Nazi retreat would take place without clashes, guarantee there was order in the city, avoid that the irregular troops would take over and provide for the continuity of the Royal government, as long as the Italian people wanted it to stay.

Alberto took the message and under Oddone's signature added in his own hand: "To Admiral Ferreri: the troops entering the city are Americans. Occupation of the Ministry and Annex are to take place immediately. Please send liaison officer who has not yet arrived. Also please send liaison officers to sectors: 1. At the home of wounded soldiers in Piazza Adriana; 2. Financial Guards barracks at San Lorenzo in Lucina. The military headquarters will be at San Giuseppe College until dawn tomorrow and will later be transferred to the Campidoglio."

The clandestine Military Front was in radio contact with Badoglio and the Allies, and had always known what it must do once liberation was at hand. Colonel Montezemolo was appointed officially from Brindisi on October 10, 1943 by cable: "Transmit whether Monte can take direction of organization. Stop." He answered yes, and in order to keep that pledge his men had risked and often lost their lives. In a sign of reverence, or perhaps revenge, Alberto reminded everyone of the origins of those orders by signing his dispatch with the name "Montezemolo." The SS had murdered the Colonel in the cowardly massacre of the Ardeatine Caves, but on this night he was the real winner. Then Alberto added: "The Germans are retreating without offering any resistance. Streets and roads are open to easy access."

The Nazis were fleeing to the north without putting up a fight, because of their agreement with the Vatican and the Allies to spare the city of Rome, despite the mines and booby traps that had been set up everywhere, that the men of the Military Front were rushing to deactivate. But on the roads in the outskirts of the capital the Germans were still killing people. A truck with fourteen detainees from the prison of via Tasso stopped at La Storta, located on the via Cassia, where every one of them was shot in cold blood.

Other news reached Alberto at headquarters that the Military Front would have preferred not to hear. A partisan shot a Customs guard that the Americans had appointed to maintain order: they did not know each other and both opened fire at the same time. But the most serious threat came from the spies that the Nazis had clearly left behind. They had to be identified and eliminated, before they could cause other damage or prevent the hunt for the former occupiers who were on the run.

General Mark Clark's American Fifth Army had meanwhile overtaken the British under Field-Marshall Harold Alexander and was now occupying Rome. With them also arrived the new Italian Army reorganized in the south. The American General called a press conference at the Capitol to announce to the world the fall of the first Axis capital. But Alberto had other matters to attend to, instead of going to hear General Clark.

He ran to 145 via Tasso, where furious crowds had broken down the wooden doors and freed the last unfortunate people that the Gestapo had forgotten in the jail. He entered a cell thinking that it could have been his, if the inner strength of Montezemolo, Giovanni Frignani, Maurizio Giglio, Simone Simoni, Angelo Ioppi and so many others hadn't triumphed of the beatings and torture inflicted upon them by the Nazis. In cell number two, where General Sabato Martelli Castaldi had been left bleeding, Alberto saw written on the wall: "Once your body shall be no more, your spirit shall be even more alive in the memory of those who remain. May it serve as an example." He was the one left, the one to keep alive the memory of that battle and of the thousands of people who were still alive. Alberto's eyes were filled with tears, when on another wall scratched with finger nails he read: "Whoever dies for the homeland lives forever. Long live Italy."

* * *

To return to normalcy also meant taking the past into account, reorganizing the military structure and putting an end to some strange habits. One issue for example crossed Alberto's desk as a memorandum: "Mr. Michele Coppola was a member of the underground Navy's Secret Information Service. He served without considering the risks to himself, facing dangerous and extremely difficult circumstances with enthusiasm, focused only on accomplishing the mission at any price. According to the orders received he enrolled in the German SS, ready to endure the consequences of being in such a position. Indifferent to any possible surveillance he never ended his connection to the underground S.I.S. providing information that was useful to the organization. Having discovered the preparation of important operations, with patience and cunning he was able to join the personnel involved. He managed to take part in the attack on Allied Headquarters at Anzio, ensuring that it would fail while crossing the allied lines by sea."

Therefore Coppola wasn't lying and he had succeeded. But Alberto already knew it because of the BBC signal "Francesco and Franceschina have arrived." During the night of the attack, while he was on the small boat that was to take him behind the front, Michele had brandished a hand grenade revealing that he was part of the S.I.S. underground and threatening to kill the others on board. Then he forced the real saboteurs to row toward the shore and give themselves up to the Allies. He made it, but at a price:

"Since he lost his entire wardrobe due to the complicated activity of the mission, he is requesting a reimbursement."

Coppola was lucky to have only lost his clothing, that Alberto was now agreeing to pay for: "Overcoat lire 5000; handkerchiefs 350; suit 5000; light colored pants 1500; shirts 1500; shoes 2000; sweater 800; underpants 120; socks 300."

Federico helped with the receipts since everything had to be accounted for. They also had to give extra pay to the colleagues that remained in Rome to fight the Nazis:

"Admiral Malceri lire 15000, Captain Giulio Sandrelli, Carlo Resio and Giovanni di Sangro, 15000. Captain Luigi Podestà 12000." And then also Luigi Tommasuolo, Mario Florio, Franco Pillone, Dario Paglia, Giuseppe Scordino, Vero Roberti a journalist at *La Stampa* daily, Giuseppe Libotte, Franco Di Donna, Luigi Filasi, Aldo Cippico, Mario Vespa, Guido De Finetti. The list went on down to the sailor Donato Bevilacqua who received 6000 lire. These names didn't not mean much to those who weren't aware of the Navy's secret service, but they were all part of Malceri's secret unit. Vespa was arrested in Genoa and ended up in the Nazi concentration camp at Mathausen, but still managed to survive.

It was necessary to record and remember all those who risked their lives: "The members of the Petrucci group will receive a document attesting to its activity." The group included 52 men, from Lieutenant Commissioner Francesco Petrucci to the Private Giuseppe Aurilia, who kept on fighting the Germans in the underground.

But there were also some accounts that had to be settled with those who had betrayed:

"I am doing my duty to myself and my comrades during nine long months of sacrifice and suffering, to explain the following regarding the Captains of the C.R.E.M. Antonino Attinà and Saverio Ragno, both part of the personnel unit at the Ministry of the Navy. Attinà and Ragno collaborated with commanders Chinigò, De Moratti and Di Domenico in compiling a note presented on December 4, 1943 that included the names and addresses of those officers who were present in Rome as of September 8. The note included about 1400 names and was handed to the German commander. Then the praiseworthy Attinà and Ragno went around boasting in the offices of the ministry, even earning the praise that the Naval commissioner offered to the officers assembled in the Marble Room. I ask for an immediate act of justice regarding these two. I also add that incidentally these two zealous informers of their own comrades in arms are still being given practically free living quarters in the buildings belonging to the Royal Navy at the cooperative Nazario Sauro."

Alberto read the three pages of the report dated June 12, 1944. He remembered the last will and testament clawed on the walls of the via Tasso by his comrades, who had been murdered at the Ardeatine Caves. He thought that just nine days before he was also living underground, hiding in the tiny streets of Rome's center to avoid capture by the Nazis. Now in the halls of the ministry he could very well be crossing paths with someone who had put his name on a list and handed it to SS chief Kappler.

Perhaps that was the reason why he didn't feel any remorse or sadness when a colleague from the military front contacted him. They found one of the names on the list that Dinah had given him, and his fellow officer said: "He was walking around unassumingly, but he was one of the spies the Nazis had left behind. He was carrying a pistol and we therefore had to defend ourselves. For him there would be no trial."

Then there was Dinah, of course. There were other days and nights that had not all been taken up by guerilla war. Nights when the fear, the cold, the curfew, and the desolation of the deserted city, the noise of Nazi boots on the pavement, the noisy fascist patrols forced you to seek some human contact. On those nights filled with the risk of no longer being alive the following day, he listened to the flesh, seeking the physical proof that he was still alive and present to the world. Those desperate nights went by as if there were to be no tomorrow. But they remained vividly unique and engraved in his memory.

He was seeking Dinah in his thoughts as soon as he found out that Allied troops had entered Rome, but the emergency forced him to do his duty first. Then he went looking for her in the streets. He really didn't know what he wanted with her, and in truth he hadn't known from the beginning. He didn't even know her name, her real name, and she didn't know his. They had met by accident, collaborated out of necessity and ended up in bed because of need. Two ghosts in a ghost town, with no identity and fundamentally without a future.

Yet he was attracted to that dead-end kind of mystery, where there was no possibility of escape. First it was her determination, and later the tenderness that he could see rising in her day after day, that forced him to surrender. She was much too young for him. A girl, sure, but also a woman, marked like the streets of this city now finally free. With Rome liberated, it became legitimate to think about the future. But Alberto was having trouble imagining it without that ghost that constantly accompanied him when death was their daily companion.

He went around town quickly, to the usual spot where he would leave the agreed signal used during the Resistance to set up a new appointment. She didn't appear and he began to laugh. What an idiot! The usual signal at the usual spot? But why did they get rid of the Nazis if now they couldn't even find one another like civilized persons? Where could he start looking? An assumed name, an unknown address, no telephone. For two people who had survived madness, only madness could serve as a common thread through the labyrinth of a normal way of life.

Alberto felt hollow in his stomach, the same feeling he would have when he was in a panic where there was no way out. Where should he look for her? She could have returned to one of the safe houses they shared during the Resistance and left a message for him. So he went to each one on foot, but found nothing. He couldn't even ask the neighbors for help: not because he was still seeking to remain in hiding, but simply because they had never even seen him and didn't even know that he existed. Two ghosts in a former ghost town that was now in a hurry to return to the business of living and no longer had any time for them.

There wasn't even a comrade they shared for him to turn to: he would hide his friends from her, and she wouldn't reveal her friends to him. Out of caution towards their colleagues, more than suspicion towards themselves, because no one could predict how they would react once they fell into the hands of the torturers. It was therefore best for everyone to not know, and have nothing to reveal. Alberto went back in his mind to all those months together, trying to find openings among those memories where a clue could have slipped inadvertently. He was proud to be able to say that they survived because of the caution they had exercised–at least that's what he thought–but now all that cleverness was of no help to him at all.

The only risk, the only dangerous moment, came during their first meeting. It was of course the mere fact of having trusted Don Ferdinando. He could have betrayed them both at the right time. He was the only one to know about them, then and now. Alberto almost ran to the parish located in the center of the city, with the speed of someone unable to control his impatience. He pushed his way past other pedestrians because he could think of nothing else. When he arrived, he found the same smell of incense and peace that he remembered from the first visit, as if a war hadn't even taken place in the outside world. He saw the parishioners kneeling and waiting in line to see the parish priest.

"It's a pleasure to see you again" said the priest when he recognized Alberto at the entrance of the rectory.

"The pleasure is all mine Don Ferdinando" he answered shaking hands.

"Something tells me you are in a big hurry."

"Yes, that's true."

"And what is it you are looking for?"

"Dinah."

"Who?" asked the priest looking puzzled.

"Dinah, the girl you introduced me to during the Nazi occupation."

"Oh, yes. So that's how she told you to call her."

Alberto nodded, suddenly feeling rather foolish.

"A clever girl, obviously. I think that name had some relation to the holy scriptures."

"Do you know where she is?" asked Alberto.

"Why do you ask me? Weren't you in contact?"

Alberto felt even more puzzled.

"Yes."

"So why ask me where she is?"

"Because after the liberation, I couldn't manage to find her anymore. I was busy with the arrival of the allied units and had no time."

The priest then answered:

"Now Rome is free and your mission is accomplished. Why see her again? Perhaps you want to offer her a job at the ministry?"

Alberto felt even more embarrassed, because he couldn't help blushing like a small boy, and mumbled without a clear answer. Don Ferdinando answered:

"In any case, I don't know where she is. Truthfully, I haven't seen Dinah for days. She has disappeared."

18.

"The Camp Commander and the authorities have decided to be very liberal and allow mountain climbers to visit the mountains. With these special permits small groups will be allowed to leave the detention center for ten or fifteen days as they climb the mountain chains around us. Last year passes were handed out up to 40 to 50 days and therefore they we issued to those who took part in large scale climbs on the mountains of Lahoul, Spiti and Lakha, besides the frequent other climbs in the area of Dhola Dhar that towers 17,000 feet just behind the Camp. While at the beginning the group of mountain climbers included twenty members, now it has increased to almost 600."

The new Red Cross delegate A. de Spendler was satisfied, when he sent his report to Geneva on May 2, 1946. It meant that one way or another, some kind of life was returning even in the prison camps at the foot of the Himalayas. "The noteworthy element of this group is that from the start it never caused any problems. The Italian organizers of the excursions like colonel Righi, who has returned home, were careful to not include any-one who could cause problems. I took part in one of the Sunday excursions on the Dohla Dhar and even a five-day trek in the Kulu Valley with four officers who were POW's. About half way from the mountain chain, or some four hours on foot out of the detention center, they built a base camp. The groups can in turn stay there for seven or ten days at a time. During those stays the prisoners go skiing (with rudimentary skis they made themselves) while in the summer and fall they climb with pick axes that they also manufactured. These trips are without a doubt very important for the physical well being of the participants, but they are also even more beneficial to their mental health. There were no reported cases of insanity among the mountain climbers. A detailed report with photographs will follow." While reporting on those mountain adventures, the Red Cross inspector would also add other important information. "Given the expected prisoner returns this summer, in the future the permissions will not be given for more than ten days and only to go to the closest chain of Dhola Dhar."

So it was true: one year after the fighting ended in the rest of the world, the war was finally ending also in India. "Of the 10820 men at Yol, 2001 officers, all of them from camps 26, 27 and 28, returned home during my visit." The forgotten men of Kangra Valley were finally returning home. All except for those in camp 25.

"Lieutenant," Vito complained while he was sitting in the mess hall, "they have forgotten us. They forgot that we still exist. The British forgot, so what. But the Italians have also written us off, as they only focus on survival, and let us rot all the way up here."

"Why, what did you expect? Did you want a medal for bravery for having rejected the swindle perpetrated by the King and Badoglio's followers?"

"Lieutenant, I really don't know. Colonel Nardozzi was telling the men in the other camps that we Italian soldiers fought well, but it was for the wrong idea: Mussolini, fascism, the Empire."

"So he had the right idea: surrender, lower your pants and accept British and American propaganda. But Vito, do you actually expect them to let us go free? The democracy they are promising is just a trick: its purpose is to divide us now and turn us into a colony later on, once the war is only a distant memory. They even gave the Maltese a booklet listing the ways to screw us. The title is "The Background of Fascism": in a few words, it teaches you how to turn us into the obedient subjects of their King."

"I'm not saying that I have any regrets, Lieutenant. But we are the only ones left here: it's enough to drive you crazy. There's a poor devil in the hut next to mine who wakes up every morning before they fly the colors. He ties up his cardboard suitcase, salutes everybody politely and goes to the main gate because—he says—he has an appointment to meet his wife to return to Italy. The sentries don't even pay attention anymore. That's what he does, every day God gives us on this earth. I wonder what will be left of his head, when they will finally load him on to the ship."

Vittorio asked Vito, teasing him:

"And what is there left in your head?"

"Fortunately there was always very little, Lieutenant. That way at least I don't have much to lose."

The days at Yol had become even more hopeless. The camps were being emptied, but only those prisoners who had agreed to collaborate with the British and the new Italian government were leaving at any moment. The prisoners had all stopped taking care of their huts, of the roads and the courtyards. Up to six months before the camp had seemed to be eternal: the new house they were supposed to get used to. Now it was like purgatory and, because of this, it became even more unbearable every day. It was like living suspended between the past, symbolized by Yol like a time capsule, and the future, that was already starting without waiting for the forgotten men of the Himalayas.

Camp 25 was the only one that remained surrounded by barbed wire and armed sentries. There was even less food since the British now had different priorities and India had other issues. Vito and Vittorio were two people that history had simply forgotten: excess baggage abandoned on the side of the road, while you wait for the time and the opportunity to go and retrieve it.

However, in spite of all this, the "25s" continued defiantly to uphold what had become their identity. They would wake up early and fly the colors, maintaining the rituals of a regime that the rest of the world had eagerly relegated to history. They even organized a kind of prisoner Olympics, the "Sports competition", to show the enemy that they were still active and alive. Their attitude remained "hostile", as the British dubbed it. Stubbornly hostile to an enemy who no longer was against them; opposed to history, that simply had skipped over them, and to a future that they rejected.

"Well, Vito, are you really that anxious to get back to Italy?"

"Well, I do miss the village and my fiancée, Lieutenant."

"Actually I don't know what we will find. I don't mean your fiancée: she'll be there waiting for you and you'll get married, I'm sure of that. But in the meantime Italy has changed without us. The whole world has changed. I wonder how they will look at us. Who will understand what we've been through all the way up here? And who, I ask, will even be interested?"

* * *

Vittorio was no longer getting any mail for months, and was therefore amazed where they called out his name at the mail call that day.

"Lieutenant Conte, news from home."

The world was remembering him and was coming back. He ran back to the angareb at the hut, because he wanted to be alone for a brief moment. He wanted to open the envelope and read it, as if there were no more India surrounding him.

There was a single sheet, written on the usual Red Cross form letters, with a single line: "Father deceased after a short illness." The rest, if it existed, had been erased by the censors. Vittorio returned to the envelope looking for something more, perhaps a second sheet he'd missed in the excitement to open it. Nothing: "Father deceased after a short illness" was all that it contained.

He put the letter on his bed and walked a few nervous steps inside the hut. He wanted that piece of paper to disappear, he hoped that the recipient was the wrong person and that he'd never taken it at the distribution of the mail. But that unmovable line remained fixed on the paper and everything else was erased. What precious information could it contain, if it just explained the loss of a parent? What could still require to be hidden from a forgotten prisoner?

Vito couldn't resist the curiosity, since he was hoping that the mail would also have something for him.

"What does it say, Lieutenant?" he asked as he walked into the hut.

"My father died."

Vito stopped at the door, covering his mouth with his hand. He was turning to leave.

"No, come in. Come inside," Vittorio invited him.

"Jesus, Don Luigi. Are you sure?"

Vittorio nodded, pointing to the letter.

"How did it happen?" asked the orderly.

"I don't know, it doesn't say. The letter says a brief illness but the rest was erased."

Vito made the sign of the cross and then asked:

"What was erased? A Christian up here doesn't have the right to know how his father died?"

"The date stamp on the envelope says it was mailed eight months ago. Who knows how many hands had to handle it before it could reach me. And I have been living here for eight months, on the other side of the world, without even knowing that my father was sick and dying."

Vittorio didn't even remember how to cry for a grief that was so old, like the crumpled paper that was meant to announce it long before. His father was dead and buried: a new tragedy to him, but already an old one to all the other family members. Who knows how the person who wrote those lines, erased by the censor, was feeling now. Vittorio remembered the last time he saw Luigi: in March 1941, just before shipping out to Africa. Almost six years ago. His father had looked at him with his stern eyes, through those small eyeglasses with the gold frame. He didn't say any of the words you expect from a father who sees his son going off to war, and he didn't do so out of affection. Just as he'd done when Vittorio went to Naples to study at the university. It was his silent way to give him strength, support, to make him understand that there was no break: they would be seeing one another again, as always. There was nothing so extraordinary that could break their bond. The rest was just weakness that was not worth displaying in public.

"I wonder if he was proud of me when he died?" asked Vittorio out loud.

* * *

One November morning the British appeared to be getting serious. They were in a big hurry, as it hadn't happened in months in the laziness of the almost empty camp. The others had almost all gone home: 26, 27, 28. They were the last ones left at the foot of the Himalayas, the "25s," hanging between punishment and oblivion. On other occasions the British counted them, lined them up, and had them get ready. But then each time they would return them to their huts, as if that were the last cruel game to break them, just for the satisfaction of bending their backs even though no one cared any more.

On that morning, though, the British were not fooling around. Gurkha sentries were posted around the camp during the assembly with their rifles at the ready. Ram was also there as straight as one of the pillars of the camp fence. "Come on, let's go!" screamed the quartermaster. Once the Italian commanders ended the count, the quartermaster explained very quickly.

"It's your turn now. You are going home. The ship that will take you back to Italy will arrive at Bombay in five days and you therefore leave tomorrow morning to be ready for the rendezvous. Between now and the second count this evening, you must prepare your baggage and line it up at the entrance of the huts. One piece per man and nothing more. At dawn tomorrow the trucks will take you to Nagrota. Have a good trip."

What do you do in such cases, jump for joy? The 25s decided not to, the British didn't even deserve that final satisfaction. The commander ordered them to stand at attention and they answered with a stubborn "To us!"[*] Then, for the last time in the Kangra valley, there sounded the final call in Italian to break ranks.

"Lieutenant, is this for real?"

"How should I know, Vito? What could change now, anyway? Let's get ready and see what happens."

The Gurka sentries took the prisoners to the hospital for a final check-up before they left, under the watchful eyes of the Red Cross delegate. As Vittorio got off the scale, the doctor dictated to his assistant for the clinical record:

"Second Lieutenant Conte. Age: thirty one. Height: one meter and eighty centimeters. Weight: forty seven kilos." Vito burst out laughing:

"Gosh Lieutenant, seen from the outside you looked chubbier than that."

---

[*] "A Noi!" was the fascist war cry.

"Maybe it was the dirty water that blew up my stomach, you jerk."

Vittorio's baggage was an old wooden soap box, painted over in green. He had written his serial number and address Corso Garibaldi 26, Lucera. Just in case it got lost. Inside there were his books, the drinking glasses Vito had made by cutting bottle ends, a drawing of the stone hill by an artist fellow prisoner, a few rags and various objects that were just mementos. Because now that was the main issue: to make sure nothing got lost, especially not inside.

All of a sudden those huts, those rocks and mountains were part of a story that couldn't be forgotten, it wasn't something that you could just turn your back on. Those who were in charge inside the barbed wire fence would become something different the moment they stepped on the train. What would become of the 25s once the gates of the camp closed behind them for the last time?

For five years Yol had become a society that appeared to be eternal and unchangeable, with its iron clad rules and detailed regulations. It even had its own dead, who were buried in camp 29 and who would never leave those mountains. Rossi, Viale, the Captain of the Alpini who hanged himself, Leonida, felled by tuberculosis at Dehradun. And now? In twenty four hours they would walk away and it would be all over? And what were they going to find back home? That night there was an unusual silence in the mess hall that no one had ordered. Too many thoughts were crowding the mind to be able to think each one of them through. There were so many, in fact, that they prevented you from falling asleep, under the starry nights of late autumn that had chased away the clouds of the last monsoon.

Dawn came quickly for all those who were wasting their time summing up their lives, and perhaps it was better that way. This time the British were not playing games and there really was a line of trucks waiting at the end of the road, at the gates. Vittorio straightened his uniform and looked at the empty flag pole. He could smell the aroma of the pine trees in the fresh air of the Himalayas, that came down from the mountains where as he followed the quick pace set by Ram he had rediscovered the will to survive. He loaded his soap box on his shoulders and walked to the gate.

The Gurkha sentries were waiting beyond the barbed wire, lined up one last time with their rifles and Kukris. Ram stood at attention but looked as he went by. Vittorio came up to him.

"How are you man?"

"Well, Sir."

"It looks like we are really going this time, Ram. What will you do?"

"I have decided Sir: I'll go to the Academy. I want to become an officer for the New India."

Of course, the New India. This was home to them. A place where life would go on, even after the Italian prisoners had disappeared from the horizon.

Vittorio offered his hand, that Ram shook with a smile. Then the Gurkha presented him with his Kukri, and stood as rigidly as possible at attention, with his right hand at his forehead in the most martial salute he could give. Vittorio took the Kukri and saluted him back, probably the last time in his life that he would salute militarily.

On the truck Vito gave the rocky surface of Yol one final look.

"Feeling nostalgic?" said Vittorio, attempting to provoke him.

"No Lieutenant, no nostalgia. But you are only twenty years old once in your life, and we spent those years up here."

19.

"The real purge never took place. A few tough customers were punished, but only because during the inquiries it became clear that some of their ideas were not welcome to the higher ups. The main guys obviously managed to save their skin."

In his office at the ministry Alberto reread the 12 page report that he had just finished writing. It was entitled *Basic Criteria for the purge of the Navy*, and was addressed to Admiral Malceri and other high ranking officers. It was tough, extremely tough. But the fact was that the old fascists were coming back and he decided the time was right to sound the alarm.

The report began:

"Right now Navy personnel is subjected to two different criteria: one military, to ascertain their behavior during the armistice and immediately after; the other of a more political nature according to existing criteria for the purge. That kind of double attempt, that could appear to be harsher at first, is resolved in the end in the most comfortable way to avoid engaging in the purge, that becomes a trap for idiots."

A single example will be enough: "The case of the suppressed Commission for the examination of the Admirals in command of naval units, created by the hierarchy to further in the views of a single member, the Grand Admiral himself. We don't need to add that the venerable old man immediately proceeded to absolve everyone."

According to Alberto the consequences were disastrous: "The only Admirals to be purged came as a result of the Council of Ministers of January 29, 1945, but the decision was never actually implemented and they remained in their positions with the related administrative and personnel consequences. Having come down from the north they remain at their posts, are received by the various commissions, and at times by the minister or his chief of staff. They are still officers with their former rank." Alberto considered this situation to constitute a serious threat to Italy: "In the Navy there are very few cases of official fascism or hierarchy worship. To be very clear, a small number of elements could be called fascist (March on Rome, lector's scarf or squad member.) This could lead to the conclusion that there were few fascists in the Navy, which would be an accurate statement. But within the upper echelons of the Navy there was and still exists a hidden and violent form of fascism."

The purges should be based on an obvious set of principles: "1. After September 8 the Germans perpetrated acts of aggression and offenses to the honor and prestige of the Italian Armed Forces of such violence, that everyone should feel duty bound to respond to the aggression and the attack by every possible means. 2. As of October 14, 1943 the legal Italian government declared war on Germany, so that after that date no soldier could harbor any doubts regarding the attitude he should have and had to at the very least engage in forms of passive resistance. If the period from September 9 to October 14 can be considered as belonging to the armistice, any assistance given to the Germans or the neo-Fascists after October 14 would have to be considered as the most serious form of treason." These were the very lines of conduct that, according to Alberto, many clever officers were trying to get around:

"Too many certifications of underground activity are being handed out, to the point that soon there will be 45 million partisans in Italy. It becomes necessary to proceed with caution when accepting such documents, also out of respect for the victims of partisan warfare."

Alberto was recommending clemency for sailors in the lower ranks, except for those who joined the black brigades, the X flotilla MAS and the assault units that took part in operations against the Italian Armed Forces and the partisans. For the higher ranks he demanded the most severe punishment.

"In Rome there were many high ranking officers with their hangers on; careerists, political climbers and the most fiery fascists, among them. They were able through multiple stratagems, contortions and compromises to slip across the treacherous waters of republican neo-fascism, to which they were tied through past connections. We shall mention the most egregious of these cases."

Alberto then openly attacked the high command: "We mention those high ranking officers with important positions at the time of the armistice who were clearly derelict of duty. Given the large numbers, rather than dealing in generalities we prefer to single out their names and the episodes with the profiles that we intend to provide."

The attachments were even more damning than the report itself. The top Navy brass was being accused point blank on very specific issues:

"Divisional Admiral Bruno Brivonesi is the most blatant example of cowardice and collaborationism out of fear. In November 1941 he was removed from the command of a naval squadron because of his shortcomings. On September 8, 1943 he was at La Maddalena. The naval base is located on an island replete with heavy artillery and is ideal location to stage any kind of defense. Our sailors, under Captain Avegno who died heroically in action at that time, disarmed the German garrison and pointed the artillery weapons toward Sardinia where the attacks were originating. Brivonesi instead immediately reached an agreement with the Nazi commander, surrendered to him and under an escort of German soldiers toured all the gun emplacements on the base, ordering that the prisoners be released and that all Italian sailors lay down their weapons. A group of sailors who viewed the Admiral as a traitor opened fire on him but unfortunately missed. Others who were misled, obeyed and lay down their arms, allowing Nazi troops to occupy the small island. These actions came with enormous consequences since the island of La Maddalena, with the cooperation of the units in Corsica, allowed the Germans to transfer their troops out of Sardinia. Those same units were to fight later on at Monte Cassino. Brivonesi's responsibility during that incident was obvious and related to that of Generals Basso and Castagna who are now standing trial. Brivonesi instead is being given special tasks at the Naval ministry."

The second attachment also cut another Divisional Admiral to pieces: "Gaetano Catalano Gonzaga is without a doubt and by far the greatest thief the Navy has ever seen. A real artist when it comes to piracy, his activity was dedicated mostly to trafficking in foreign exchange, precious metals, jewelry, furs etc. His most fruitful period was in Greece (1942) where he served as naval commander in that area. He used warships to smuggle his contraband, that was being carried out openly and in such large amounts to warrant a special investigation by Under Secretary Riccardi. Although he was implicated in the much larger "Geloso scandal", he was simply transferred to Corsica as punishment, where he managed to have the Italian government spend some ten million lira to "beautify" the headquarters and then resumed his trafficking with Sardinia and southern France. He used Italian Navy speed motorboats to travel between cities just to be fitted by his tailor.

On September 8 he was still in Corsica under General Magli's command, who had 85000 men facing only 6000 Germans. In order to prevent Italian sailors from firing on the Nazis he ordered that the artillery pieces be disabled or dumped into the sea. An inquest was held by the Naval high command regarding the events in Corsica and Catalano's behavior avoided reaching any judgement by deferring the matter to the military court. He is now in command of a naval squadron and is continuing to carry out his smuggling operations undisturbed."

Alberto then moved on to accuse a squadron commander: "Admiral Ettore Sportiello is one of the dirtiest officers in the Navy. He is well known for his ignorance and for using the Navy to his own ends in traffic and smuggling. As the top commander of the C.R.E.M. in 1942/43, he would pry on the wives of the younger officers who came to him for various reasons. It is well known that only those who were the most pliant, out of love or because they were forced to do so, obtained appointments to the most comfortable assignments or destinations in the service thus depriving the honest ones. This will give an idea of the moral character of the man.

At the start of hostilities against Greece he was as a divisional admiral in charge of the Navy in Albania. Somehow he managed to get into the good graces of General Cavallero who made him part of the honors of victory, even citing him in the speech that Mussolini gave on that occasion (the speech of the "broken back".)* That was how he was promoted as commander of a naval squadron. Actually he had been unanimously voted as not deserving a promotion. Despite his past history and his moral and professional baggage, and even though his case is clearly of the kind that is referred to as one of "career

---

* Mussolini said in a speech "We will break the back of Greece!"
** MAS stands for Motoscafo Anti-Sommergibile or anti-submarine patrol boat.

advantage", Sportiello is now President of the superior council of the Navy."

Finally Alberto attacked those who usurped their medals:

"Right now Lieutenant Emilio Legnani has been completely exonerated by the Commission of Inquiry of the Ministry of the Navy. His case is the most egregious example of nepotism. Even though he was actually at war for only two weeks, and spent the rest of the time convalescing, he was awarded the gold medal which he obtained as follows. Through bluff and bluster, in the spirit of adventure that existed on our assault boats in the Black Sea, he was able to obtain the command of a MAS** in that theater. He took part in only one single naval action, together with another boat commanded by Captain Castagnacci. At night they saw a black shadow and mistakenly thought it was a Soviet cruiser. Castagnacci's MAS attacked and hit the enemy ship with a torpedo that managed to stop it. Legnani's MAS went against a target that couldn't move, fired its torpedoes and declared to have sunk the Soviet cruiser.

He immediately returned to Italy to collect many honors and the ministry of the Navy put his name up for a gold medal, while Castagnacci received a silver medal. The Central Commission for awards didn't accept the proposal and sent the request back to the ministry. The response came back with a motivation signed by Under Secretary Riccardi written in his own hand, but that was also rejected. Finally the Duce himself had to get involved so that he could obtain the gold medal. The scandal was such that Captain Castagnacci, who would later lose his life in combat in the Sicily Canal, offered his resignation to the S.P.E. and returned his medals to the ministry.

After September 8th Lieutenant Legnani followed his father, who had been appointed undersecretary of the fascist Navy so called, becoming his aide de camp until his father's death. We don't know what he did later on but his family benefited from the advantages that Mussolini bestowed upon it."

20.

Naples once again, it was incredible. I had become accustomed to the idea that I would never see the city again, ever. It would have been more logical to die in the French campaign, on the ships taking us to Libya off the coast of Malta, under the British bombardment in the desert of Cyrenaica, while traveling from Egypt during the long trip to Bombay, or in the camps at Derhadun and Yol. When I left India even His Britannic Majesty's doctors were amazed, since I didn't weigh much more than a small boy. Enough to fizzle out like a spent candle during the return trip: twenty days in steerage over the Indian Ocean, the Red Sea, Suez and the Mediterranean.

Instead here was Naples, the Gulf with its colors and Vesuvius. Who knows why I managed to make it back here. Who knows what I can expect to find on the pier and what kind of Italy I will discover. Perhaps my sisters and my mother Annita, with her hair getting whiter and her sad and tender smile, or maybe Alberto. The last time I saw him he was showing off his officer's insignia on his blue uniform of the Royal Navy. My brother was always the best, the most intelligent, brilliant, congenial and unpredictable of them all. And good looking as well.

But what has happened to all of us? Those were Vittorio's thoughts when on November 29, 1946 a foreign ship took him back to what in the meantime had become a foreign land.

The water of the Gulf was filled with debris inherited from a war that was not yet erased. All around the ship were little boats filled with beggars asking for alms.

Vito nodded and said: "We are doing better and better, Lieutenant. These fellows are begging to us, the returning prisoners who have nothing but an empty box of soap."

He remembered the images at the time of his departure, six years before, when this was the proud harbor of the imperial Navy. Or at least the city enjoyed that illusion. On the pier Vittorio saw a small band dressed like for the San Gennaro festival that was playing little marching tunes.

"What the hell are they doing? Celebrating what, Vito? Are they cheering the defeat?"

The 25s looking over the ramp made obscene gestures at the band. The musicians didn't understand. They stumbled, missing a few notes, stopped playing and inquired: "But why are they so mad at us?" A POW yelled out from the ship: "What the hell are you playing those happy tunes for? Don't you have a good funeral march for Italy?"

The little band, amazed at the reaction, quietly moved away while the sailors on the British ship were throwing the moorings. Vittorio went up to the gangplank:

"We have fallen pretty low. Here they are celebrating treason."

Someone, perhaps in the new administration financed by the Allies, had lined up a few tables on the pier with food, water and fruit. The first 25s that landed didn't even stop:

"Why don't you go screw yourselves, you and your trinkets. We didn't beg for soup while we were dying of hunger in front of the British, so now you want us to fall all over your charity? These people don't understand shit or what?"

As Vito went down the ladder, he was the first to notice the uniform of a naval officer among the families and bystanders that were curiously hanging around the pier area. So he stepped aside without too much fanfare.

"So, Lieutenant, we'll see each other tomorrow in the village."

Vittorio didn't understand his haste but agreed.

"Certainly Vito, you can count on it."

He patted his orderly on the shoulder.

"Don't forget that you asked me to serve as best man at your children's wedding."

"First as godfather at the christening, then the wedding Lieutenant, as God decides."

Vito had already disappeared into a military truck that was loading the prisoners, when Vittorio also recognized the uniform. He understood who it was and recognized the look, but Alberto didn't recognize him. He was standing conspicuously in uniform in the crowd looking at the prisoners, but couldn't tell one from the other. A long line of refugees with thick unruly beards, emaciated faces and patched up uniforms.

For the first time in six years Vittorio felt as if he were looking at himself in the mirror and not seeing the same person. He imagined a face that had aged and been marked too much to be remembered. Yet he made an effort to go up to Alberto and touched his arm.

There were words that had to be said, questions and explanations that had long been thought through to be attempted. But silence remained the most eloquent statement for many seconds, filled with a strong tight embrace as it had never happened while they were kids. Yet the silence was immediately replaced by a recovered intimacy.

"I really am ashamed, I almost didn't recognize you," said Alberto.

"Don't even mention it. I must look really awful."

"Well, to tell you the truth, you never were that nice to look at. But when you look like this you would never find a girl who would take you, even if you kissed a pig's ass."

Vittorio was surprised to be suddenly laughing:

"Why, do you have some gal you can introduce me to right now?"

The sleeve with the stripes of a naval officer went up to give him a whack on his neck, over the back of his tattered shirt.

"Damn it, even the war didn't change you one bit, did it?"

"Oh, if it's only for that…But let's not even discuss it."

Vittorio's eyes lingered on that sleeve:

"What are those stripes? I don't recognize them."

"Oh yes, they promoted me to Major," answered his brother.

"So I must address you with "voi"."

"No. "Lei" is good enough right now."

Alberto pointed to a car that thanks to his uniform he was able to park close to the pier. He was shocked and saddened because his brother looked like a shriveled up old man, but he managed not to let it show.

"You know about Dad?"

"I found out eight months after you mailed the letter" answered Vittorio.

"I'm sorry. We mailed it through the Red Cross but by then nothing was working any more."

"All it said was that he died after a brief illness. The rest had been erased by the censor."

"Idiots," said Alberto.

"But what happened exactly?" asked Vittorio.

"It was his heart. He didn't suffer because it all happened very suddenly. He was very weak during the final period. Weak and sad."

"I still have trouble accepting it: Dad had been dead for so many months and I didn't even know it."

"I remember how he saved the newspaper clippings about you on his desk."

"Which clippings?"

"Oh, of course, you wouldn't know anything about that. The local paper in Lucera was always publishing news articles about your wartime exploits."

"Exploits?"

"Yes, like the time you stopped a whole column of tanks by yourself. They awarded you a cross of military valor for that action. You didn't know that either, I bet."

"I was a prisoner in India. We barely knew that we were still alive."

Alberto looked straight down the road in front of the car and nodded:

"We were kept informed through the Red Cross but it was very little. At first they said you were missing at Tobruk. It almost took a whole year to receive confirmation that you had been taken prisoner."

"And you? I don't know a thing about what happened to you." asked Vittorio.

"Nothing heroic. After 1941 I was transferred to Naval Staff headquarters at the Ministry. I am still there. I'm sharing an apartment with Federico on the Lungotevere. As soon as you feel up to it, come and see us in Rome."

"Federico and Giuseppe, damn it! How are they?"

"Federico left the Navy and wants to transfer to the ministry of the interior. Giuseppe became a judge."

Life had started up again, even though Vittorio couldn't make heads or tails of any of it.

"And mother?"

"You'll see her as soon as we arrive. She suffered for Dad, but she remained strong because she wanted to see all her children around her again. Silent and determined, as always.

She's very capable of giving you another slap because you wandered too far away from her."

When Vittorio arrived in Corso Garibaldi however there were no slaps in the face. His mother took him by the hands with tearful eyes and walked him to his room. Everything was exactly as he had left it as a young boy. She patted his face and kissed him on the cheeks. Then, in silence as she had welcomed him, she left the room so he could be alone. She wanted him to get accustomed to a normal life once again, without being watched like an animal in a zoo. There would be enough time to speak later on. "We must tread very carefully," said Alberto as she came back downstairs.

"I know," she answered.

"First of all no trocchioli, orecchiette or pot pies: any of it would kill him. He weighs only forty seven kilos and hasn't had a decent meal in six years. You must bring him back a little bit at a time. Only weak broth and light foods at first."

"I'll take him to the doctor when he will feel like going out." "Certainly. The other very important thing is to give him space. Don't crowd him too much with too many questions and too much affection. He will talk when he'll feel ready to do so."

Annita nodded, as Alberto went on.

"And don't feel slighted if he is not nice and behaves rudely. He's back from war and the prison camp, and his nerves are frayed. Make him feel that you are close to him but let him be. He will speak in due course."

His mother understood:

"He said that for the moment he only wants to see me. I'll be the one to bring him his meals."

"All right."

"Then he asked to visit his father's study. I left it untouched just for him."

"Fine. I must return to Naples to matriculate him at the university. He'll have to start over and do something as soon as possible. Then I'll quickly drive back to Rome because I have some work related things to do."

Alberto was still involved in the purge of fascists from the Armed Forces, while he kept on looking for Dinah. He never stopped in his search, following up on every trace, no matter how improbable it could appear. But now his brother came first, ahead of everything else: "I'll be back in a few weeks to see how things are coming along."

Vittorio stayed in his room for days refusing to see anyone. "Mother, I don't feel like it, I don't want to," he would always answer his mother when she would ask him to come out. He would wait for her to climb the stairs with his meal, smiled and left everything in his plate.

Annita finally thought it necessary to have the doctor come to the house because Vittorio didn't want to move. The doctor said: "Your health is good enough, taking into account what you went through. But you should do me two favors: first, eat some raw onions to build up your vitamins; second, have a bit of red wine to get your stomach fluids flowing again."

So every day his mother would go up with a glass of wine and a few slices of onion. He would send everything back and she would try again the next day, without asking questions.

When Alberto returned Annita couldn't help crying:

"He doesn't do anything all day. He eats very little and drinks even less. He hasn't left the house once since he's been back."

"Did you try talking to him?" asked Alberto.

"A few sentences, nothing serious. He's nice, affectionate, but it's as if he were absent. I wonder if we are really helping him like this or if we are losing him."

"I have to go upstairs."

"No, Alberto. The only thing he insists on is that he only wants to see me."

"I understand, but I must go upstairs anyway."

Alberto touched his mother's arm to prevent her from saying anything else. Then he went up the staircase, entering without knocking. Vittorio was looking out the window.

"I just got back from Rome. How are you doing?"

"Well," answered Vittorio without turning around.

"You've never left the house?"

"No."

"You are also not eating?"

"I don't feel like it."

"And you don't speak with mother."

"Better for her and for me."

"And you feel good about this?"

"Yes."

Alberto shook his head.

"Vittorio, I understand you. I have seen hundreds of soldiers coming back from the war and prison camps, but this will not work."

"What do you understand?"

Alberto didn't answer.

"Do you understand what it means to come back to a country you don't recognize? Do you know what it's like to be hungry for five years, while defending a dignity that everyone here has forgotten?"

Alberto continued to stare at his brother without answering.

"What would I do outside in the street? People would look at me as if I were crazy. Why didn't you come back earlier? What were you doing in India, guarding empty barrels? You have all gone back to living it up as if nothing had happened. I remained with my comrades who died in Libya, or those who hanged themselves at Yol in order not to lose themselves, while you were already smoking American cigarettes."

Alberto went toward the window with his arms crossed over his chest.

Vittorio went on:

"To think that I was convinced of defending my honor and that of my country. But which country is that going to be? In your eyes I had to be some kind of fool, in the best of cases. In the worst case I was an accomplice to a criminal regime. But all this comes after I was sent off to fight for Italy, after being wounded and being held as a prisoner of war. I did my duty as a soldier and they almost killed me. But to the people out there I'm just some kind hoodlum. Can you understand this?"

Alberto went up to his brother, put a hand on his shoulder and began talking to him quietly:

"You're saying some pretty silly things that I don't even want to listen to. You survived the war and the prison camps, and now you feel ashamed because of the way people look at you in the street? Who are they to judge? Furthermore, who gives a damn about what they think?"

Vittorio didn't answer and Alberto went on.

"Or perhaps you are staying locked up at home because of the contempt you feel for those who didn't live their lives the way you did? But then you are a rather conceited person. Each one acted according to what he believed in or was able to carry out. Correct or incorrect, doesn't really matter in this discussion: if I told you what I saw and continue to see. What's most important is how you feel. If you think you did your duty, if you believe you were right, if you know you can hold your head high, go in the outside world and start living again. If you stay locked up in here then you are only a weakling. And, quite frankly, I didn't remember having a brother who was ready to piss in his pants!"

* * *

Two days later Vittorio was on the train to Naples. Alberto got him an appointment to return to the job he used to have at the bank before the war, when he worked part time to make some pocket money while attending courses at the university. He shaved, combed his hair back with gel, and wore one of the elegant suits his mother had saved for him. She cooked him breakfast as if he had never left home for the last ten years and nothing had happened.

The trip was a journey into the past, when going to the city meant having fun. Vittorio saw his memories go by from the train window. At the main office at the Banco di Napoli one of the big shots, the head of personnel in fact, agreed to see him. He was clearly a very busy man in a hurry, but remained friendly enough.

"Please sit down."

Vittorio took a chair in front of his desk.

"So, you have just returned from being a prisoner of war?"

"Correct."

"I'm sorry for what you went through."

"I'm not."

The manager cleared his throat and shuffled some papers on his desk.

"Let's see now. I notice that before the war you used to work at our bank. You were well placed to begin a career, while you studied for a degree in Economics and Business."

Vittorio nodded.

"Correct."

"So now you would like to have your job back."

"If it's possible, while I get my degree."

"So you did not graduate yet?" asked the head of personnel.

"For the last seven years I was at war, not on vacation."

"Understood, understood. But, if I may ask, why didn't you come back before?"

"I was being held prisoner in India."

"Yes, I understand. But you see, this is a problem. In the last few years the bank has made a lot of progress. Business, if I may say so, is rather good, so that now there are other people who have filled your old job."

Vittorio kept silent as he looked at the manager who went on.

"Of course your brother is a Resistance hero, so for him we could make an exception...I mean, your brother is well known and we would therefore be pleased to help you. However the position you used to have is no longer available. You would have to start all over again, from scratch."

"Look, I didn't come here seeking favors. I am only asking to have the job I left when I went to war back."

"Yes, it makes sense. The problem is that the job you used to have no longer exists."

"But weren't you supposed to hold it, by law?"

"Well, so many things changed since then, don't you know? Even the laws have changed."

Vittorio got up out of his chair:

"I went to fight even for people like you, who stayed at home to tend to their business."

"There is no reason for you to get upset, Sir. And I wouldn't use such a contemptuous attitude when speaking of our business."

"Well, I think I have a good enough reason, because while they almost killed me you were warming your chair with your behind, busy making money. You were in business, as you people say, because some asshole like myself was doing the fighting for you."

"How many excuses will we discover relating to this war, Sir. Now, it's all water under the bridge. I'm just trying to help you, but you must also be realistic. You see, while you were wandering around the world engaging in your adventures, some of us stayed behind to work at rebuilding Italy. You can't just re-appear suddenly, and demand that those who sweated it out for you should now step aside and bow when you walk."

Vittorio was already standing up, so he didn't need to move that much. He put both hands under the top of the desk and rediscovered the strength he had lost in Libya and India, as he turned the big desk over the director of personnel.

As he screamed for help and yelled that he was crazy, Vittorio readjusted his elegant suit, smoothed his hair back with his pocket comb and went out the door. Something inside made him smile.

21.

When Federico returned home to the old apartment on the Lungotevere Flaminio, Alberto's desk was piled up with his reports. He was holding a letter from Don Fedinando in his hand, asking that he contact him as soon as possible since he had important information about Dinah. He put the envelope back in his pocket when he heard his brother entering.

"Any news from Vittorio?"

Alberto looked up from the papers.

"Yes, mother said that a few days ago he went to Naples."

"Good, so he finally got out of the house."

"He visited the headquarters of the Banco di Napoli to ask for the job he had before the war."

"Excellent."

"Yes, except for the fact that he flipped the desk over the director of personnel."

"No kidding. Why would he do that?" asked Federico.

"I think the director insulted him about the war or his being a POW."

"So he's still at it? Do you think he'll ever overcome this feeling of his?"

"Yes, of course he will, don't worry. I see it as a rather good sign: I'd rather have Vittorio getting angry than being depressed."

"Instead, you look like the one who's depressed. What are those papers?" asked Federico.

"Just reports." answered Alberto.

"Reports about what?"

"The purges."

"But how can this be? Hasn't Togliatti decided to give amnesty to the fascists?"

"That's what the politicians have decided, yes. But someone has to preserve the memory."

"Excuse-me but doesn't this matter also involve Vittorio?" asked Federico.

"No, not at all in fact. He was a mere soldier and a POW far removed from everything. He made the kind of choice he felt was the most logical, one that also turned out to be the most dangerous. Vittorio paid a price. I am talking about the big shots here in Italy. Those who had all the necessary information to choose the right path, but who, instead, preferred to look out for their petty interests."

Federico looked at the papers on the desk and read the first few lines.

"My God, this is heavy stuff! But aren't you taking a big risk in attacking the Admirals so openly?"

"Real scoundrels, is what you mean. During the war these people sank the Navy because of their incompetence. Then they kept hanging on to the Italian Social Republic, hoping to save their privileges and their trafficking. Now they are appearing in Rome once more and want to order around the people who risked their lives under the Nazi occupation."

"All right, but they are still powerful. Maybe they were the same ones who were trying to put you on trial for the battle of Matapan."

"Maybe, I don't know. Some of them accused the Navy of being monarchist and therefore of having betrayed fascism."

"So now they will have even more reason to seek revenge, if they can."

"Of course, but what can I do about it? After fighting the Nazis in the underground resistance, I should now bow to those deserters?"

22.

Don Ferdinando was taking his leave from the last parishioners who stopped in to say good bye after mass. At the entrance of the rectory he saw Alberto. He let him inside and shut the door.

"I got your letter that said it was urgent," Alberto began.

"Yes, thank you for coming. But please sit down."

The priest took two wooden chairs from the table and placed them near the window. Then, holding both hands together, he said:

"I must confess that I had lied to you."

Alberto looked up and was staring at him in silence.

Don Ferdinando went on:

"I know you wouldn't expect such an admission from someone wearing the cloth. But I had to because she asked me to."

Alberto continued to look at the priest, and remained silent.

"As I mentioned in my letter, this about Dinah. That is, the person you knew as Dinah."

The priest hesitated for a moment, so Alberto encouraged him to go on:

"Keep going."

"When we met for the first time I had told you that she was Jewish."

"Yes, I remember that very well."

"What I did not tell you was the reason why she was in my rectory. I did so to protect everyone's security."

"I understand."

"Dinah's family, her father, her mother and brothers were deported by the Nazis on October 16, 1943 during the raid on the Ghetto. She saved herself by a stroke of luck since that day she was not in Rome but at the house of friends. I was a friend of one of her father's colleagues at work who told me her story and asked me to protect her."

Alberto was leaning on the chair and kept on listening intently.

Don Ferdinando said:

"I know very well all the rumors that are going around regarding the behavior of Church hierarchy during the Nazi occupation: God will be the judge. But I can guarantee that scores of priests like me did what they could to hide people at the risk of their own lives. To save the Jews that had escaped the raid. And in most cases we were acting with the full knowledge of the leadership of the Church."

"I know."

"So Dinah was one of those who escaped, but she didn't want to just hide and wait. She wanted to be reunited with her family. She felt a deep love for her parents and brothers and she couldn't accept the idea that they may be all dead. She was not seeking revenge, because she didn't accept the possibility that she may have lost them. But she was convinced that by helping in the liberation, she could possibly find them. In some way, don't ask me how, she had good connections and was able to obtain useful information. That was why she asked me to contact the Resistance and the reason I introduced you to her."

Since Alberto continued to remain silent, the priest asked him:

"But she had told you nothing?"

"We didn't discuss the past and even less the future."

"Yes, during those months we could say that we were barely living in the present. But she had to be thinking about the future since she was intent on finding her family. She was obsessed by the idea. That's why I had to lie to you."

"About what?" asked Alberto.

"Regarding what happened after the liberation. I remember that you came to see me because you were looking for Dinah and I said that I knew nothing about it. It wasn't true. As soon as the Nazi troops began moving out of Rome, Dinah ran away. She went north to join a partisan unit, always hoping to find some trace of her family. She knew that the deportees had been taken to the camp at Fossoli, near Modena, and she thought that by getting closer to that area she would be able to gather information."

Alberto remained silent.

"Dinah asked me not to tell you. She had begged me not to do it."

"Why?"

"She was convinced that you would have attempted to stop her and she wasn't sure that she'd have the strength to say no. But when she thought things through calmly, she always came to the conclusion that her only duty was to find her family. That's why she decided to run away in secret."

Alberto couldn't feel any anger toward the priest or Dinah. He only felt a huge void, like the nights he spent underground when he didn't know whether he'd see her the following day.

Don Ferdinando had trouble hiding his emotion as he said:

"I didn't call you before to let you know because I honestly had no information. You must believe me this time. As soon as I was able to find out something I wrote you that letter."

Alberto listened and didn't have the courage to ask any questions.

"Unfortunately there was no news of Dinah's family: out of the one thousand Jews deported from Rome barely a dozen returned. But she did join that partisan unit I mentioned before, fought with them and died."

Alberto looked out the window, lowering his head holding his chin. The priest said:

"If you wish, I can give you the address of the people that informed me. They were with her during her final moments."

He answered without acknowledging the priest's offer:

"She was one of the few reasons that gave me hope during those days."

Don Ferdinando clenched his rosary tightly in his fist.

"I don't know how to express my regret because I lied to you, but, in good conscience, I don't think I had much of a choice. Sometimes I think I was mistaken and that I should have been the one to stop her. But then I'm not sure I would have succeeded."

23.

All the reports Alberto had prepared turned out to be useless. The top brass hid them somewhere, as though they were the symptoms of a contagious disease that had to remain hidden under thick makeup, and they just muddled through. Fascists, deserters and careerists remained at their posts, more self assured and powerful than before. Alberto felt isolated but he also sensed that he had no choice. Therefore he started to write once again. He wanted to put on paper the history of the purge that failed, and this time he pointed his finger directly at the former Navy minister de Courten.

"It is already a well known fact, since we have been uselessly repeating it, that the purge of the Navy was a complete failure. The High Commissioner for sanctions against fascism pointed this out in a report with a decision by Sidney Prima Ricotti [What happened in the Navy seems absurd. One more reason to have these Admirals retire–Pietro Nenni.]"

He lost faith in justice.

"Already on other occasions we attempted to identify the reasons that prevented a thorough cleansing of the ranks. We shall repeat once more, for the last time, that the roots are to be found in the bad faith and incompetent behavior of a few members of the Naval Office of the High Commissioner, and the obstruction that was carried out on a grand scale starting with the Naval Minister and those who were part of the cabinet of Minister de Courten, a reactionary who excels at underhanded maneuvers."

His words were no longer measured and he had thrown any caution to the four winds. The apathy and lack of interest that his father had worried about before the war had been transformed into deep-seated rancor. Alberto felt betrayed and surrounded, and he singled out his enemies by name:

"The Naval Office of the High Commission was always poorly served by the various directors that were called upon to manage it. At first it was headed by the Lieutenant Colonel in permanent service Gino Scotto who today says that he is a communist but who until July 25, 1943 was openly proclaiming his vocal approval of fascism. During the Nazi-fascist occupation he was a collaborationist since he continued to receive his regular salary as an inspector. This sad individual who should have been forced to pay a price for his sins, was instead placed as chief of the naval office filling the functions of prosecutor and judge…with the results that one can only imagine."

There was, it appeared, a conspiracy to obscure everything and turn the purge into a joke: "Following Scotto came Nicola Amendola who, as head of the office, took a similar position during the German occupation and was only given a simple reprimand by the inquiry commission. He always wanted to act with extreme diplomacy where the purge was concerned, and created a paternalistic atmosphere in the office. He made every effort to save both sides: his superiors and himself."

Every appointment confirmed the objective of avoiding to lay the blame on anyone's doorstep:

"The third one was Major Giovanni Vassallo who couldn't inspire confidence because of his intellectual failings, his crass ignorance of even basic facts, his complete lack of balance and less than straight character. Witness the little masterpiece in the indictment of Major Commissioner Mario Adinolfi, a well-known thief and collaborationist in the Navy. He now goes out of his way to proclaim himself a communist, even though he knew absolutely nothing about the most fundamental tenets of communism. He follows only the rule of favoring his friends and trying to hurt other colleagues in the service, exclusively for his own personal advantage."

The mistakes continued to the end—as Alberto pursued his denunciation. "Major Vassallo was to be replaced as the director of the office by the Lieutenant Colonel in permanent and full service Armando Desoindre, another individual whose non-purge cannot be fully understood (or is really totally comprehensible). He was at the ministry of the Navy under the fascist government up to December 15, 1943 as the officer in charge of the liquidation section within the general commissioner's office. For that kind of behavior the military commission of inquiry only gave him a simple reprimand. The only merit Desoindre can point to is as the brother in law of Dr. Scalise, who is the head of the cabinet of Pietro Nenni."

The spider web had managed to insinuate itself into every corner:

"As for the civilian dependents we should single out Judge Dr. Tommaso Fortunio, councilor of the various office heads and the extremely faithful servant of Admiral de Courten's cabinet. He was also a Lieutenant Commissioner in the reserves and being of deeply monarchist faith, he followed the dictates of his ideas to save those officers who shared his politics. He had the daily use of an automobile that belonged to the cabinet with which he traveled around Rome even to attend to his private business. He was attempting to obtain credit for an imaginary role as a partisan fighter that he never had."

Alberto ended his report by attacking those who turned the laborious process of the country's rebirth into a grotesque farce: "The incompetence, bad faith and mistakes on the part of the highest authorities of the office managed to totally paralyze the purge that was required in the Navy even more than in other branches of the public administration. Added to the inherent faults of the naval office was the well known obstruction that remained systematic within the ministry, making it obvious that the entire purge was nothing but a colossal joke. The lack of good faith and uniformity of those in charge produced the greatest injustice mostly toward the lower ranks and among the non-commissioned officers."

Admiral Malceri had Alberto's report on his desk, when he asked him to come to his office at the ministry. His secretary announced that the Admiral wished to meet with him for an urgent piece of information.

"Good morning Major Conte, it's always a pleasure to see you."

"The pleasure is all mine, Admiral," answered Alberto as he took a seat.

"I'll get right to the point. Don't think that I didn't read your denunciations; they describe the reality very well and I am in complete agreement."

"But they fell on deaf ears."

"You are right about that. You know very well which side I am on and I am sure you don't doubt my good faith. The politicians have made a decision however, and we must obey."

"Certainly."

"But I have asked you to come here about a different issue."

Alberto listened intently as Malceri went on.

"I don't know whether there is any connection to your reports, but the ministry has decided to reopen the inquiry into the events at Cape Matapan and you are being investigated. This is a confidential piece of information that very few people are aware of, but that I felt duty bound to warn you about."

"How can this be? Years have gone by."

"The excuse, since I am convinced this was the reason, came with the return of captain Bregnola from his POW camp. He was the second in command of the *Pola* and survived during the night of the battle of Matapan. He was rescued and taken aboard the cruiser *Jervis,* where he made a surprising discovery: on the bridge he saw Admiral Cunningham's orders, where he had the full details of our operation that was theoretically to remain secret, when we started it off the Greek coast. The orders were dated March 26, 1941 and the British knew everything long before we sailed out of Italian ports."

Alberto felt rage rather than fear welling up inside. "But Admiral, now we know that they were able to decrypt our communications through the Ultra system."

"Of course Major, you and I know this very well. But the truth is irrelevant at this point. When Bregnola returned from the prison camp he revealed what he saw aboard the *Jervis* and did so in complete good faith. But, Major Conte, your enemies seized the opportunity. Those who didn't appreciate your reports took advantage of the news to reopen the inquiry and accuse you."

"Too bad for them, we will prove what the truth is and shall finally nail them."

"Yes, we can show the true story, but by the time we do that it may already be too late."

"What do you mean?" said Alberto.

"The gambit is much more complex than you think, Major. The people who reopened the inquiry into Cape Matapan couldn't care less how things actually took place: their sole objective is to destroy you."

Now Alberto listened in silence:

"I am convinced of your innocence, so don't misinterpret what I am saying. I have some clues about Ultra and believe that the new relationship between Italy and Great Britain will allow us to bring the true facts to light. But in the meantime the inquiry into your actions will become official, and this will be enough to allow our enemies to focus on their objective. From then on every word, every report, every denunciation for the purges that were never enacted will be deprived of any value. In the halls of the ministry the only talk will be about the fact that you are being investigated for high treason. In the end we will be able to prove the truth. But by then the damage will be done. Your reputation will be destroyed and nothing is more difficult to rebuild. Your enemies will have avoided the danger of being nailed for their responsibilities during the fascist period, and who knows where they will be by then."

Malceri's last words diluted themselves into the room without eliciting an answer. Alberto got up and shook hands with the admiral:

"I understand. Thank you for the warning."

After the meeting he left the ministry and went home. It was the Carnival time of the year and he had promised Federico to go out with him to a masked ball. Life had to begin once again.

24.

Federico found the body. He cleaned off the blood and called his mother Annita. He told her it was pneumonia, a sudden illness that can hit you with lightning speed. What else was he supposed to tell her—the truth perhaps? And what would the truth be anyway? He looked for it in a note, a detail, a diary. But there was nothing. He looked for it in his last words, his gestures, even the way he looked at you. What was the truth?

When he would think about it and stop to repeat to himself that Alberto committed suicide, he wasn't sure he understood the true meaning of the words. A gunshot to the head in the bathroom, at home. It sounded so strange that you had trouble believing it.

But Federico fell and rose again, just as his father would have expected of him, since he considered him the most reliable of his children. He told Vittorio:

"It's Alberto, you must come here right away."

He held back his tears and told his younger brother to calm down, because when he got to Rome he wanted to bust open somebody's head. Vittorio yelled:

"You have to tell me what happened. You must tell me the truth. Because as much as there is a God, I have already killed in the course of my life and I am ready to do so again."

"Alberto shot himself, Vittorio. Who do you want to kill? We went to the Carnival ball together. Then I lost sight of him. When I got home he was lying in the bathroom. He had shot himself in the head and the weapon was close to his hand."

"But why? Why?"

"I don't know anymore than you. I looked for a note, a clue, something that would help me understand. But I found nothing."

"You were living with him, you must have sensed that something was wrong."

"He was obviously disillusioned, depressed and feeling hopeless because of the way things were shaping up after the war. He felt betrayed but to think he would commit suicide... I for one, was unable to see it coming. Forgive me"

The powerless pain felt by his brother brought Vittorio to his senses. He hugged Federico:

"No, you should forgive me."

Federico then went on:

"Alberto wasn't just a commissioned officer in the Navy. He also worked for S.I.S., the naval secret service. His commanding officer was Admiral Malceri, an officer he had known since the Naval Academy."

"Go on" said Vittorio.

"In 1941, about the time you left to go to Libya, there was a large operation off the Greek coast. Several Italian ships had sailed to intercept British convoys that were bringing supplies up from Egypt to Athens. The attack failed and several of our ships were sunk. You must have heard about the battle at Cape Matapan."

"Yes, of course. But what does it have to do with Alberto?"

"On the way back some Admirals, who were probably trying to hide their responsibility, expressed the suspicion that someone had to have been spying for the British, since they were able to find our ships much too easily. The ministry decided to begin an investigation and Alberto was the target."

Vittorio looked amazed:

"And why him, of all people?"

"The fascists were always suspicious of the Navy and were convinced that it was full of monarchists. Alberto spoke good English, knew many things, and everyone knew he had a mind of his own."

"What does that mean?"

"Simply that he didn't hesitate to level criticism openly when necessary. After the war began, I can assure you, there were many more reasons to be critical of the regime."

"Was what they claimed true, then? Did he betray?"

"Vittorio, you knew him as well as I did: does that seem possible to to you?"

"Unfortunately I have seen even worse."

"No, I am convinced that he had nothing to do with it. Alberto would never have betrayed, even more so if it meant sinking his friends who were still on the first ship where he had served as an officer. The Admirals were only looking for an excuse to cover their own incompetence. In any case the intelligence service, after the investigation by Admiral Malceri, discovered that perhaps the British had managed to break the Italian codes."

"How did the investigation end?"

"It was never brought to a conclusion, because in the meantime the war was going badly and there wasn't any time to waste on such issues."

"So it never was given an official explanation?"

"No" answered Federico.

"I still can't understand how all this could have anything to do with Alberto's death," said Vittorio, as he looked down at the Lungotevere from the window.

Federico explained:

"At the time of the armistice I was with Alberto at the naval ministry. The chiefs were running away and the officers at sea were asking for instructions. We helped them reach Malta and other destinations, as stipulated in the peace agreement. Then the Nazis occupied the city. Alberto decided to remain faithful to his allegiance to the King and tried to defend Rome."

Federico stopped, expecting Vittorio's reaction as he remained at the window. He added:

"I can guarantee you that this was an awful situation. The Nazis were conducting raids and were killing people in the streets. A Colonel named Montezemolo and Admiral Malceri had set up groups of military resistance and Alberto had joined them. He had chosen to go underground, risking to be shot every day that went by."

Federico paused and smiled:

"You may not believe this, but in that tragic situation he even fell in love. He had met a Jewish girl who had managed to elude the raid on the Rome Ghetto and joined the Resistance." Federico's voice became more serious.

"I smile only because it was a beautiful and incredible thing, that out of his usual modesty he was trying to hide from me. But I knew him too well to not understand."

"Well, can we meet this girl? Maybe she can help us understand."

Federico shook his head:

"She is dead. She was killed by the Nazis while fighting up north with the partisans. After Rome was liberated Alberto went looking for her, but she had run away to find her parents who had been deported: she was still hoping that they had survived."

After a brief silence Federico went on:

"In any case Alberto continued to work at rebuilding the country. They placed him in the office in charge of purging the Navy. I'm not just talking about low level fascists, but about the big wheels of the Navy. Those incompetent Admirals who had grown rich thanks to the regime, but expected nonetheless to discredit it and remain in charge once it was gone. He wouldn't accept that, he found that it was a huge injustice to the living and to all those who had died. He would spend his nights writing reports where he would denounce deserters, thieves and careerists. You can read them if you wish. Some of them are still in the drawers of his desk." And Federico pointed to the piece of furniture at the other end of the living room. Vittorio didn't move and Federico went on:

"You can imagine that a lot of people were displeased by his accusations. When Togliatti became minister of Justice and extended amnesty to the fascists, his decision effectively ended the purge. But Alberto went on writing reports. He kept on saying that we had to maintain at the very least the memory of the facts. He had even ended up attacking former naval minister de Courten, accusing him of closing his eyes. He put down on paper all the names and the pro-fascist Admirals had sworn to have him pay for it. At one point they managed to reopen the investigation into Cape Matapan, denouncing him for high treason. Malceri told me the whole story when I talked with him after the suicide. You can imagine Alberto, who had risked his life in the underground resistance against the Nazis: he was being accused of treason by four scoundrels who benefited from fascism, and who didn't even have the courage to admit their responsibilities."

Vittorio remained silent, still looking out the window, and Federico concluded:

"Well, to tell you the truth, I don't know what pushed him over the edge and made him squeeze the trigger. No one can tell.

But this was the story and it is important that you know the facts."

Vittorio remained silent. He was leaning on the side of the window without asking questions. What was there to ask? It was a familiar feeling: his war was still very much going on, and didn't stop. The difference was that it was hitting closer than ever before. The bombs were still continuing to drop. To have survived in Africa, in the Indian prison camp and the sadness of his return. It was all useless. The war was still going on and demanded its price: it didn't give any truce, it never promised to.

* * *

A few weeks later Malceri contacted Federico asking that he come over to the naval ministry with Vittorio. He wanted to meet him and speak to both brothers face to face. As they went up the steps, both Federico and Vittorio were still wearing the black armband of mourning as was customary back home.

The Admiral welcomed them both very courteously in his vast office overlooking the Tiber River. The lights of a Roman spring were streaming in, contrasting with their sad faces. Malceri shook hands firmly with both brothers, placing his left hand on their shoulders. His gestures were direct and informal. Then he told Vittorio: "I knew your brother since the days of the Naval Academy."

"I know the whole story, I was told all about it." Vittorio answered dryly.

Malceri replied:

"Good. Well, I also know your story." Sitting on the edge of his chair, the Admiral went on: "As an old soldier, let me tell you two things. First, that I feel a deep respect for the coherent choice you made as a prisoner in India. Second, that your brother risked his life and unfortunately lost it to save our homeland. I can't advise you on how to reconcile these two facts in your conscience, since they may appear to contradict one another, but I can say that both of them are true."

Vittorio felt his tension easing up and wanted to speak, but stopped, letting his face illustrate the sorrow. Malceri placed his elbows on his desk: "I am sure that in a British POW camp the easiest choice was to collaborate. I can therefore understand that to have honor, dignity, coherence and love of country to you meant not giving in. But here in Rome, with our streets occupied by the Nazis, things were very different. The most dangerous choice was the one your brother made, to stay behind the lines and fight the enemy in the underground resistance. Do you know how many just like him were shot by firing squad because someone talked? Do you know how many of them were tortured in the via Tasso? They were our colleagues, our lifetime friends. It could have happened to us. If we didn't die it was because of a stroke of luck, a quirk that threw the Germans off, or a mistake on their part. You'll have to accept the possibility that your idea of honor and that of Alberto could be identical as to principles and feelings, even though they clashed politically or as to the choice of which side you were on."

Vittorio stared at the Admiral and kept silent. Malceri went on: "It will seem absurd, but I became convinced of one thing: had you been in each other's shoes, you would have also played each other's part. Knowing Alberto, I can say that had he been a prisoner in India he would have also chosen to not cooperate with the British. Now that I met you, I doubt that in a Rome occupied by the Nazis you would have decided to stay on the German side." The Admiral opened his drawer as he spoke: "But these are obviously only my assumptions."

He took out an envelope and placed it on the table. Then Malceri said, also looking at Federico:

"Whatever the case may be, I asked you to come over for two reasons. First, to inform you that the investigation into Cape Matapan is closed: there were no traitors at work that night.

Maybe there was Ultra. But there were no Italian traitors who passed on intelligence to the British enemy. The second reason is in this envelope."

The Admiral gave the yellow envelope to Vittorio who opened it. Inside there was the official decree of a military valor cross given by the Republic of Italy to Alberto Conte. The motivation was drafted as follows:

"As a naval officer, caught by surprise by the armistice in territory that was under enemy control, he took part in creating the military front within the resistance inside the Royal Navy. For many long months of indefatigable and generous activity, he supported and assisted his fellow soldiers in the struggle with high ideals and quiet faith. Even in the most serious circumstances he provided an example, with his firmness and fearlessness in the face of danger, motivated only by a high sense of duty and deep attachment to the national cause. Occupied territory 9 September 1943–4 June 1944. Decision of 5 June 1944, on the battlefield."

Vittorio made a decision as he was reading. When he returned to his own life he would have a son. He would call him Alberto.

Afterword

Alberto and Vittorio were, respectively, my uncle and my father. I changed their family name in the novel, using only that of my grand-mother Annita, to avoid the distraction of having the main characters with the same last name as the author.

The main facts in the book are true, including the epilogue. Alberto was a naval officer assigned to the office of the Chief of staff who decided on September 8, 1943 to join the military front of the Resistance, and who was awarded the war cross for valor because of that activity. Vittorio was an officer of the Bersaglieri sent to a POW camp in India, who decided to refuse to cooperate with the British on September 8, 1943, after the armistice. However this is a novel and many parts of the story are a work of fiction. I decided to use fiction because my historical memory of these events has many unbridgeable interruptions, due to the death of the protagonists that I had to fill by using my own invention. The character of Federico is also inspired from a brother of Alberto and Vittorio, who was also a military officer during the Second World War.

Admiral Malceri is closely inspired by Admiral Franco Maugeri, who was the real life commander of the Naval Intelligence Service (S.I.S.) during the war. After September 8, Adm. Maugeri turned the S.I.S. into a cell of underground military Resistance where Alberto played a role. The character of Vito is inspired somewhat from Vito Livrieri, who during the war was actually Vittorio's orderly. They remained friends for the rest of their lives.

All the documents, letters, diaries and reports on the Resistance cited in this book are authentic and are part of the family archive, along with the military decorations. The diary by Father Romualdo Formàto on Kefalonia is authentic and was in my Uncle Alberto's papers, as were the lists of those who collaborated with the Nazis, that were compiled following the bombing at via Rasella and the massacre at the Ardeatine Caves. The same applies to the denunciations regarding the failed purges in the Navy. These documents were all transcribed verbatim from the originals and reflect Alberto's views at the time.

The texts of the International Red Cross regarding the conditions of Italian POWs in India are the original reports written by the inspectors at the time. My research benefited from the excellent collaboration I received from the Red Cross and I must thank Mrs. Marija Feug and historian Fabrizio Bensi for their help. During the endless tragedy of the Second World War that claimed the lives of millions of people, a few Red Cross representatives found the time to follow the personal ordeal of my father Vittorio, from the time he was wounded in Libya to his prison camp in India, providing accurate news on his condition.

Some sixty years later it only took two weeks, after I mailed an ordinary letter to the Red Cross in Geneva, to receive all the documents relating to Vittorio that had been carefully filed in the archives of that organization. The same kind of cooperation came from the Italian Defense Ministry, the Navy and the Defense Ministry of the United Kingdom, that helped me reconstruct the moments in the lives of my father and my uncle. A special thanks to Captain Emanuele Bottazzi and the entire staff at the Ministry of the Navy, that helped and facilitated this complicated research.

I traveled to Libya where the scars of the Second World War can still be seen. In Acroma, where Vittorio was wounded in battle, there is a military cemetery for British, Australian and New Zealand soldiers. On the rocky desert outside there are still pieces of barbed wire, the foxholes where the men would dig in, and spent shells lying around. Near Tobruk the trenches and concrete pillboxes built by Italian military engineers remain intact.

I also visited India, and went to Derhadun and Yol, where I saw the former prison camps. At Yol I met an old Gurkha Major now retired, Ram Bahadur Gurung, who as a boy was friendly with some Italian prisoners. I thank Italian diplomat Giorgio Starace who helped me organize the trip.

Roberto Santachiara believed and supported this project from the start when it was only a vague idea far from reality. I thank Paolo Zaninoni for having listened and I am indebted to Giuseppe Laterza. Gianni Riotta always encouraged me, read the proofs and provided valuable suggestions. Marcello Sorgi, Giulio Anselmi and Maurizio Molinari of *La Stampa* gave me the time and opportunity to do the research and write the novel. My conversations with Mario Calabresi were useful in erasing my final reservations. Paolo Signore agreed to undertake the first critical reading. I thank Robert Miller, the publisher and translator for deciding that this story deserved to be told to the American and English speaking readership worldwide.

But this work would not have been possible without the help, understanding and support of Giovina, Alberto, Flavia, Stefano, Federico, Marianna, Simonetta, Michele, Giuseppe, Filomena, Anna Rosa, Carmela and Annetta, all of whom I also warmly thank.

Bibliography

Sergio Antonielli, *Il Campo 29*, Editori riuniti, Roma 1976.

Mainardo Benardelli, *Yol: prigioniero in Himalaya*, Edizioni EsseZeta-Arterigere, Varese 2006.

Rosario Bentivegna, *Achtung Banditen: prima e dopo via Rasella*, Mursia, Milano 2004.

Ferdinando Bersani, *I dimenticati: prigionieri italiani in India*, Mursia, Milano 1975.

Gabriele Bigonzoni, *Ex uomini*, Tiber, Roma 1956.

Flavio Giovanni Conti, *I prigionieri di Guerra italiani 1940–1945*, Il Mulino, Bologna 1986.

Alfonso Del Guercio, *Campo 25*, L'arnia, Roma 1951.

Leonida Fazi, *La repubblica fascista dell'Himalaya*, Edizioni Settimo Sigillo, Roma 2005.

Carlo Grande, *La cavalcata selvaggia*, Ponte alle Grazie, Milano 2004.

Angelo Ioppi, *Non ho parlato* (edizione esclusiva per le Forze Armate), Roma 1945.

Robert Katz, *Roma città aperta: settembre 1943–giugno 1944*, Il saggiatore, Milano 2003.

——, *Morte a Roma*, Net, Milano 2004.

Antonio Lisi, *Gioacchino Gesmundo, l'altro martire di Terlizzi*, Associazione turistica pro loco Terlizzi, Rieti 1993.

——, *Don Pietro Pappagallo: un eroe, un santo*, Libreria moderna, Rieti 1995.

Gabrio Lombardi, *Montezemolo e il ponte militare clandestino di Roma*, Quaderni del Museo storico della liberazione di Roma, roma 1972.

Franco Maugeri, *Ricordi di un marinaio. La Marina italiana dai primi del Novecento al secondo dopoguerra nelle memorie di uno dei suoi capi*, Mursia, Milano 1980.

Alessandro Portelli, *L'ordine è già stato eseguito: Roma, le Fosse Ardeatine, la memoria*, Donzelli, Roma 2001.

Gianni Riotta, *Alborada*, Rizzoli, Milano 2002.

——, *Fucilate gli Ammiragli. La tragedia della Marina italiana nella Seconda Guerra mondiale*, Mondadori, Milano 1987.

Lido Saltamartini, *10000 in Himalaya, 1941–1947: tesori, orsi, idee, fughe*, Humana, Ancona 1997.

Elios Toschi, *In fuga oltre l'Himalaya*, Edizioni del Borghese, Milano 1968.

Gaetano Tumiati, *Prigionieri nel Texas*, Mursia, Milano 1985.

100 scatti sulla nostra storia: dalla dittatura del fascismo alla democrazia republicana, Capitolium-Anpi, Roma 2003.